HIRED KILLER

HIRED KILLER

CRYPTID ASSASSIN™ BOOK ONE

MICHAEL ANDERLE

LMBPN Publishing
PMB 196, 2540 South Maryland Pkwy
Las Vegas, NV 89109

First US edition, January, 2020
eBook ISBN: 978-1-64202-700-6
Print ISBN: 978-1-64202-701-3

Thanks to our Beta Readers

Jeff Eaton, John Ashmore, and Kelly O'Donnell

Thanks to the JIT Readers

Dorothy Lloyd
Jeff Eaton
John Ashmore
Diane L. Smith
Dave Hicks
Peter Manis
Jeff Goode

If we've missed anyone, please let us know!

Editor
Skyhunter Editing Team

CHAPTER ONE

The recruitment poster claimed the operation Taylor had suited up for was the heaviest armored group to ever head into the alien-monster-infested tar-ball called the ZOO.

Although everyone except the rookies knew better.

There seemed to be an unspoken consensus to simply pretend what brass said was true was true.

Part of Taylor resented the fact that they skirted the terrible reality and let it be overshadowed by the hype generated to lure in the numbers they needed. At the same time, he was relieved that no one contradicted the claim.

Mention of it would lead to inevitable demands that he tell those going in all about the first tar-ball mission with a large force he had been a part of.

Taylor would far rather not think about it.

That might have been a little hypocritical of him but he was, after all, the only one who had lived it in the group.

He'd earned the right to his silence.

One thing was certain. No one would be able to suggest

that this mission was undermanned. Not only that, it sure as fuck was the largest team heading in they had ever been a part of. Except him, of course.

He was the only one from that first clusterfuck left at the Zoo now.

It didn't really matter, he told himself over and over again. The point of it all was that people simply wanted to be a part of something that appeared to be bold and noble, something out of the ordinary.

If anyone who'd been there for a while recalled the past events and recognized some similarities, they made no effort to challenge the wisdom of such a large force.

Taylor simply kept his knowledge and misgivings to himself and allowed everyone get on with it.

Whoever sponsored the mission obviously had deep pockets. No one knew who it was, exactly, but the fact that it was split more or less evenly between official armed forces from the American and French bases, supplemented by outsider mercenaries, indicated hefty financial and political clout.

With that said, Gunnery Sergeant Taylor McFadden didn't like it. Not one bit.

He had been called in—as one of the soldiers with the most trips survived into the Zoo—to fulfill a leadership role. His first run into the jungle had been four years earlier—what people called the early days now. It seemed like a long time ago, no question about that.

It had been something of an initiation by fire.

They called it the Gulch of Armageddon Battle these days—if people mentioned it, which was seldom—but it seemed more like a massacre in his memories.

He'd been a part of battles during his time with the Corps and none of them had been anything like his memories of the GoA. Two weeks in the hospital and a purple heart somehow seemed to earn him a reputation as a lucky charm.

Some people were stupid enough to call him a leprechaun, thanks to his bright red hair, but only a couple were stupid enough to call him that to his face.

Of course, he made sure those dumbasses never repeated the mistake.

Eighty-three trips into the Zoo later, he couldn't help but think they might have had a point. Not about him being a leprechaun since he was about three and a half feet taller than what they were supposed to be according to his grandmother, but about being a lucky charm.

Not all his trips into the jungle had been successful and he'd lost a number of good men, women, and friends over the four years he had been there.

But, on average, he'd brought his people out alive so maybe it was less about luck and more about competence. Or maybe he had been lucky enough to go in with folk who knew what they were doing.

That counted as luck too, right?

Then again, there was a motto in the Marines—*Fortis Fortuna Adiuvat* or that fortune favored the bold. And he was bold. There was the Semper Fi motto too, but that was more for all Marines.

That notwithstanding, he still didn't like this walking fustercluck. The nagging itch had surfaced between his shoulders.

There was a *reason* why teams were kept on the small side when going into the jungle.

The monsters tended to escalate when they realized their home was being invaded, and the only way to avoid the mass assaults directed in retaliation was to push them back and get the fuck out before the rest of the alien mutant cryptids could find them.

With a crew that consisted of a total of fifty-six people in full combat armor—and with some in the personal power mech suits—the Zoo would have to work hard to counter them.

While true, it was equally true that the Zoo would throw everything it had against them.

He knew that because he had the experience to prove the fact. The last time he had been in there with a large force, it had been far more people who headed into Armageddon Gulch.

Eight teams—which together made a total of seventy-two men—headed in independently to rescue the young, up-and-coming scientist, Genesis Banks.

Only three people escaped alive that time.

The Zoo had decided to get creative about how it killed humans, and if it had been an actual battle run by humans, it would have been considered the kind of failure that Stalingrad had been for the Russians. The bodies of humans and beasts had piled up but the Zoo eventually overcame the humans when they ran out of bullets.

This time, there was an air of confidence those in leadership seemed to affect that he questioned, and not only because he was cynical.

He'd noticed that Team Heavy Metal was conspicuous

by their absence, which both made sense and should have waved a warning flag. They were generally regarded as the most successful and the most competent and professional of all the merc teams, possibly in the entire Zoo area.

If Heavy Metal didn't participate, it wasn't due to a lack of courage or resources. It was because they knew the expected outcome and chose not to be a part of something likely doomed from the start.

Those who had signed on, however, seemed to have forgotten a few basic truths and had included a few full-sized combat mechs. By now, brass should know those things had no place in the Zoo—like most vehicles.

The jungle had the uncanny ability to identify the biggest threats and learn their vulnerability. It would target those first, and God help the men inside if the mutants managed to topple them. These massive machines had a role and could be very effective at the wall or outside the flora area but in his opinion—which he'd shared with little effect—they would be more of a hindrance than a help in the jungle.

Sometimes, human arrogance meant you died before some useless lucky asshole learned from your mistakes, because your dead ass certainly had no use for the knowledge anymore.

"Hey, ginger," one of the men called on the open communications channel from the other side of the line he was leading. "Do you think you'll be able to rub some of that luck of the Irish over us?"

"That's Gunnery Sergeant Ginger to you, Corporal," Taylor snapped in response with mock-sternness. "And while I'm sure no one wants to see you and I rub anything together," he continued, "you should know that my luck comes from Scotland, not Ireland."

"Scotland and Ireland are basically the same thing, aren't they?" the corporal asked.

"Let's see if you still think that when the IRA bombs the shit out of your house, shit-for-brains," he retorted and flexed his shoulders to ease the stiffness.

It was a good idea to maintain the banter between his men. Not all of them were the veterans he and others were. While they were professional soldiers and would act that way until the pants-shitting terror descended on them, it was good for them to see the veterans chatting about it like it was no big deal.

It would calm them and hopefully give them confidence that they would make it out of this situation alive.

It might not improve their chances of survival that much, but being calm would improve their chances of being useful if there was a fight.

And with a team this large, fighting was essentially a given.

"Why would my individual retirement account bomb my house?" the corporal asked.

"That's not what he meant, dummy," one of the other veterans of the Zoo interjected. "And do you guys mind keeping this inane debate off the open channel?"

"You could always simply turn your shit off," Taylor pointed out.

"Sure, and miss it when we're getting torn to pieces by a horde of alien monsters?" the man—a captain going by the name of Pearle—asked.

"Seriously? It's not like it's an easy thing to miss," Taylor responded sharply. "They're alien monsters and they'll attack. Folks will shoot at them. That's honestly a big red flag if you know what you're looking for."

"Fuck you. Keep this channel clear," Pearle grumbled.

"Something crawled up your ass and it wasn't the luck of the Irish," the corporal commented.

"Scottish," Taylor corrected.

"Whichever lucks of many origins," the man laughed. "But get your collective undergarments untwisted and let us banter for crying out loud."

"I'm not saying you can't banter. I'm merely saying keep it off the open channels," the captain retorted. "We're all working on this together, and with the different teams, there is a need for open communications that doesn't involve the two of you talking about—"

"Bantering," the corporal corrected.

"Bantering about nothing," he finished.

"Excuse you, but we are having a very important conversation about…about…" The corporal mumbled under his breath as he attempted to come up with something important about the previous conversation.

"Retirement money," Taylor said and came to the man's rescue. "Um, Irish terrorism during the eighties, as well as the origins of the members of our team. Incredibly important topics."

"What the fuck ever," Pearle said dismissively. "Keep it down."

"You're not my superior officer."

"We have movement in the southeastern quadrant," one of the commanders of the mission called crisply. "Gamma squad, could you look into that?"

"Who's Gamma squad?" Pearle asked.

"That's us," Taylor said and his voice immediately became serious. "Give me an update from your scanners, squad."

The collective data streamed onto his HUD and gave him a decent view of the area surrounding them. Sure enough, there was movement in the quadrant but it was headed away from the group.

"Alpha squad, there is movement in my quadrant but it's moving away from us," Taylor reported.

"Roger that, Gamma leader, stay frosty," the commander ordered.

"Roger that, Alpha Leader," he replied.

"Alpha Leader, this is Delta leader. We have movement in the northwestern quadrant," said another man. "It looks fairly big too—no, wait, they're moving back now."

"I don't like this." Taylor looked around.

It felt like the Zoo was testing their reaction times and trying to get them to move out of the formation they had held for the past six hours of marching in an attempt to find a weakness.

People said it was impossible for creatures to be capable of strategic tactics and calculated assault, but given that they talked about mutants spawned from goop of alien origin that had also produced a very aggressive jungle—in the middle of the damned Sahara—he wasn't willing to rule anything out.

He'd seen too much intelligence in the attacks to be able to dismiss the idea that they might be testing their defenses. There was something happening in the Zoo, and it definitely *wouldn't* allow a group this large to advance through the jungle without powerful resistance.

Almost without thinking, he disengaged the assault rifle from his back and synched it to his HUD while he continued to scan for anything that might resemble trouble.

"Do you think we'll be involved in imminent violence, Gunny?" one of his men asked.

"The Zoo doesn't like us to interfere with what it's doing Dorson," he replied. "Whatever the fuck that is. For the moment, though, it'll look for a weak place to attack and then…well, we'll be fucked or we won't be." He noted his people had all begun to respond. "There's no middle ground here."

"Fun times," the man responded and immediately began to prepare his weapon.

The rest of the troop appeared to think the same thing. The veterans knew better than to assume the Zoo would simply leave them alone, and the rookies followed their lead. There was no chance that the jungle would catch them with their pants down.

Taylor didn't turn at the sound of gunfire from the rear of the group.

"Report, Foxtrot," came the order from the Alpha team.

"We have movement in the back of the line," Foxtrot leader called. "Hordes of critters…they look like the hyenas — Oh, shit, we have one of them killerpillars."

"What the fuck?" Taylor said and finally turned to look. Sure enough, through the motion sensors, he could see one of the massive monsters that never failed to make his skin crawl.

It was backing away, however, and Foxtrot squad chose to give chase.

"Stay in formation, Foxtrot," Taylor said and usurped the role of the Alpha squad leader in giving orders. That was why they wanted him in this mission, right? To act on his expansive experience in the Zoo?

"Negative. We'll give chase," Foxtrot leader said. "If we can show them a little force, they'll decide to back off more."

"What-ever in the fucking history of the jungle gave you that idea?"

The monsters there could practically melt into the tree cover in seconds. That aside, backing away usually meant regrouping for a more powerful attack.

He grimaced when he realized that Foxtrot was one of the merc teams. They tended to run operations their own way and didn't like to play nice with military groups.

And they didn't like to take orders either.

"Fucking hell—" Before he could even complete the expletive, the Zoo came alive in reaction to the attack from the team's rearguard. Suddenly, with a roar he recognized as coming from one of the albino gorillas, the jungle erupted. Foxtrot was almost instantly surrounded and they circled their leader—one of the idiots who controlled a heavy combat mech and used it to provide a limited area of defensive ground together with the other two mechs in their team. Taylor realized then why they'd been so damn sure of themselves.

God help them.

"Dawson, take two and hold the rear until Foxtrot can regroup," Taylor commanded and opened fire on the monsters that now surged toward the hole in their defenses.

There was no time to question the orders and certainly no time to wonder if they shouldn't simply leave the mercs behind for being dumbasses.

Dawson was quick to respond and hastily pinged two men from the Gamma group, whom he led to where Foxtrot had moved out of the defensive line.

It wouldn't be enough but it would buy them a little time, at least.

Taylor unhooked two grenades from his belt and slipped the first into the launcher under the barrel of his rifle. He delivered them in quick succession into the swarm of beasts that attempted to overwhelm the temporarily weakened human resistance.

"What the...where did these locusts come from?" Dawson demanded. "I never heard them fly in!"

"Nope, they're jumping from the trees," Taylor confirmed.

He'd been in the Zoo enough times to know that they could easily fly above and below the canopy and could glide fairly efficiently for short distances when things were heavily overgrown. They could also scuttle and leap at incredible speeds on the ground, but this was the first time he'd ever seen them attack from a stationary position in the trees.

Despite the heat of battle, it was still interesting to watch. There had been almost no movement from the canopy until Foxtrot broke formation and now, the bugs launched their ambush from the higher position.

It meant they had hugged the trees and were still high enough to not be seen in the motion sensors.

Now that was some terrifying shit. There had to be hundreds of them pressed up against the tree trunks all around them that had simply waited for some kind of signal for them to attack. They clearly made up most of the numbers of the assault but certainly weren't the only ones.

"Do we have any way to clear to Foxtrot?" asked Alpha leader. The entire team had formed up into defensive positions when they were attacked from all sides.

Alpha squad was made up mostly of the higher-ranking officers of the group, and they were armored almost exclusively in heavy mech suits. They were already hunkered down to provide secure positions for the teams around them to make use of their enhanced abilities as well as provide covering fire.

Taylor assessed the situation.

Foxtrot had almost completely isolated themselves by their precipitous pursuit of the enemy, and they definitely wouldn't make it back without an offensive push from the rest of the team.

"Not without sacrificing this position," he called. The *brak brak brak* of his weapon muted over the comms while he continued to provide covering fire. The rest of his men worked to seal the gap in their ranks.

"Shit." Alpha leader growled with obvious irritation. "All right. All squads, withdraw to Foxtrot's position and provide them with covering fire while flanking the attackers."

"Flank them?" asked Bravo leader. "How to you flank something when they're all around us?"

"This won't end well." Taylor allowed himself a low curse of frustration before he called on the team comms. "Form up. We'll hold the position indicated."

He highlighted the area where Dawson and the other two already stood their ground, yanked the last two grenades from his belt, and fired them to clear the area for his troops to advance. The team was coordinated enough to fill the path the explosives caused without actually being caught in the blasts.

They worked in unison to eliminate all the monsters before they advanced to where Dawson and his two teammates awaited them.

A ground-shaking roar bellowed above the sounds of battle, the kind Taylor could feel in his bones and even through his armor.

"Oh shit!" one of his men called out.

"Bathroom break later, Williams!" Taylor snapped.

He had been around the Zoo long enough to know what the fuck those were.

Still, he needed to look to see the living, walking fossils that would soon assault their line. Having dinosaurs in the world again would have been far more awesome if they weren't ready and able to swallow people—in armor no less—in a single bite.

And this time, there were three of them, perfectly alive and terrifyingly angry.

"Fuck me," he whispered as the building-sized creatures lumbered toward the combat mechs that still tried to stand in defiance, apparently convinced that they had the wherewithal to overcome the titans.

It took only a single blow from each of the massive

heads to topple the mechanicals. They fell, one after the other, and while the limbs moved immediately to push them off their backs, they were too heavy and cumbersome to recover quickly. The dinos lunged to take advantage of the heavy mechs' vulnerability.

The yelling was crowding the comm's on all sorts of channels.

"Take this you tit-fucking lunatic!"

"Lead poisoning works every time!"

"Godammit! Someone shoot that big sumbitch!"

Massive teeth savaged the reinforced armor that had been developed exactly for this kind of an attack like it was cardboard.

The spectacle was terrifying and haunting, yet a little impressive. It was like the Zoo had evolved these creatures specifically to destroy what mankind had engineered to defeat it.

Terrifying and haunting soon won out, though. The screams of the men inside the mechs were the worst as they were still connected to the commlinks with the rest of the teams.

Thankfully, the tortured sounds cut abruptly but left those alive visibly shaken.

A colossus swung ponderously from the mangled remains of its victim and turned its focus to the officers in their powerful mech suits. The other two followed—driven, it seemed, by an uncanny ability to target their leaders and the strongest resistance. They bulldozed through the desperate fusillade that greeted their approach and appeared utterly untouched by the assault, even with chunks of their flesh blasted off their hides.

With relentless efficiency and an almost casual disregard, they proceeded to systematically obliterate the line while shrieks and gunfire erupted around them.

"Fuck—form up." Taylor yelled and assumed the mantle he had known would fall on him eventually. He merely stepped into the position before things were too far gone. "If you motherfuckers want to survive, you form up now!"

The remaining men rushed to comply and organized their lines of fire to keep the massive monsters at bay for the moment. They were too busy with their savage attack for them to turn and face the barrage directly.

He knew that shit wouldn't last, though.

Foxtrot was being pulled back into the fold, but they had taken casualties over and above the leaders in the mechs. If they wanted to survive, they had to force a path back and find a way to put some distance between them and the horde.

"Collect the claymores and place them to give us a perimeter to fall back to," Taylor said quickly while he worked some alterations into the assault rifle.

He liked tinkering with his suit and making changes with the applications. With the help of some of the tech experts in the US base, he had made himself a suit that would outperform most of those they had worked inside during past runs.

And from the looks of things, he would need every one of the improvements to work flawlessly if they had any chance to get out of there alive.

The teams knew that leadership was needed, and they moved to follow him in carving out a path for them to work with, laying the mines in a semi-circular pattern that would allow for a retreat.

Taylor looked at the enormous mutants that had now totally obliterated the heavy defenders and tried to think of a way in which he could handle them. He had been around long enough to know how the jungle would react if they burst the blue sacs of fluid in the larger creatures' spines.

"Don't shoot the spines!" The current battle was a pale reflection of what they'd bring down on them if that happened.

He would need a way to keep them at bay until they were able to pull away behind the mines.

There were enough mutants ranged against them that he knew they would not have a clean getaway. It would be a start, though.

"Pull back!" he called as the dinosaurs began to rush their defensive line. He refitted the launcher under his barrel with a double shotgun barrel, already loaded and ready to fire.

It was called a shotgun but might as well have been twin barrels of grapeshot cannons.

The thought that he would have to buy the engineers in the base a few drinks brought a grim smile. He pulled the triggers and felt the kick all the way to his bones as he was knocked back a step.

It was effective, though. The two massive-gauge rounds drove into the closest dinosaur's head and knocked it away with an earth-shaking roar. After a couple more steps, it collapsed with a shudder and convulsed in its death throes without damaging the sacs.

Thank God.

His moment of elation was shattered when the remaining two attacked the formation and walked through their concentrated fire like it was a swarm of friendly mosquitoes.

They trampled the front line with the ease of a giant wading through toy soldiers, seized the men in larger mech suits, and crushed them in their massive jaws. From what he could see, only Pearle had managed to evade them.

"Fuck." Taylor gasped and forced his mind to focus. "Set the mines off! Now!"

His roar over the comms elicited an instant reaction. The earth shuddered beneath his feet as the powerful blasts lit the forest up enough for him to see exactly how many mutants there were around them.

And how many of the original team were left. There wasn't much in the way of visible bodies, which wasn't unusual, but the HUD in his helmet told him that only ten members were alive.

"Fall the fuck back!" he shouted and opened fire on the mass of beasts that surged into a renewed assault. He couldn't tell one from the other. They were merely an amorphous blob of death and hunger sweeping down on him and his men.

Pearle stepped out in front and pushed the supports on his suit into the earth as a massive rocket launcher on his shoulder activated, locking over his shoulder. A stream of rockets seared into the advancing horde.

"Get on my back!" he called over the comms. "The mini-gun's automatic fire control is fried, but there's a manual override that'll let you shoot it anyway."

"Sounds good," Taylor replied while Dawson tried to gather the survivors into an organized troop to return to the edge of the Zoo.

It soon became apparent they wouldn't get far. The killerpillar had returned and it clearly had no intention to back down this time. It claimed two victims before it curled and let its carapace absorb most of the bullets fired at it.

This version of the mutant was a far cry from the stories he'd heard of the original creatures. Those had been fast but cumbersome and had attacked in tandem, each latching onto their prey with huge mandibles that remained locked until the next gained hold. They would move up the body, usually starting at the legs, until they reached the vital organs and slow and excruciatingly painful death was inevitable.

These, however, were fast, worked alone, and had evolved into a formidable creature that had the ability to simply protect itself by curling to shield its vulnerable parts. It was fearless and difficult to kill in a hurry.

"Turn the rockets on that big bastard," he called to Pearle as he took up the mini-gun. "I'll hold the front."

"Good plan," the man replied and complied while Taylor targeted the front line, opened fire with the powerful machine gun mounted on the mech's back, and supplemented it with a volley from his assault rifle.

It was good enough to hold the beasts back, and once Pearle had successfully annihilated the killerpillar, he turned his attention to the heaviest area of the attack.

The rockets had more explosive power than the claymore mines that had ripped a little clear space for them.

Launched in the rapid-fire technique he now used, they were enough to turn the jungle around them into a burning wasteland.

Before too long, the monsters chose to beat a hasty retreat. They weren't supported by the larger beasts, and there were no longer enough of them to sustain an effective attack.

Which was for the best as the team had begun to run low on ammo.

"Okay, people," Taylor said and jumped from the back of Pearle's mech. "We need to double-time it to the edge—"

He paused and looked at the group that now consisted of Pearle, Dawson, and himself.

"Sorry, Sarge," the corporal said and looked distraught. "I... They..."

Taylor had nothing to say. He wanted to speak and felt like something needed to be said for the death of so many of his friends and comrades, but nothing came to him. Fifty-three dead. His brain somehow couldn't move past that single fact. It was somehow made worse by the fact that he'd warned them and the whole clusterfuck could have been avoided if they'd only listened and used their goddamn brains.

While he'd never been much good at this bullshit anyway, it still felt shitty to simply leave them behind without even a word of recognition.

The reality, though, was that they had to run. It wouldn't be long before other creatures found their way in to see what all the commotion was about and they would have to face another attack.

"We have reinforcements due southwest," Pearle said

and looked like he tried to not let what he was looking at affect him.

All the explosives had demolished and felled the trees in the area, which gave them only too clear a view of the aftermath of what had transpired. Something for Pearle's video cameras to take back to headquarters.

"Let them know we'll rendezvous with them as soon as they're within range," Taylor said. Something choked in the back of his throat and made his voice thicker than it needed to be. He wanted to curl in a ball like the fucking killerpiller and wake up with all this as nothing more than a dream.

But that wouldn't happen. There was no clicking his magic heels and wishing himself home.

"Let's go," he said roughly and tried to push the feelings down. They would have to wait until they were in the clear again.

CHAPTER TWO

There were people who told him he really needn't have bothered with the whole song and dance of therapy.

Those were the kinds of people who didn't know about the internal workings of the military.

After the fighting and the mission during which he had lost forty-three men in a trip into the Zoo to collect seismic data? That sounded like bullshit to him.

However, he still had no idea who it was who wanted to find out about the earth rumblings around the jungle. Nor, for that matter, why it was so important that they threw caution and common sense out the window in what was arguably one of the stupidest missions of all time.

Still, whoever they were seemed moot. They had been more than willing to throw cash at the survivors of the trip and the families of those who hadn't made it out.

There were things people simply couldn't buy back, though.

Taylor had been trapped in the hospital while he recovered from numerous smaller injuries. He had no idea why they had held him there until he received his psyche eval.

Not fit for duty.

That psyche eval was one of the most difficult reads of his life, and it had led to hard decisions. These included accepting a medical discharge with all kinds of honors and full benefits after four tours of duty.

He could now add medals and a speech from the commandant of the US base—telling him how much his honorable service to his country had inspired thousands—to add to his resume.

Amazingly, that didn't really help, given that hundreds had died while he had been in the Zoo with them. He was one of the few who made it out alive—and with one hell of a pension, thanks to four years of collecting the money from the Pita flowers over and above his payout from the military.

But even then, the medical discharge was not enough. They wanted to make sure there would be no option for him to eventually sue them for damages and would therefore wait for him to be cleared by a professional in the US before they released him to go be a free man.

Whatever the hell that meant with his darkness.

Overall, it was a nice thought, even though it was purely budgetary in the end. Besides, while he waited for the wheels of medical bureaucracy to turn, he was able to live on one of the bases near DC, not pay any rent, and be with the people he actually knew and felt comfortable around.

Four tours had taken up most of his adult life. There wasn't much out in the world for him unless he wanted to make it for himself. Thankfully, he wasn't the type to whine and kick his heels and had already accepted the challenge.

It was his turn and he would forge a future beyond the military.

The only downside, of course, was that Taylor needed to pay a visit to a shrink who would determine whether or not he would be a danger to himself or others.

How the hell could someone actually determine that kind of shit anyway? It wasn't like they had a test for it. Well, they had about a hundred, but none of them were conclusive enough for Dr. Jane Bedford, apparently.

It wasn't a long way from the base to her office and it was a nice drive through some of the better suburbs around the nation's capital. It ended with him stepping into the small, three-story building where he would spend the next hour or so.

Taylor no longer felt comfortable in civilian clothes. He had even tried to grow his red hair and beard to make him fit in a little better.

For some reason, that didn't really work when you were six-five and built like an ox. Kids pointed and stared at him while he did his shopping and walked around town, thinking he was a part of one of the local professional wrestling franchises.

It had been an interesting idea but not one he had put any serious thought into. Those who participated put themselves through too much training and too much pain for it to be worth it for him. He was large enough to be a linebacker on a football team but probably too old.

No, there were other things for a man of his particular

skill set and mentality to get into if only the good doctor would sign off on him so he could get the hell out of the military.

The good doctor in question waited for him at the door of her practice and smiled broadly in a way that made her cheeks flush and her eyes light up.

He wasn't sure if it was a well-practiced smile for all her patients or if she was genuinely happy to see him.

Instincts suggested it was the latter.

Either one was suspicious enough for him to not trust her. It was better to be wary until he had his signed discharge in hand.

Nevertheless, he faked a smile as well.

"Dr. Bedford, it's nice to see you again." Taylor shook her hand.

"It's nice to see you again too, Taylor," she replied and grasped his hand firmly. "You know you can call me Jane, right?"

"I don't think I will, Doc, but thanks anyway," he replied affably. There were some relationships that should be kept professional. He was still the patient here, after all.

"Please, follow me into my office," she said and guided him through the first two rooms and away from the secretary, who eyed him curiously, until they reached the larger office in the back.

He sat across from her and simply allowed the silence to wash over him. Some people felt uncomfortable with silences. Not him.

Taylor could stand to not speak or listen to anything someone had to say, especially when he was about sixty percent sure that what came from their mouth was bullshit. It was a distraction from what he really needed to pay attention to.

The doctor was uncomfortable with the silence. She shifted in her seat a few times and tapped something into her tablet before she turned her attention to the man seated across from her.

"Well, what do you want to talk about today, Taylor?" she finally asked, a hint of desperation in her voice. "The hour is yours, as you already know."

"Well, fuck me, Doc," he said and shrugged. "The weather? Maybe sports?"

"The weather has been nice this week," Bedford said, her head tilted although he couldn't read her expression. "And the Redskins are looking at making a championship run this season."

"Not if my Packers have anything to say about it," he replied. "Our wide receiver corps will be hard to stop, and you know that the Pack is a factory for Hall of Fame quarterbacks."

"I don't really want to talk about sports, Taylor."

"I thought you said the hour was mine." He chuckled and rubbed his cheek idly. He liked having a beard. It made him look like a biker and he decided he liked the look. Maybe he should actually get a motorcycle to complete it.

"I'm not here to talk about sports, Taylor," she repeated. "I thought we had real breakthroughs in your therapy over the past few weeks. I *do* care about your progress."

"I'm fine," he said for what felt like the hundredth time during the therapy journey. "I've told people that for the past five weeks and yet, no one believes me."

"Because you went through a genuinely traumatic experience and there were very real signs that you weren't dealing with it," she said and leaned forward. "For one thing, if you're as fine as you say you are, why do you fill the prescriptions I give you? Why do you arrive at my office at the correct time—on the dot, I might add—every Tuesday and Thursday for our sessions?"

"Because I'm taking everything seriously," Taylor replied. "It's the only way I'll get my pension. I may be thought of as a loose cannon but I'm not stupid. I want to leave here without any ties holding me back from my future."

"Right." The doctor leaned back in her chair. "What kind of future do you see for yourself? Where do you want to go once I sign off that you have completed these mandated therapy sessions?"

He followed her example and leaned back into his seat. Finally, she'd raised a topic he was willing to talk to her about.

"Well, I thought of moving to Vegas. You know, where the business laws are loose and the women are looser."

"Do you want to start a business?" she asked. "That sounds exciting. What kind of business?"

"I've learned numerous skills along the road," he explained. "I've worked with combat suits and mech suits for the duration of my tours, topped off with a degree in engineering, and I'd like to invest that knowledge into building and repairing the same. It's a niche market, I know, but there aren't many businesses here in the States that do it. Since this is where most of the parts and pieces come from, I'm sure I could undercut the prices of the companies running things in the Zoo. I have seed money to get me started, but I won't want to invest all of it so I'll probably take out a loan. Thanks to my work in the Zoo, my credit score is fantastic, so I think it would be a great start to my life as a civilian."

Bedford's eyes were open, her mouth slack for a moment before she closed it and smoothed her features. ""Well…" It was the longest he had spoken to her in any of their sessions. "Wow, it sounds like you've put considerable thought into this."

"It's my life." He smiled. "Who else will think about it but me?"

She nodded, shook her head, and retrieved a sheet of paper which she quickly initialed in a few places before she added her full signature at the bottom. "I don't want you to think that I approve of how well you hide your emotions, Taylor, but…I have the feeling you'll be able to process them better without being forced to talk to a therapist."

"That's really insightful of you, Doc." He stared at the paperwork that would officially release him from the therapy and let him go about his life. "So…does this mean you're not my therapist anymore? That I'm not your client?"

"Patient," she corrected him, nodding as if to herself. "But…yes."

"So, if I were to ask you out for a drink tonight when you're finished working here, your answer would be yes, correct?" he asked.

Her eyebrows raised sharply. "I… Well, I'd have to think about it."

"How much is there to think about, Doc?" he asked and leaned forward. "I can't imagine there are many guys who like to date someone as smart as you. Dumbasses like to pretend their partners are dumb and weak. It helps them to get a hard-on. You know I'm not like that. It seems like we could both use a drink."

She regarded him with a somewhat bemused expression. "It sounds like you've put a fair amount of thought into this."

He shrugged. "It's my life, Doc. And yours too."

"Pick me up here at seven." She smiled. "I'll need to go home and change first."

"That sounds like a plan," he said, stood quickly, and took her hand in a firm shake. "And I think this will be the first time you and I actually look forward to seeing each other."

"Well, I have looked forward to seeing you over the past few weeks," she admitted.

"I know," he replied smoothly. "That's why I asked."

He tucked the release paper into his coat pocket and headed to the door, tipped an imaginary hat to the secretary on his way out, and whistled what he thought was a jolly tune to cement the impression of a normal man who was pleased with the outcome.

As soon as he was out the door, he stopped as the weight of it seemed to collapse on top of him. The breathlessness that had plagued him since he'd left the Zoo had returned to remind him of the way he woke up some nights gasping for breath and thinking those damned vines had crawled around his neck and squeezed tighter than a constrictor.

It lasted until he reached his car, where he sat in the driver's seat, grasped the steering wheel, and stared blankly into space while he counted the beats of his bounding heart.

That was a way to calm oneself down, right?

The seconds passed slowly, and he gradually relaxed with the tick of each one. His hands were still shaking but he took the vial of pills from the glove box of the rental car he'd used during his time there, took the two prescribed pills, and washed them down with a bottle of lukewarm water he had in the cupholder.

The doctor's question about the meds returned to startle him. She had a point, and he decided it was time to look at weaning himself off them. Once he set his plans in motion, he'd have enough to occupy him and feed his soul to give him what he needed to hurdle this last obstacle.

"You're fine," he mumbled to himself in the rear-view mirror as he started the car. "You're fine, kid."

Niki sighed softly and stared at what felt like a mile's length of paperwork she needed to review. They had told her that taking responsibility for this part of the job would do wonders for her career.

Having her own taskforce was like putting rocket boots on her promotional track.

They had also mentioned there would be mountains of paperwork—the kind that consisted of actual paper. She could type at one hundred and ten words per minute when she was in the groove, but actual writing? On paper? That sucked far more.

But still, it was something that needed to be done if she wanted to climb the ladder.

"Good morning, Special Agent Niki Banks," chimed a soft, feminine voice from her computer.

She tensed, closed her eyes, and clutched the pen in her hands a little tighter. "Goddammit, Desk. When will you ever learn to stop startling the hell out of me? Can't you simply pop up on the desktop or something?"

"I've tried that for the past five minutes with no response," the AI replied.

She turned to look at her computer screen. Sure enough, there were fifteen unanswered messages.

"Damn, you got me there," she admitted. "How can I help you?"

"I've been alerted to the recent availability of one of the prime candidates for your CA task-force. The agent opened the file of the man she was talking about that had been attached to one of the messages.

"Oh, right, I remember him," she said and studied the man's bright red hair and beard, his powerful build, and the vibrant green eyes, along with the half-smirk he seemed to have in all his official pictures. "Yeah, I guess eighty-three stints in the Zoo does make one a prime candidate for the CA position, but... Have you looked at his psych record?"

"He's been signed off by his civilian medical adviser," Desk pointed out. "He's cleared for this kind of duty."

"Yeah, well, pardon me for not taking the word of a government-paid shrink," she said. "There's so much shit they don't look for in these kinds of people, and I have to pick up after them."

"Forgive me for saying this, but I do think McFadden is a prime candidate to bring my operational capabilities into the field." There was a measure of insistence in her tone. "You have said you'd like someone else to manage your freelancers on this. That is the reason I was brought on board."

"I don't know," she grumbled, folded her arms, and flicked her dark hair back so it wouldn't cover her eyes. "He's volatile."

"Which of your freelancers aren't?" the AI challenged.

She paused and grimaced. "You got me there, I guess. I'll need to clear it with him, of course, but if McFadden is on board, he's all yours."

"I appreciate the vote of confidence," Desk replied and cut the line.

"It makes sense that he's the one you'd choose," she whispered under her breath.

CHAPTER THREE

There were a handful of things a guy usually looked for in his truck.

The first was what was important for most vehicles, really—the power of the engine. Some people looked for the kind of gas mileage that would last them for a long time between filled tanks, and Taylor could see why that was a priority. Others would want the kind of engine that would make impressive noise and generally make them look like an ass to everyone and anyone they encountered. Of course, those cretins also always seemed to generate plumes of black smoke which they thought, for some reason, was super-cool.

Taylor didn't think of himself as belonging to any of those categories. He liked having a powerful engine but leaned toward the hybrid type in which the well-built engines were the kind that, while not quite electric, were still efficient enough with combustibles to make them last a while. He'd selected a truck that was known for its efficiency and long-lasting engine and fitted it out in the way he had been taught to do all his life.

With a dad who ran a mechanic shop outside of Madison, Wisconsin, he had grown up around cars and their paraphernalia and so knew what to buy, what was needed, and what wasn't.

A powerful engine was necessary, especially in light of what he carried in the back. The vehicle had been purchased on a police auction and subsequently adapted into a masterpiece of raw power. It had taken him considerable time to tweak it the way he wanted it, but the end result was totally worth it.

Admittedly, painting it black wouldn't be the best choice in the middle of the Nevada desert, but that was based more on his personal aesthetic preferences. He was a metal-head to his core, and there was nothing he owned that wouldn't be painted as black as his soul.

A couple of his buddies—the few who were still alive—questioned his decision to relocate to Vegas. Their opinion was that the only people who lived there were the kinds who were either gorged from or sucked dry by the casinos that made up most of the state's economy. Given that he had no intention to be a go-go dancer or a professional loser on the casino floor, no one thought he should start his new life there.

With that said, when it was pointed out that the business licensing laws had intentionally been kept loose in the state for the past solid hundred years, they admitted that it wasn't a terrible place to set up a new and budding business.

Besides, Taylor had seen the kind of shit that happened

in the Sahara. He wouldn't say the shit still terrified him—aside from the dreams that appeared out of nowhere when he least expected them—but the shit was *still* terrifying as an overall reality.

People who thought otherwise were ignorant. Given how quickly the Zoo had spread in the Sahara, he could only imagine how rampantly it could expand in areas that were already lush with vegetation and populated by towns and cities as a handy larder for biomass.

While he knew it was contained by the ongoing wall construction, he had no real confidence that humanity would be able to halt its progress indefinitely. He'd seen the kinds of unbelievable things the Zoo was able to create and manage and had to concede that maybe, just maybe, it would come up with a way to break free of the constraints humanity struggle to impose on it.

If that ever happened and the alien jungle invaded Earth with a vengeance, he wanted a solid chunk of desert between him and any impending Armageddon that might head his way. He wasn't sure what he would do if the shit ever hit the fan, but it was better to have a buffer—and hopefully a little time to prepare or whatever—than not, right?

Besides, there was business to be had. The most common complaint he'd heard from his merc friends had been about how they hated the fact that the larger corporations ran a veritable monopoly on repairs to the suits used in the Zoo, as well as keeping all the skilled mechanics out there under their employ. They needed someone who would work for them and Taylor was willing to be that someone.

He accepted that the larger companies wouldn't like him to impinge on their business like that, but it was part of the reason why he chose to set up shop in the States. The Zoo had no monopoly laws, but the country did.

Those would protect him from outright retaliation. He hoped. Well, that was the plan, anyway.

Things were looking up. Taylor felt good about his life as he drove along the highways toward Sin City. He didn't trust the radios in the area very much and relied on the head-banging repertoire provided by his own playlist that currently delivered Five Finger Death Punch's iteration of "Rock Bottom."

"I refuse…to be your type…have you lost your *goddamn motherfucking mind?*"

While he had never been the greatest of singers, when you sang the death growls that were typical of his kind of music, being skilled wasn't really a criterion. Especially when he did so in his car and Taylor had turned the music up so loud he could only feel himself sing.

It did make his throat hurt after a while, but it was still a great song to head-bang to while on a long, boring drive.

The motions weren't too enthusiastic, of course. He was driving and while he had better instincts and reflexes than most when it came to operating heavy machinery and the vehicle did most of the driving anyway at this point, he was still transporting close to a million dollars' worth of equipment in the back of the vehicle.

There were his tools, of course, collected during his time at the Zoo—the kind that made working with the suits and mechs used in the jungle easy. Well, they were used outside of the Zoo too, he reminded himself.

Reports of private armies marching around the Middle East, Southeast Asia, and even South America using the shiny new mech suits flowed in.

On top of that, he had the one he'd used in the Zoo himself. He had purchased his own rather than rely on those in stock for the military men and women who went in.

The load included two extras he had used for parts initially but had since rebuilt to perfect condition. The three were easily the most costly pieces of tech he had ever owned and would likely be the most expensive he would ever own.

He'd scavenged the two from the Zoo itself under the salvage rule—basically, this meant that anything you found was yours if you could retrieve it. His suit had been acquired at a ridiculously low price from the widow of one of the mercs who had accompanied him on a trip in. He'd suggested payment terms with a hefty deposit, but the woman had simply wanted to get rid of it.

She'd assured him that the pension payout was sufficient blood money.

None of the companies in the US would ever confess to selling to drug lords and oil barons and Sheikhs, but no one denied that billions of dollars were in it for them if they put their morals aside for a while and "lost track" of one or two shipments. He didn't really want to explore the kind of financial finagles that obscured those deals from both the government and the public.

It wasn't the kind of shit that made the newspapers—at least until there were pictures of war-torn areas where men in power suits towered over destroyed villages that stood in the way of a new oil pipeline.

People simply didn't care until that kind of tragedy occurred. Then, they were all over it.

The music was turned down automatically when the ten-inch screen stereo that had been set up free of charge showed that he had a phone call.

Why was it that someone always seemed to call when he had better things to do or was simply in his groove?

He was tempted to simply reject the call and let the music continue, but there was always a chance that it was something important. Still, he hated the notion that everything had to stop because someone wanted to chat. He had no idea why no one bothered to simply send him a text so he could respond to it eventually when it suited him.

"Someone had better be dead," Taylor grumbled under his breath. "Or someone will be."

He pushed the call details to the HUD on the windscreen and narrowed his eyes. His frown became a grin before he tapped the button on the steering wheel that would answer the call.

"My man, Bungees. How the fuck are you?" he asked and very quickly came to terms with the fact that he would have to talk to someone today anyway. In this instance, the fact that he wanted to speak to the man certainly eased the process.

"Not too bad," Bungees voice came back at him from the speakers. "It's as hot as fuck out here but still not too bad. How about you?"

"I'm sitting in my truck with the AC on full blast,

driving along the highway, and listening to some tunes," he replied. "I don't have a thing to complain about."

"So, what's this I hear about you coming to Vegas?" Bobby—aka Bungees—asked. "Is it only to see me or do you plan to lose all your hard-earned cash at the craps tables? Because I'm happy with either one."

"I had a business proposition I wanted to run by you. It's kind of the reason why I chose Vegas, actually. The business, that is. The fact that you are there is merely a happy coincidence if I'm honest."

"Are you sure you didn't choose Vegas because the girls are looser than the tax laws in the Cayman Islands?" the man retorted.

"It's not...*only* that," Taylor said and tried to stay honest to himself and his long-time friend. "It's the fact that the Zoo needs more biomass. At least in the desert, it won't have a city-full of people sitting on flora it doesn't have to change to jungle to swallow like it would in fucking New York or LA. With that said..."

"Loose women is a close second?" The other man completed his statement for him.

"Well, yes, sure." He changed lanes to pass the minivan that looked like a family road trip from Missouri. "After everything that went down and sudden death, I'm not looking for anything long-term anyway. If the both of us or hell, all three of us agree to be adults and be in it for simple human comfort, I'm all for that shit. I know, it's not very politically correct of me in this day and age but hey, if they don't want to be involved at all, I'm down for that too."

There was a pause on the other end. "It sounds like you've thought this shit through."

"What can I say, I like planning ahead in most aspects of my life." Taylor laughed, leaned back in the comfortable seat of the truck, and watched as the miles ticked by on the odometer. "So, what do you say, man? I know you have a job there, and from what I found out through flicking through the cable channels, apparently your own TV show on the Auto-TV channel as well. So if you're not interested, I completely understand."

"I don't think you do," Bungees replied. "But I'll forgive you for that without you even asking me. See, the owner of the auto shop I work at gets all kinds of money from the TV contract, but we don't see much of it trickling down to us. Not only that, the kind of stress that goes into making the audiences happy...well, it's not as good as you might think."

"Fair enough." Taylor grimaced when his imagination expanded on the idea of having to pander to the public. "Look, I'll pull into town in a couple of hours. Do you want to have a drink when I get in?"

"I have a late shift tonight, my man, but maybe some-time tomorrow?" He sounded genuinely regretful. "I'll call you and let you know the when and the where."

"That sounds good to me. I'll still get a drink, though. There's nothing better to wash away the feeling that you get from driving all day."

"Why didn't you fly?"

"Do you think I'll trust my livelihood to the hands of movers?" he asked. "Now I know you're crazy."

"Yeah, yeah, whatever." His friend laughed. "Anyway, it'll be good to see you again, Taylor. It'll be like the old days."

"Not too much like the old days, I hope," he responded. "Talk soon, Bungees."

The line clicked and the moment of silence that came over him before the music kicked in again was one of careful thought.

He couldn't help but wonder if he had made the right decision in coming out there.

But FFDP came on and soon, he rocked out to the metal that was loud enough to lock out any other emotions and thoughts other than those conveyed by the people on the other side. You know, those with the musical talent.

There weren't many views that were more overwhelming than the sight of Las Vegas as the sun began to set. Say what you wanted about the place, it was a monument to the stubbornness of the people who set up a huge tourist city in the middle of the fucking Mojave Desert and made that shit work.

Essentially, they'd carved out a place in human history that would last for a long, long time.

All the glittering lights and brilliant views of the city weren't quite his scene, though, and while he did have money to spend, he knew better than to let any be funneled down the drain created by the local casinos and hotels.

Taylor cruised slowly along South Las Vegas Boulevard and grimaced, relieved that he'd opted to avoid the hotels crammed almost shoulder to shoulder. Instead, he'd chosen a smaller hotel he considered a safe and comfortable distance away and so was a little more affordable. Still, one had to at least see the Strip if you visited Vegas—which he'd done so had that out the way.

If it hadn't taken thirty minutes to go five blocks, it might have been less frustrating.

Once out of the mess, he followed his GPS to Boulder Highway and Sam's Town, relieved to watch the over-whelming neon fade into the distance in the rearview mirror. The three-star hotel complex obviously included the Vegas-requisite gambling hall with enough tables and slot machines to guarantee a good income, but he wasn't there for any of that. He needed somewhere to park his truck off the street and a room to spend the night before he met the realtor he'd contacted the day before to begin his search for a place to settle down in.

Check-in was quick and painless since they were a few months removed from the prime tourist time of year. He had hoped to be able to sleep in the truck but it had proven to be a bad idea. In turn, it meant he'd needed to find stops during his drive from DC to Vegas, and it had been tough going for a while.

But there he was in the hotel he thought he might maybe call home—for a while, at least. It smelled a little of cigarettes. There couldn't be that many people who still smoked in the world, but they seemed to congregate there. The sounds of slot machines trying to lure people in to spend their hard-earned quarters were easy to resist as he completed check-in and headed up to his room.

Taylor wasn't sure how long he'd need to wash the four-day drive off him, but however long it took him, he was left with the positive feeling that it was gone. He could focus on the next chapter of his life without looking back too far unless he chose to.

He stepped out of the shower, dried off quickly, and

draped the hotel towel around his waist before he moved through the cloud of mist caused by the long shower and wiped his hand across the mirror.

His reflection revealed a certain gauntness to his features he didn't really like. It was as if a haunted look lingered around the man in the mirror and Taylor didn't actually feel that way. It was a little annoying but not enough to give him pause.

By force of habit, he rolled his shoulders and his neck in quick succession. He felt a little drained but not tired enough to warrant an early night.

"I need a fucking drink is what I need," he grumbled.

Even though he had no one to join him, it still felt like the way to go and he wasn't in the mood to raid the over-priced minibar. He would ask the front desk if there were any sports bars in the area. That way, the attention would not be directed at any newcomers. He'd simply be one of a crowd.

CHAPTER FOUR

When he approached the woman at the front desk, she was willing to help. While she clearly wasn't thrilled to hear that he wouldn't spend his money at their particular establishment, they did have recommendations in the area around the hotel that might be more to his taste.

The clerk seemed very keen to push him toward one in particular. A pleasant little sports bar could be found around the next corner, she said. It had a kitchen so would see to any of his drinking, eating, or gambling needs. She even had a pamphlet that would give him fifty percent off his first drink at Jackson's Bar and Grill. It was a decent enough offer.

"Thanks, I guess," Taylor said and his gaze studied the coupon she'd handed to him, which included her signature. He logically assumed that the clerks who worked there might have the coupons on hand and would be offered free drinks or food for however many coupons with their signature on were handed in at the bar.

It was a neat system that many hotels and bars worked to help each other, and since it was mostly based on rewarding employees for good service, he was all for it.

There was also the part about having half off his first drink that definitely had appeal.

"No problem," she said with a broad smile and tilted her head to look at him with a smile. "I hope you enjoy yourself."

"Yeah, me too." He left the hotel and made his way toward the street.

As the sun had almost completely set, he could feel the temperatures around him drop sharply. He had felt the same thing out in the Sahara, where the lack of humidity in the air meant the heat that would bake anything beneath it dissipated quickly and temperatures fell to almost freezing sometimes.

Of course, the city around him and all the asphalt would hold onto the warmth for a few hours more, but it would could get hellishly cold before midnight.

He didn't mind, though. There was more than enough time to return to the hotel for a nice long rest before it became uncomfortable.

For now, though, he looked forward to getting slightly buzzed without the worry that he had to drive anywhere.

The establishment didn't look too impressive from the outside, but he didn't need it to. Stonework decorated the exterior with the name emblazoned in bright red neon above the entrance, along with advertisements for food, spirits, and video poker over the wooden awning.

A portrait of President Andrew Jackson was prominent beside the name, a little to the left. It seemed a little odd, especially when he realized that it was the same portrait as the one used on the twenty-dollar bill. They were clearly looking to make the name count and he decided he couldn't fault them for that.

Taylor wondered if there was actually a Jackson involved in founding the business or if it was merely named after the president, but it seemed like an inane question and he shrugged it aside.

He strode through the entrance and the small lobby curved to the left to lead him into a room that was surprisingly well-lit for a bar. Or maybe he was simply used to the darker, more pub-like establishments they had around the Zoo.

It was a pleasant surprise to see that it was a Packer's bar, as evidenced by the helmets on display and the small shrine to the team on his left. The sight triggered one hell of a kick to the nostalgia bone he'd thought he kept well-hidden.

That alone was enough to encourage him to make a note to himself that he would return often if only to pay homage to the home team.

As he turned to the bar itself, he saw it was manned by only one bartender—a younger woman—and looked a little abandoned. It wasn't entirely unexpected given the hour and the season. It would probably fill up with a vengeance come football season or maybe during the weekends when sports were on.

For the moment, they played a few reruns of the baseball games that were happening around the country, preseason games for the most part although a few triple-A games were already deep into their seasons.

The bar itself had screens that enabled the patrons to indulge in the advertised video poker. An area in the back was designated for people who wanted to focus more on either the sports or the food aspects of the establishment, whereas the front was dedicated to drinking and gambling.

President Jackson made a few more appearances around the bar, as well as the same stonework he'd noticed on the outside, which gave it a nice, sturdy aesthetic.

Taylor was probably unlikely to do much gambling, but if he was still in Vegas come football season, he would definitely return for the opening game.

For now, though, he would simply have a drink or two.

The bartender smiled as he dropped onto one of the stools, grabbed a rag, and ran it across the bar top as she strode over. "Evening, stranger, how can I help you?"

He withdrew the coupon from his pocket and placed it on the bar top. "I don't suppose this is still valid."

She laughed, took it, and studied it carefully before she placed it in the cash drawer. "It sure is."

"Then I think I'll have a whiskey sour," he said. "And, for a drink that won't have half off, whatever you have on tap."

"Coming right up," she said, still smiling. It didn't feel fake, at least not to him. She seemed to enjoy her work. Maybe she would rather be at home in comfortable clothes and shoes but she didn't mind being there.

Or perhaps she was merely happy for the distraction from boredom. There were five, maybe six people in the entire establishment he could see and none of them looked like they had any real interest in keeping the bar busy.

"So where are you from?" she asked as she handed him the beer first.

"You can call me Taylor," he replied and took a sip from the stout that she put in front of him. "And I do hail originally from Madison, Wisconsin, but all over the place after that."

"That sounds fun," she replied. "I'm Alex, by the way. I'm a Green Bay native, myself."

"A woman after my own heart," he quipped with a chuckle, and he meant it too.

The girl was slim but not overly so, and her mostly flannel and jeans clothes left enough to the imagination to make her interesting.

She wore her straight, black hair short, barely shy of her shoulders, and the right side was shaved to reveal a couple of tattoos. One, in particular, trailed down to her neck. It looked like a black snake with wings draped down the body.

He was curious as to whether it was supposed to mean anything. He had a couple himself. One on his back read *Semper Fidelis* in strong black letters and his shoulder boasted his regiment's shield. There were a couple more here or there, mostly work he'd chosen without thought while he was drunk and then regretted it almost immediately.

Still, they were remnants of what he had done and been in the past and he'd never looked into removing them, no matter how embarrassing they might be. He was who he was, mistakes and all.

"So, how come you're with us here, Taylor?" Alex asked as she finished the whiskey sour and wiped her hands on a washcloth.

"You have all kinds of questions, don't you?" he asked

with a small smile.

"Hey, I make most of my money on tips and people tip better when the cute bartender is talkative," she replied smoothly like she had expected the question. "So, will you answer the question or do you prefer that I ask another?"

"Nah, I'm good." His smile remained in place. "Well, I'm here to start a business. I only arrived today and I'm in the mood for a drink. How about you—what brings you out to Vegas?"

"Would you believe that I was shooting for Hollywood and landed in Vegas instead?" she asked and leaned closer.

"I have no reason not to believe you." For once, he phrased his words carefully. "I would be curious to hear what you hoped to accomplish in Hollywood. Or maybe still want to accomplish. You look like you have the will to succeed in what you're interested in."

"Well, thanks for that." She laughed. "Anyway, I lied. I have a scholarship to finish my bachelor's degree in econ at the University of Nevada, Las Vegas, and I'm here merely to pay the bills before I graduate."

"Well, I guess you could still make your way to Hollywood and make a name for yourself as an ass-kicking economist or…uh, entrepreneur, something like that," he said, then took a sip of his beer first and another of the whiskey sour. "It depends on where you want to end up, I guess."

"How about you?"

"Well, I won't go too deep into my past, but I do have a degree in mechanical engineering I intend to use."

"Paid for by the GI bill?"

"How'd you know?"

Alex shrugged. "I know a military man when I see one. It's like you guys look uncomfortable in clothes that aren't uniforms."

"Fair enough, but the Corps paid for my degree between tours," he explained. "They liked having someone who knew what they were doing running things from the front."

"I can understand that." She tilted her head and smiled her wide, genuine smile. "Did you see any action?"

"You have no idea." He deliberately stopped at that. It was better to keep some mystery and avoid the subject of where he'd seen the action. His train of thought was broken, however, when the entrance doors were yanked open and the ruckus the new arrivals caused in the parking lot spilled in.

They brought it quickly into the bar. There were six of them with expensive suits, haircuts, and watches and looked like they had left drunk behind about three hours before and were very good friends with stupid drunk.

"Hey, man, they can kick us out of the party," one of the frat boys shouted. "But they can't kick the party out of us!"

"Hey, barkeep," another shouted and swaggered to the bar. "I'll need shots of tequila for my boys, and if you're willing to add strip club to this bar, there'll be one hell of a tip in it for ya."

The way he grabbed his crotch clearly indicated that he didn't mean a gratuity. The others in the group laughed uproariously. One fell back to land on one of the nearby stools and managed to topple it and a handful of others to the floor in a loud clatter. It only served to make them laugh harder.

"Fucking hell," Alex muttered and shook her head. "It would have to happen when my bouncer's out for the night."

"Murphy's fucking law," Taylor agreed and watched the group head toward one of the nearby tables. "Do you guys have rules against overserving in this establishment?"

"Of course," she said, still scowling. "They'll start getting rowdy if I don't get them out of here now, though."

His gaze followed the bartender's hands as they inched slowly toward something under the bar and out of sight. The way her wrist arched told him there was more than likely a shotgun there, and one probably sawed off.

He didn't need to see it to know it was well short of the legal minimum.

"There's no need for bloodshed here tonight," he told her softly and kept his gaze lowered. "There's too much paperwork for everyone involved in something like that. I'll toss them out for you."

Alex eyed him. "Are you sure?" She looked uncertain.

"Don't worry about it," he said. "You might want to call the cops first, though."

She nodded and retrieved her phone from her pocket as he turned to face the six men who still hadn't realized that they wouldn't actually get their drinks. They probably wouldn't notice it for a while.

He would still throw them out. There was no way to enjoy his drink when other patrons made assholes of themselves.

"Hey, do you have our shots?" the man who had placed the order asked. He looked at Taylor and adjusted the sapphire cufflinks he wore.

"Do I look like I'm carrying shots?" he asked. "No. I'm here to escort you and your friends off the premises. Go home and sleep it off. You guys will have a killer hangover as it is."

"Come on, you can't throw us out. We just got here," the man said, pushed to his feet, and stood. Taylor winced when he smelt the gin the guy had clearly swilled all night from a foot away.

"I can and I will, but I don't have to if you and your friends leave nicely," he said, his stare unyieldingly.

"You can throw six of us out?" the drunkard asked and laughed derisively. "You look like a red-headed Jason Momoa—you know from the Aquaman movie? But...uh, shorter." He leaned forward, his eyes squinting. "With freckles."

He had no idea what was funny about that, but the man's cronies clearly did.

"Hilarious," he said and his voice dripped with sarcasm. "Tell it to me again on your way out."

"Look, buddy." the drunk said placed his hand on Taylor's shoulder. "You won't throw six of us out. We'll beat the shit out of you and stay. So go ahead and get us our shots and remind the bartender about the tip I have for her."

"Yeah, she's steaming."

"I want to see her pick a beer cap up with her cheeks."

He shook his head. "Your call, bubba."

The man barely had time to blink before the volunteer bouncer snapped his forehead forward into his nose with a loud and satisfying crack. The drunkard stumbled back and blood seeped between the fingers that clutched his nose as he screamed in pain.

A second man tried to surprise Taylor from the right. He pivoted in place, arced his elbow out, and drove it against his attacker's cheekbone hard enough to break the skin.

That would inevitably be annoying to clean up, he realized. He made a mental note to maybe hold off on the kinds of wounds that would make them bleed.

A third tried to stand from his seat, but a quick shove on his head thrust him down again. The three others charged simultaneously. One of them had picked up a pool cue from the nearby table.

The closest assailant was off-balance and needed only a snapped punch to the jaw to fell him. He sprawled against the table, stunned. The second tried to deliver a blow that sailed hopelessly wide of where Taylor stood without him even needing to dodge. Clearly, he had underestimated how inebriated they were—as had they, apparently.

He hammered his fist into the man's gut and scowled darkly when the idiot with the cue thumped his improvised weapon across his back.

Taylor looked over his shoulder and raised an eyebrow. "You know you'll have to pay for that, right?"

The would-be attacker tried to back away but tripped over one of his fallen comrades and landed hard with a groan.

"Pathetic," Taylor grumbled, shook his head, and turned to face the one who was still unscathed and more or less conscious. "Get up."

The man simply gaped at the ginger Momoa in terror

from the seat he had been pushed into and shook his head vigorously.

"Get up or I'll pick you up and carry you out. I'll have to carry these five dumbasses out too and would appreciate the help, so get the fuck up or I'll toss you out first, then these fuckers out on top of you. ".

The young man stood hastily, reached down to help one of his bleeding friends to his feet, and dragged him toward the exit. He lasted until the door but when he tried to open it, he lost his balance and collapsed under the weight of his comrade.

"Fucking useless." Taylor grasped two of the men who were still conscious. He had a little help from them churning their feet as he hauled them to the door. When he reached it, a police car drew into the parking lot.

An officer stepped out, confused by what he saw. He looked from Taylor to the guys he could see. "What happened here?"

"These are drunkards you can book on drunk and disorderly charges if you like," Taylor replied. "Although from the looks of their seven-thousand-dollar watches, I'd say their bails will be paid by morning."

"That sounds about right," the cop said. "Who are you again?"

"Hey, Hank," Alex said and stepped over the unconscious characters on the doorstep. "Sorry about this. Meet Taylor, our temporary bouncer."

"Huh," Hank said. "It's nice to see you're okay, Alex. What happened to Marcus?"

"He had a family emergency," she explained. "His kid

had an allergic reaction and he needed to drive her to the hospital. Taylor here offered to fill in while he was away."

"Oh, okay then. Tell him if he needs anything to call, all right?" The officer gestured to his partner to help him drag the frat boys out of the bar and toward the cruiser. "You all take care now, ya hear?"

"Thanks for your help, officer," Taylor said, his arms folded over his chest in true bouncer style.

"Hey, call me Hank. Any friend of Alex's is a friend of mine."

"I appreciate that, Hank. Have a nice evening."

"You too." He sighed. "I'll be up all night with the paperwork on this one."

"Good luck with that." Taylor turned and returned to the bar when a second cruiser pulled up to take the other two.

Alex grinned from ear to ear. She'd already cleaned what had been spilled by the frat kids. "Thanks for your help, Taylor."

"I only want to be able to drink in peace," he replied.

"Well, if you're in the mood, I think I can talk the kitchen into whipping up a thank-you meal," she said. "They owe me various favors I can cash in."

He eyed her. "I'm always in the mood for free food."

"Awesome. Sit and enjoy your drinks and I'll be right back."

CHAPTER FIVE

I t wasn't a particularly long night.

He hadn't originally intended to stay too long, but he stuck around the bar for a few hours and told himself it was to make sure Alex would be okay while the bouncer was out. Eventually, they had word that the man would be at the hospital all night and they would close Jackson's early since there wasn't that much happening anyway.

Most of the time was spent getting to know Alex. She was a sharp character, much more than merely a pretty face, and she had skills behind the bar too. For a while, she had tried to push him into taking a few drinks for free, but he'd been a little more insistent on paying his tab as well as a generous tip.

In the end, she hadn't resisted too strenuously. She had a scholarship but being in college was still expensive and she couldn't afford to be too generous.

Besides, she'd arranged a meal for him on the house, and damned if it hadn't been one hell of a meal. Taylor was a fan of the classics, and a plate of medium-rare steak, baked potato, veggies, and a side of fries left him more than satisfied.

Not only that, she had been good company. It had been a fun night despite the fact that it ended with his return to his hotel room alone to sleep it off. He would definitely return to Jackson's in the near future.

They had a breakfast menu that seemed worth exploring.

But that was probably not an option today. He had business to attend to and he was supposed to meet with the realtor who would show him a list of possible locations where he would be able to begin to establish his little business.

He still had no idea what he would call it, but various ideas floated in his mind. Most involved some kind of mech-based pun—the kind that would get a kick and an eye-roll out of the guys who worked on and in the mech suits themselves.

Taylor was up at seven in the morning, wasted no more time than necessary in the shower, and adjusted his hair and trimmed his beard into something that looked at least somewhat respectable. He still resembled a ginger lumberjack but that wouldn't change anyway, so there was no point in any effort to portray himself as something he was not.

Before long, he was dressed in a blue button-down shirt and slacks that matched the dark brown of his boots and already waited outside with sunglasses in place to escape the glare of the early morning sun.

He was precisely on time—eight in the morning—after a hurried indulgence in the continental breakfast provided at the hotel.

The realtor was not on time. He knew he couldn't expect civilians to subscribe to the same time standards as military folk, but there was still something of a tick in his right cheek when she finally arrived ten minutes late, driving one of the newer Lincoln MKZ models.

She slid out of the car and circled it to greet him. The woman was tall and looked like she had once had aspirations of being a model. The idea stuck because it possibly explained her blonde hair done in a perfect ponytail, her expensive glasses, and the tan pantsuit that was supposed to both display her professionalism as well as show off a little something else. The outfit was completed by five-inch heels.

Taylor checked his watch pointedly as she joined him on the sidewalk.

"I know, I know. I'm sorry I'm late," she said and adopted the flustered look she was obliged to. "Morning traffic around here is hell. I'm Heather—Heather Mills. It's nice to meet you."

"Taylor McFadden, and don't worry about it," he replied, took her hand, and shook it firmly.

"Wow, that's quite a grip you have there, Mr. McFadden," she said and laughed. "Well, we can get started right away unless you want to get breakfast or coffee first?"

"I'm good, thanks." He strode toward the passenger door.

"Yes, you are," she said under her breath.

He called over his shoulder, "What was that?"

She smiled. "Nothing. Let's get going. I have a few prime places I think you'll really like."

He stepped into the car and settled into the comfortable leather seat. "Well, I'm yours for the day so we might as well get started."

She sighed softly as she slid behind the wheel, pulled the vehicle out onto the road, and began to talk him through the list she'd made.

The first few places she showed him were clearly those on her docket with the highest price range that she needed to get out of her way as quickly as possible.

They were offices, for the most part, and while he didn't doubt that they were built for business, there were probably all kinds of problems that wouldn't be listed until after papers were signed. Not only that, they simply weren't suitable for what he had in mind.

Either way, Taylor wasn't interested. He preferred the places that would be cheaper to get his hands on outright so he would have a say in how they were remodeled later. It meant he would look at a long list of locations he wasn't interested in before they reached the metaphorical meat of the deal, but he didn't mind. Heather was good enough company.

She had the look of a former cheerleader about her as she moved quickly and tried to keep his attention on her the entire time, even when discussing the property itself. She had jokes that were marginally funny and a solid, confident way about her that he enjoyed.

It might have been a practiced look for her, one that made her successful enough in the industry and allowed her to work on helping businesses get set up instead of showing off houses and the like.

They took a quick break for lunch before they headed

into some of the less popular locations. He told her he was mostly doing research for the moment, which allowed him to simply say he wanted to move on after taking quickly scribbled notes on the various premises.

He had a firm idea of what he wanted, however, and if he saw it, he would take it, research be damned.

"How is it that you settled on the idea for this business of yours?" Heather asked as they drew into their third location of the afternoon. "Obviously, inspiration strikes any one of us but it seems like you put both time and energy into what you have in mind."

"I can't say it wasn't always a dream of mine to own my own company and be my own boss," he responded almost before he had time to think about it. "The idea, though, is that I've worked with these mech suits before and I know my way around them. It's a growing market that has considerable room for expansion, one I have a very particular in on."

"How do you mean?" she asked and put the parking brake on.

"Well, the kind of in that many people look for is a conversation starter with the clientele," he replied, opened his door, and stepped out of the car. "Once you have that, there's an opening to already break into the market. Given that I know many of the people making and repairing the suits where they're actually used the most, there's my in. All I need is a supply for their demand, and I need a location for that."

"You seem like you have it all worked out," she said and donned her sunglasses.

"There's no point in pushing into something like this if you don't have your steps planned carefully," he replied.

"Well, this property isn't quite like the rest." She returned to business. "Which makes it unique, I guess. Here on the East Side, you'll have much more space for a lower rate, but there's a fair amount of gang activity in the neighborhood so you might want to think about that. The insurance will go through the roof if you have issues."

"I need the space and I can look out for myself," he said with a chuckle. "Space large enough for the workshop, maybe room to set up living quarters for myself and maybe someone else."

"Interesting," she replied.

It was a strip mall, basically, with what appeared to have been an erstwhile grocery store next to a defunct car shop.

There was more than sufficient space inside, and while it did look a little run down, the foundation was solid and the building made mostly of prefab, so many people wouldn't like the aesthetic.

Having been around buildings like it for the past few years, though, he had absolutely no problem with the appearance. In fact, it had definite advantages.

Prefab buildings looked like shit but they were durable, which explained why a building that appeared to have been abandoned for years was still standing and in good condition.

"I like this one," Taylor said after his inspection. "There's a good feel about it. It's a little run down, obviously, and could use a little polishing, but I think this is the one for me."

"Really?" Heather looked a little bewildered. "I should tell you that whatever you bring in here will probably be stolen at least twice a year. No matter what you save, anything around here will cost you at least twice as much."

"I understand that and again, I can take care of myself. It has potential. I'll buy it."

She smiled, blinked, and paused when she realized what he'd said. "Do you mean rent it?"

"No." He turned and fixed her with a firm gaze. "*Buy it.*"

"Oh." She made another hasty study of the property as if that would help her make the mental adjustment. "I'll...uh, look into that. I think I need to make a call to my office first to see if the owners are willing to sell rather than rent."

"Anything you need to do," he turned back and focused on the interior. The potential was high and as long as he set up a solid defensive perimeter, he would feel comfortable having his little shop there.

The other benefit was more than enough space for expansion.

The realtor stepped outside into the sun, pulled her phone out of her purse, and hurriedly dialed what he assumed was her office number. He had no doubt that the owners would want to get this place off their hands for a single cash payment instead of having to deal with folks who didn't know how to protect themselves from the criminal element and who would leave as soon as the lease expired, if not before.

He moved closer to the window to listen as she began to speak to someone on the other end of the line.

"He says he wants to buy it," she said. "Yes. He looked

me dead in the eye and wanted a price to purchase the whole property. No, I'm not kidding and yes, he… Well, he looks respectable, anyway. He has that look about him."

Huh? What look?

"Yeah, I guess he's hot but he has the body to show for it too if you know what I mean," she continued. He grinned and assumed she didn't know he could hear the conversation. "He's a redhead and has a nice beard too… No, I don't know if the carpet matches the drapes. *Yet.*"

Taylor tilted his head, a little surprised. These people must have one hell of a solid working relationship if they were willing to talk that way.

Or maybe they were simply good friends. Still, he didn't mind it so much as he was curious about what she meant by "yet."

"Look, text me the details on what the owners want… Oh, okay, I think he'll like that," she said. "Anyway, text me the details, and I'll see if I can close on the deal today. He seems like that kind of guy, yes… Yes, on a date. A girl has to eat after all. He's staying in a hotel, so maybe I can be a kind of good Samaritan and offer him a place to rest his head for the night… Yes, both heads. I'm not that good a Samaritan."

That *did* sound like a plan. He grinned

She hung up and entered the building again. Her flushed cheeks looked like she had a decided touch of the desert sun.

"Okay, I had a chat with my office," she said, still oblivious to the fact that he had listened in. "Anyway, the owners are interested in selling, and their standing price for the whole property is around one-point-five million."

"That's no good," Taylor said. "There's potential but I'll cover the insurance and repair costs on virtually everything out of pocket—unless they want to pay for that too? We're talking seriously basement prices here."

"I'm sure I can get them down to one-point-two—" she started to say, and he shook his head again.

"I know they want to get rid of the place as quickly as possible without trouble from the local zoning folks and before I can even have an inspection team in here," he said, moved closer, and placed a hand on her shoulder.

She uttered a small sigh as she removed her sunglasses and looked into his eyes.

"What did you have in mind?" she asked, her tone breathy.

"Tell the owners that if they're willing to sign the papers today before the close of banking hours, I'll have a wire transfer of a solid million in their accounts before the day is out."

"Huh... A million?" she asked and still looked a little distracted.

"I'll bet you make about six percent on the commission of these sales, right?" Taylor asked, and she nodded. "That's sixty grand for you. Not bad for a day's work, especially since it looks like it's been a fucking long minute since they've been able to get any money out of this place. This is good for you, your clients, and me too."

She nodded. "I'll get them on the phone and see what I can do."

Exactly as he'd suspected, the owners were in a desperate hurry to offload the property.

Judging by the call Heather made, they leapt at the

opportunity to get it off of their hands, even for what could only be described as a garbage price.

The two of them headed to the realtor office where paperwork already waited for signature, and it wasn't long before hands were shaken and keys exchanged hands.

It was, he decided, a very good day.

And it looked like it would be a good night as well. The business concluded, he and Heather moved on to enjoy a dinner at a higher-end steak joint.

When the time came for the bill to be paid, she quickly collected the small leather holder containing his half of the bill.

"It's a tax write-off," she explained and proffered what looked like a corporate credit card to pay for the meal, which had included a full bottle of red shared between them.

"Are you sure?" he asked.

"Absolutely," she replied. "Do you have a place to spend the night? Should I drop you back at your hotel?"

"Well," Taylor said and grinned. "I wouldn't decline if a Good Samaritan were to offer me a place to lay my head for the night."

Her eyes widened and her mouth dropped open.

"Yeah, I was listening," he said with a small smirk. "So, will you offer me a place to lay my head?"

She bit her bottom lip and toyed with her hair before she nodded slowly.

"You'd better ask them to bring your car around then," he said, stood lazily, and offered her a hand to stand when the waiter returned with her card.

"That sounds like a plan," she whispered breathlessly.

CHAPTER SIX

Although a long night, it wasn't altogether unproductive. Heather did have a nice apartment to match her luxury car, which confirmed exactly how effective she was at her job. He didn't want to make any assumptions.

Besides, it wasn't like they spent much time examining the decor. It was a quick drive from the restaurant to her home.

From there...well, there wasn't much talking either.

With that said, it was a pleasant night for them both, but when morning came, Taylor woke before her. A quick glance assured him that she would sleep in for a while. He was both disappointed and smug at the idea that she needed time to recover.

That aside, she would celebrate closing a rather large deal, whereas he still had business to attend to.

She was still asleep when he finished his shower and there was no point in waiting for her to wake up. What would he say? That he wanted to see her again and they had a special connection?

The choice really was an easy one. There was no alteration to the plan. If she wanted to have fun, he was all for that, but he wasn't there for a long-term commitment.

And from the look of the ring he had seen on the floor when he woke up—he assumed it had fallen out of her pocket when they were undressing the night before—she already had a commitment, although he wasn't sure how long-term it was.

No way would he have moved forward had he known of the ring.

He was out before eight in the morning and used his phone to call an Uber. His truck was still in the garage of the hotel but he didn't want to drive around with all his most expensive belongings in the back. He might have to rent a car or maybe find a lease vehicle that gave better mileage in the city.

On impulse, he chose not to head directly to the hotel. Instead, he made a quick trip to a nearby diner that had a special on waffles.

"That sign looks permanent," the Uber driver said as they pulled up in the parking lot. "It seems like they've had a special on waffles for the past three or four months."

"Then they're probably good at it. Thanks for the ride, man."

"Hey, be sure to leave a good review," the young man said, and he nodded although he hadn't known there was a way to leave reviews. He had been out of it for a while and there were quite a few things he wanted—and needed, apparently—to catch up on.

"Uh...yeah, sure. Thanks again." He patted the kid on the shoulder before he exited the car.

He would leave a good review for him. There weren't too many things he liked from the people who were in the driving business. One of them was keeping their mouth shut for the duration of the drive, and the kid had fulfilled that to a T. People needed to be rewarded for that shit.

Taylor stepped into the diner and gave it a cursory inspection. It had a distinct eighties feel and even the waitress' uniform had the right look.

"Hi there, darling. Are you looking for breakfast?" the woman asked in an accent that was distinctly from Georgia. He couldn't tell if it was faked or not.

"Yeah, that's what I'm here for," he said. She sounded a little too perky this early in the morning. There was enough time for him to have coffee, and while he was energetic enough, he certainly wasn't a morning person. A little caffeine was definitely in order.

"Well, we're having a special—"

"A special on waffles I see," he said. "I'll go with that, plus bacon, eggs, and coffee."

"Coming right up, sugar." She smiled, turned, and passed the order on to the kitchen behind her before she poured coffee and left it on the counter for him to add sugar or cream as he liked.

He ignored the brew for the moment. It was the waitress who had his attention.

"How long have you worked here?" he asked and leaned toward her.

"Why do you ask, hon?" she responded and mirrored his movement.

"You don't sound like you're from around here, is all," he said. "I have to say, I love the accent. Georgia, right?"

"You have a good ear," she said and regarded him with a curious expression. "Savannah, actually. Where are you from?"

"Wisconsin."

"Damn, that's a good way away," she said and laughed. "How are you handling the heat around here?"

"Well, I've spent time in deserts around the world, so I think that settled me well enough in the kind of heat you guys have." He chuckled.

"Where have you been?" she asked. "Around the world, I'll bet."

"Well...Kelly," he said as he read her name on the tag on her chest, "I'd be happy to tell you about it. Maybe over dinner when you have a little more time and aren't working?"

"Oh, sugar, that would be great," she said. "There is one small problem, though. My husband works in the kitchen, see? And he would not take kindly to it if he knew you were hitting on me, a good-looking man like yourself."

"Fair enough." Taylor pulled back with a nod.

If the night before was any indication, the sanctity of marriage didn't appear to be a big issue around there, even though he didn't quite like the idea. With that said and since they were talking about the same man who would prepare his food, he decided not to risk it one way or another.

He did not want "accidental" food incidents engineered by an overprotective husband.

"Don't think you can't flirt with me, though," Kelly said

with a laugh. "A woman in my position learns to enjoy the ego boost whenever she can."

"Understood," he said with a smile. "This is some good coffee."

"I made it myself," she said with a wink.

The food was ready rather quickly, with the waffles still steaming and melting the butter next to the bacon and eggs. He couldn't afford to spend all day there, though, and as much as he wanted to spend time with Kelly and explore her unique take on being married to someone at work, he did have business to tend to.

His time would be better devoted to working on getting his little operation off the ground.

Taylor now owned the property, but he reminded himself that there was still a slew of paperwork he needed to address. The taxes needed to be looked at and there were more than enough inspections that had to be done before he could initiate the repairs. He would probably do most of those himself since he knew his way around prefab.

When he'd finished his food and his coffee, he left the customary twenty percent tip. He didn't want to seem like a stingy customer but also didn't want to appear overly generous either. She likely made most of her money from the tips, which explained her willingness to indulge in the flirting.

He didn't judge her for using those tactics but at the same time, she would have to work a little harder than that if she wanted to hold his attention.

"Come back soon, sugar," she called after him as he left. He raised a hand in farewell, his focus already on his phone to call an Uber. If he was lucky, he would get the one that had dropped him off.

Some people liked working in the field. They said heading out into the world and talking to people was a good way to get ahead in life since it developed your people skills. When you could handle people, you could suck up to bosses better.

Niki knew that ass-kissing was a legitimate way to get ahead in life, but it wasn't something she liked doing at all. It wasn't that she looked down on people who did it. Well, maybe she did, but it was more a matter of jealousy than anything else. Kowtowing wasn't in her blood so she didn't like it. It simply wasn't something she was capable of and, to herself at least, she could confess to being a little envious of those who could.

Thankfully, she was a good enough worker to push ahead on her own. It had taken a while longer than it could have, but she now had her own task force and looked at a way up the ladder if she was interested. For now, though, she kept the citizens of America safe.

Her biggest challenge was that she simply didn't like to interact too much with people.

They had all seen way too many TV shows and had the wrong ideas of how law enforcement was supposed to work, especially at the federal level. She tried to be understanding of their misconceptions and had even attempted to use that on a number of occasions to help her push forward on cases in the past.

It hadn't always gone well, but they hadn't backfired the way she had imagined they would. As it turned out, most people were more afraid of a federal agency than they needed to be and were happy to merely be left alone as much as possible. It truly was weird how the feeling was mutual sometimes.

But in this case, she needed to be out in the open. Hunting military people was the worst since they were inevitably the best at covering their tracks. Finding McFadden had proven to be a pain in her ass and forced her to go back to basics, which meant interviewing the people who had interacted with him in the past.

There was a long list—most of them in the military and who knew nothing of his whereabouts since his official discharge, as he'd moved off base.

But the woman who had acted as his therapist before he was released from military service was as good a place to start as any. Niki didn't think McFadden would do much in the way of talking to professionals, but if the woman was as good as the length of her time working with the military indicated, she had to know something about where he might have disappeared to.

Once again, she mentally cursed the various unavoidable complications that had prevented her from locating the man immediately after he'd been signed off. Desk had made her thoughts on that clear—mainly that she felt she was avoiding it deliberately, which might be accurate, at least to some degree.

But all kinds of crap had hit the proverbial fan—crap she had to deal with and couldn't delegate—and she didn't trust anyone else to approach the man and make the kind of assessment she knew was imperative.

He was...odd, and she needed to know it wasn't the kind of odd that would blow her efforts, hard work, and all she'd accomplished into the garbage pile.

That delay had led to another infernal delay while she tried to locate him. This visit to the doctor would put an end to wasted time. She had to think positive.

It was a nice little property, she noted as she studied the doctor's location. Hopefully, it would also short-cut her trail to the man she needed to find. The small building in the suburbs held a handful of businesses and offices. It seemed like the kind of venue where people set up a ballet studio for kids where parents could leave them for a few hours while they went to book club or the bar or whatever it was that suburban types liked to do.

Niki needed to find out more about what people were like—normal people, that is. If she wanted to complain about them thinking she was a walking cliché based on the most recent procedural that they happened to come across, she needed to react to them like they weren't walking clichés from the sitcoms she watched.

She sighed, rubbed her temples before she moved into the building, and removed her sunglasses as she stepped into the shrink's practice.

"Good morning!" the secretary said in a voice that was seriously too cheerful for this early in the day. "I'm Jasmine. How can I heal you today?"

"Hey, creepy greeting, Jasmine," she responded and waited for the confused look to slip from the woman's face before she continued. "I need to have a chat with Dr. Bedford."

"Do you have an appointment?"

"I do not," she replied, drew her badge out, and placed it on the desk. "I do need to speak to her, though, so if she has time to spare, I would really appreciate it. Tell her it's Special Agent Niki Banks."

"Of course, one moment, please," Jasmine said and picked her phone up as Niki moved to one of the chairs in the waiting room. If the good doctor didn't want to talk to her, that was one hundred percent all right, but the agent wanted her to be compliant.

And that would only happen if she wasn't overly pushy.

Thankfully, the wait only lasted about five minutes before the door of the office opened and a woman in a grey pantsuit stepped outside. She was attractive, Niki decided, in a kind of severe librarian way.

"Special Agent Banks. I'm sorry to keep you waiting," Bedford said, took her extended hand, and shook it. "I was finishing off an early lunch. A person in my position needs to take breaks whenever possible."

"I appreciate that—and you taking the time out of your busy schedule to see me," she said although she meant little of it. "Could we speak in your office?"

"Of course." The doctor guided her into the office she had exited. Niki took a seat and looked at her over the rather large desk.

The entire room was stacked full of diplomas and plaques of recognition, she noted. There wasn't much space for pictures of happy patients, she supposed, in the field of psychology.

"How can I help you, Special Agent?" Bedford asked.

"I have questions regarding one of your former patients," she said and pretended that she needed to check her phone to refresh her memory. "A Taylor McFadden?"

"Oh," the woman said. "I haven't been a part of his treatment for a while now. Almost two months, actually."

"Yes, I can see that. However, I have it on good authority that you maintained a personal relationship with him after you signed off on his treatment."

"I don't know who your sources are—"

"Trust me, they are solid," she said and kept her voice steady and even. "Now I'm not too up to date on the regulations surrounding doctors in your position but I'll go ahead and guess that maintaining social ties with former patients is…what's the word—unethical?"

The doctor leaned forward and her face suddenly revealed a change of emotion. "I…fine. What do you want to know?"

Niki raised an eyebrow. "How do you know that's not what I want to talk about?"

"Because the FBI doesn't investigate ethics concerns," Bedford replied. "How can I help you, Special Agent?"

"I only need to know where McFadden went after he completed his treatment with you."

"I don't know. I don't make it a habit to keep tabs on my patients after they're done with their therapy."

"Again, I have it on good authority—"

"Look, when I signed off on his therapy, he asked me out," the woman explained and kept her voice low. "We went on two or three dates but he didn't call me after that. Last I heard, he planned to move to Vegas."

Her eyebrows rose. "You slept with that hot mess? I would think someone in your particular position would have better taste."

"Better taste, absolutely," the doctor retorted. "Better options? Not a chance. How many guys do you know who want to fuck a therapist?"

She nodded. The doctor had a good point.

"Either way, we were both in it for a little connection-free fun and that was what we got," Bedford said. "Besides, I don't know if you've ever met him, but Taylor... Well, there are many redeeming qualities that go with the hot mess."

Niki stared at her for a moment, then shook her head. She really didn't want to know. "Well, there's really no accounting for taste, I guess. Vegas, you said."

Bedford nodded. "Regarding the...ethics?"

"Like *you* said, it's not the FBI's job to look into that," she said with a shrug and pushed from her seat. "Thanks for your time, Dr. Bedford. I'll show myself out."

CHAPTER SEVEN

Taylor abhorred paperwork. He hated bureaucracy in general, but paperwork was a particular pet peeve of his.

He could acknowledge that people who made their living making sure everything was up to code were the bedrock of everything that made modern society livable, and he even appreciated that.

That didn't change the fact that he hated it, though. More than a few had gone on record as saying that men like him were fossils and relics of an archaic past who were only necessary in this day and age because most people weren't stupid enough to throw themselves in the line of fire like he did. He could appreciate that too and accept that there was some truth to it.

Courage and stubbornness were often mistaken for stupidity since all three resulted in one standing one's ground against insurmountable odds or putting oneself into the line of fire, to begin with.

He didn't think their train of thought lacked merit.

In the same way, he appreciated the need for bureaucrats and pencil-pushers in the world while he hated the fact that he needed to be a part of their world in order to get anything done.

In all honesty, he felt more drained after a morning spent finalizing all the paperwork for his budding business than he had after three days in the Zoo. He needed a drink and food and thankfully, lunch was the opportunity for both.

Of course, he had more business to look into during the meal but this particular aspect was something he actually looked forward to.

As he still hadn't had time to rent a car, another Uber ride dropped him off at the Luxor, where Bungees had said he wanted to meet. He had never thought of the man as a gambler in any sense of the word, which explained his confusion as to why he had asked to meet at one of the better-known casino hotels on the Strip.

Either way, he was more curious to see what exactly his old friend was doing there than he wanted to avoid the touristy spots in the city, so he tipped his driver and stepped inside the pyramid-shaped building. He moved past the front desk with enough purpose to make sure that none of the bellboys and desk clerks had any reason to stop him. From there, he headed into the casino where he could see his friend waiting for him at one of the many, many bars to be found on the floor.

When they had been drunk on one occasion, Robert "Bungees" Zhang had defined himself as "Jet Li, but a little chunkier and with less hair." He had then proceeded to say it wasn't racist because he was a Chinese-American and used the definition himself.

Taylor wasn't a fan of the description, but it was appropriate. He did like most Jet Li films, and there were a couple of traits that matched Bobby to the man—except for the fact that he was built like a tight end with powerful shoulders and thick arms that distracted from the bulge in his stomach and waist areas.

Bungees shaved his head religiously and left only a bushy mustache to make him distinctive, which explained the second half of his description.

In fairness, it did make him hard to miss in a crowd. He was only a few inches shorter than Taylor was, and he looked bigger too. He had gotten into playful fistfights with the man and had repeatedly underestimated both the power behind his fists and the speed at which he could move.

The lesson had finally sunk in and he wouldn't make that mistake ever again. At least not while he was sober.

Thankfully, he was equally easy to see with his bright red beard and hair and his height. Bobby peeled away from the bar, spread his arms, and wrapped him in a hug tight enough to drag a groan from him as his ribs protested the strain.

"It's nice to see you again too, Bobby," Taylor grumped when he was finally lowered onto his feet. "It's been a while. What…a year?"

"A little more than that since I turned my papers in and headed Stateside," his friend said, returned to the bar, and ordered beers for the two of them. "You know, I couldn't stand to be out there anymore with people getting killed and fucked over by the corporate assholes who run the place in the background. I'd made a fucking mint while out there, helping them research their damn suits, so I bugged out."

"Fuck them." Taylor scowled, shook his head, and picked up the tall, frosty glass that had been placed before him. "Have you done anything interesting lately? You know, besides being the star of your own TV show?"

"Fuck no." Bobby chuckled. "I've gone to great efforts to make my life very uninteresting, and I intend to keep it that way."

"Is that why you're considering leaving the auto shop that has you working as the star of your own show?" Taylor raised an eyebrow.

"First of all, I'm not the star. I'm *one* of the stars," Bobby retorted acidly. He sounded like he had taken this issue up with others, and often too. "Secondly, they don't even pay us that well for appearing on the show. Obviously, the owner takes home a solid chunk of cash, but the way he's worked it out, we're still hourly and he only pays us time and a half per hour that we're on camera. And it's not like he does it so he pays us for the hours when they have the camera crew in the shop and then adds the half for everyone who was on the job. No, this bitch decides he'll actually look at the footage they've collected and literally times us to see how long we're in front of the camera and pays us for that."

"He sounds like a prolapsed asshole to me." He wasn't merely agreeing with his friend. The kind of people who underpaid their workers were the kind who deserved the same level of hell as those who answered their phone calls in the movie theater.

"Damn right." Bungees shook his head vehemently. "I've looked for a way out for a while and sure, there is any number of folks out there who wouldn't mind having someone with my resume on their team. The problem is they're generally not the kind of folks you want to work for, so I was simply waiting for the right offer to come along before you showed up."

He nodded. "Well, I would like to have you on my team. I have the property to start on the business now but I need to work on it a little before it's ready for...you know, large-scale work."

"I can dig that," the man said. "I have to say, it's good to see you out of that literal hellhole. After everything you've been through, you deserve a little uninteresting living too."

"I appreciate that." He patted him on the shoulder and downed the rest of his beer. "Now, what say you we get food and I can show you the full pitch, eh?"

"That sounds *good* to me." His friend returned the pat a little harder.

"Which brings me to my next question, I guess." Taylor inspected their surroundings, eying the slot machines dubiously. "Why the fuck did you choose a fucking casino for our lunch, anyway?"

"Excuse me!" a woman near them shouted and covered her son's ears. "Would you gentlemen please avoid using such foul language?"

Bobby laughed and shook his head. Taylor, for his part, curled the fingers of his right hand onto a loose fist and jerked it back and forth.

"The kid's not supposed to be on the casino floor anyway," he retorted. "Look at the fucking rules."

The woman was too flabbergasted to speak, and the two men decided to beat a hasty retreat before she had a case of the vapors.

"So?" Taylor asked.

"So what?"

"About why you chose a casino for our lunch meeting?"

"Oh, right," his friend laughed. "Well, casinos don't like to advertise it, but they want to make sure you spend all your money in the building. To encourage that, they make the drinks and food ridiculously cheap so you keep on gambling with as little a pause as possible. Their lunchtime buffets are the best." Bungees stopped a moment. "Well, some of them do still. Others require you to take a mortgage out on your home."

"Okay," he said and narrowed his eyes.

"Okay, where the fuck else will you find somewhere you can eat all you care to for a couple of hours for the low, low price of twenty bucks a pop?" Bobby demanded.

"Come on. The big TV star is skimping on food?" he asked, his tone joking.

"Don't hate. It's good food. I can and I will make the most of the cheap, good food they provide. Do you think it's easy to maintain a bod like this? It takes a ton of exercise and a ton of calories to keep me, and from the looks of it, *you*—well-muscled, paragon of manliness that you are— have a similar battle to maintain muscle mass."

"If you say so" Taylor shrugged his powerful shoulders as they purchased their lunch passes, which included a free pass for beer, wine, or select cocktails for only an additional fifteen dollars. They both selected that option, quickly chose their food from the buffet provided, and headed toward the tables.

It was still early enough that most of them were empty, but it was filling up slowly. The place would be packed in about an hour.

"So," Bobby said once they had made inroads on their meals. "Why don't you go ahead and give me the pitch?"

Taylor looked at him for a moment, gathering his thoughts. "It's not much of a pitch to make yet, I don't think," he said and wiped his mouth. "I intend to offer you better than what you're currently getting so will need a little input from you first. What kind of hours do you work? How much do you make?"

"Oh." The man grunted, took another mouthful, and chewed and swallowed quickly. "Again, I'm hourly, so it's basically as much work as I can get in. I've worked between forty- and sixty-hour weeks. I like what I do, and they do pay overtime at the shop, so I've made around... Well, last year, I pulled in a little over sixty grand in total."

"That's not bad. I think I can beat that, though. You wouldn't work on cars with me, though. Well, not exclusively anyway, but we could probably take custom jobs if they pay enough. We'll work on mech suits, power armor, and body armor, for the most part."

"They're the top of the current tech, so there's not really any way to beat that," Bobby nodded. "I have to admit, I've missed working on the suits, whether the entry-level ones or the power mech. Seriously, telling people how to use their fucking parking brakes while having a camera in my face all fucking day has worn on my last fucking nerve."

Taylor leaned back in his seat. "They've made the kind of advances in the tech that you wouldn't believe."

"Oh, don't get me wrong, I have kept up with the advances." His friend turned his attention to a pile of chicken wings and dug in. "They have these conventions that show off all the new tech, and I've chatted with the folks still in the Zoo to see if they have anything interesting to show me. But what kind of clientele are we talking about here? I can't imagine that there are enough people who have mech suits here in the States for you to make a living from it. At least not until those second-amendment guys get them to start selling to civilians."

"I've thought about that," Taylor admitted. "I've looked into the repair charges they have had to pay in the Zoo over the past couple of years and compared them to the prices of doing the repairs in the states. Not only are the parts cheaper to get here, but it will be cheaper for them to ship their suits and mechs out for us to work on."

"What happens when the corporations with a monopoly on what happens there lower prices to compete with you?" Bobby asked.

"I've researched it, and even if they lower the labor price, the cost of shipping that many parts would still force them to keep their prices above ours," Taylor explained. "Besides, you and I both know they make most of their money from repairing and replacing the mass orders the various governments in the area generate, so they won't bother trying to adjust for our rates. I've already been contacted by a few of my friends in the various merc companies that work out there, and they're ready to send us their suits in need of repair as soon as we've set up shop."

"That's always good news, I guess," the man said, leaned back, and folded his arms. "Where have you decided to set up shop, anyway?"

"A premises on the east side of town. Come on. I can show you."

"Are you crazy?" Bungees slapped his palm on the table and laughed. "We still have time on our lunch passes and I won't let mine go to waste."

Taylor shook his head and called one of the waitresses to bring him another beer. He had done well on the admittedly decent food, but he didn't have the appetite his friend had. If it were up to Bobby, they would have bought the 24-hour passes.

But he had a business to run and a potential employee to inspire, and he chose not to be too pushy as the man headed to the buffet to refill his plate.

Bungees understood what had happened to people in the Zoo. He had actually made a handful of trips in when they needed mechanics to move with the teams to repair the suits that constantly broke down back in the day.

His companion returned with another heaped serving of what looked like seafood this time. "Can I ask why you picked Vegas, of all places?"

"You already did," he replied, his eyes narrowed. "And I already answered."

"I wanted you to answer with a straight face and in person," the man responded and suddenly looked serious. "Was it the loose women or did you come because you missed me?"

Taylor laughed aloud. "Honestly, I want to stay as far away from any potential apocalypses as possible and hopefully scratch out a living."

His friend gave him an eye. "You know that deserts don't stop the goop, right?"

"Maybe not, but a desert is better than a lush, tropical area with tons of biomass. At the very least, it'll maybe slow it a little," Taylor pointed out. "And that's all you can really ask for. Now, finish your food. We have a full day ahead of us and I'd like to get started."

CHAPTER EIGHT

He had thankfully made sure they didn't drink enough to render them unable to drive. It was the kind of thing he had down to a science by this point. Even so, neither he nor Bobby had come in their own vehicles, which compelled them to hire someone to drive them to the hotel where Taylor was staying.

"Why didn't you bring a car to the casino?" Taylor asked when they were on their way to the hotel.

"Come on. Parking there is fucking expensive," Bobby reminded him and shook his head. "They make the money they lose on the cheap food and drinks any way they know how."

"Yeah, by having people gamble, right?" he said and looked around. His folks liked to take him and his brothers and sisters to Atlantic City and said it was as good if not better than Disney World in Orlando.

Once he was old enough, he'd actually thought about whether they might have lied to them. He'd never really reached a conclusion because part of him could see why they truly believed that might be the case.

For a kid, Disney World would be a magical experience but for an adult, the magic faded somewhat and all it was for them was a long day in the sun while surrounded by the bad costumes of beloved childhood characters. The rides could be fun, but that didn't make up for the uncomfortable heat and the thousands of people there to share the experience as well.

That wasn't to say it couldn't be a great experience so part of him also blamed his folks for lying to the kids. But he could understand why they had avoided the place. And honestly, Orlando had actually been quite a blast when he thought back on it.

But Vegas was nothing like Orlando. Well, no, that wasn't quite right. Vegas was like Orlando but turned up to a hundred, and everything came to the fore in the casinos themselves. Given where it was located in the middle of the Mojave, he had to admit it was an impressive sight.

Built mostly on money from organized crime, it was still a monument to what could be done if you wanted to make a profit without having the government interfere too much. It was the same spirit he tried to establish his own business on.

Admittedly, the laws were far more stringent now than they had been in the fifties and sixties, but there was still enough for him to work with as he headed off into this new adventure of his.

They reached the hotel, and Taylor took Bobby into the underground garage where his truck waited for him.

And there she was, as sleek and black as the darkest

darkness with the kind of improvements only people who loved machines could make.

Technically, he wasn't actually a mechanic, and his engineering degree helped him more with the delicate work that powered the armor and mech suits. Cars were comparatively antique and still retained the kind of machinery that had made the world go round in the past century.

But there was something strangely comforting when he worked on vehicles, made them go, made them work, and most importantly, made them better. The truck he'd purchased had been in a bad way, and after two months of tinkering and making her his own, she was something to see.

And Bobby could appreciate that. He uttered a low whistle when Taylor lifted the hood to give him a view of the V10 engine beneath it.

"You got your hands on a V10 diesel?" the man asked and ran his fingers lovingly over the engine. "I didn't think they made these babies anymore. They are tough to get to work but once you do, they last for fucking *ever*."

"I don't think they make them anymore either. Emission laws being what they are, it's hard for them to make anything this powerful that doesn't have an electric motor."

"Doesn't it?" Bobby sounded surprised.

"There's one in the back, but that's mostly to run all the electronics so the engine isn't overloaded," he explained. "But I think my piece de...however the fuck you pronounce that, is the transmission."

"Oh, yeah, automatic transmissions in the diesels are a pain in the ass." His friend leaned closer for a better look.

"Oh… I see what you did there…connecting a manual to the electric motor in the back, and from there…"

"Yeah, programmed as an automatic for when I don't feel like changing the gears myself," he said with a chuckle.

"Now that's… That's just fucking awesome." Bobby laughed and folded his massive arms over his chest as Taylor closed the hood again. "I bet you I could put in upgrades that would make your mouth water, though."

"I tell you what," Taylor turned to him. "You come and work with me and you'll be able to tinker with her all you like."

"Her?"

"Well, yeah. All the best vehicles have to have a name, and I decided that most ships are she, so why not her?" he asked.

"Seriously? You talk about a big black bastard that spews foul smoke and you don't think a *chick*, man."

"You've hung out with the wrong kind of chicks, then," Taylor retorted. "Anyway, I call her Liz—after Queen Elizabeth."

"That woman will outlive us all, I swear to God," Bobby grumbled. "How old is she now? Two hundred?"

"At least."

"Liz, though?" the man asked dubiously and scratched his head, his expression comically disgusted.

"What's wrong with Liz?"

Bungees shrugged as if the answer was obvious. "It's a shitty name for a car. Why not go with Liza? At least that calls up memories of a diamond in the rough kind of story around the car."

"What?"

Bobby raised an eyebrow. "Haven't you ever watched *My Fair Lady* with Rex Harrison and Audrey Hepburn?"

"I can't say that I have."

Bungees shook his head, sympathy in his eyes. "Such a lack of culture."

"Oh, and Liz is a truck, thank you very much," he pointed out, not liking the shot at his cultural sensibilities.

Both men slid in quickly and Taylor started her and pulled out of the garage.

"So, if you've had Liz all this time, why are you taking rides from strangers on the Internet?"

"First of all, strangers on the Internet have been perfectly delightful so far," Taylor countered.

"Probably because they were afraid you would use their bones to make your bread," Bobby pointed out.

"Well...that might have been it, but they were very quiet and respectful," he assured him. "My point, though, is that I have basically my whole life packed in the back of this truck. Three suits I managed to bring back with me, all my personal belongings that can't fit in a suitcase, and my suitcases too. While I have savings from my time in the Zoo, they won't replace most of that shit. Things have sentimental value."

"Is there *any chance* there's a stop between here and the fucking point?"

"What I'm trying to say is that I don't intend to drive everything I own around town like a fucking traveling circus," he snarked. "I needed a place to park it where it would be safe from folks trying to steal anything until I had a place to park it with a little more permanence."

"Oh," Bobby said. "I guess that makes sense, although

if I remember correctly, you said the place you bought for the business was somewhere in the east side of Vegas?"

"Yep," Taylor said, as they now headed in that very direction.

"Fuck me," his friend said with a smirk. "I do hope you're ready to fight for what's yours in there because you might actually have to."

"I've fought for my life and what was mine in the Zoo more times than almost fucking anyone," Taylor reminded him. "There's no reason why that should change now. Let someone come and try to steal my shit from my place and I'll crush their heads with my boots."

"I'd say you were full of shit, but I do remember that one time with the panther—"

"Was it a panther?" He narrowed his eyes as he tried to recall what had happened. "I thought it was a hyena."

"Who the fuck knows?" Bobby said. "We killed three or four zoos' worth of animals. Well monsters, the kinds that attacked us first."

"Zoos?"

"The... regular kind, not the Kudzu kind," Bobby said. "You know, lions, tigers, bears, oh my?"

"I can't remember having ever visited an actual zoo in my life, honestly. I knew they existed, of course, and people talked about it at school and the other kids went on field trips to the zoo for the day, but since Dad only wanted me to take over the shop from him, I ended up never going to one of them."

"That's some sad shit, dude."

He wasn't wrong, but although Taylor hadn't exactly

had the most traditional of childhoods, he didn't really mind.

People who had traditional childhoods went on to become lawyers and shop workers and the like. While some would say that was a good thing, he preferred his more exciting life to whatever it was that they lived.

As it was, if an apocalypse involving the Zoo ever came about, he was now outfitted with the skills and equipment he would need to protect himself and his, and that was worth exchanging the quiet life for, right?

He liked to think it was. And he knew people would agree with him once—if, he reminded himself—the armageddon in question started.

But that was a topic for another time. They now pulled into the property he had purchased and he stopped the vehicle and yanked on the parking brake.

Both men exited the truck and stood in silence for a moment as they stared at the strip mall.

He still had no idea what to name his business.

The place did not look great in the afternoon light. He doubted it would look good in any light, quite honestly, but thanks to his efforts in the morning, it had lights and running water without any problems, and that was all the start he needed.

Yes, electricity was definitely what he needed for now.

"It looks like shit," Bungees pointed out and raised an eyebrow.

"Yeah, I guess it does," he agreed. "But I own it all—the parking lots and everything, although I think I'll move the grocery store."

"The location is a crappy place to start a business in."

His friend continued with his assessment as if he hadn't spoken. "For one thing, all the clearly visible problems aside, there is an issue with crime in this area."

"I think you and I both know we can handle anything that comes our way."

The man nodded agreement.

"Think about it," Taylor continued. "Our business model is fairly unique, given that the product we sell won't require clients to come in and be impressed by our location. It'll be purely functional, and there's not that much we need for it to work itself out."

"I guess that's true, especially if we'll ship the suits out from the Zoo," Bobby concurred and rubbed idly at his chin.

"More importantly, the property came dirt cheap. And I mean dirt cheap. I persuaded them to cut a third off the price simply by offering to take it off their hands immediately."

"Do you think there might have been a reason for that?" his friend asked.

"Sure, one man's trash is another man's treasure," he replied and chuckled. "Anyway, my point is that it will lower our costs. We can do most of the functional repairs ourselves since we know how to work it and know what we need. Taxes and facilities are cheaper out here too."

"But insurance rates will go through the fucking roof."

"You're not wrong," he acknowledged. "I've looked into the pricing for this area to see what I can get that's cheaper for a location in development. I'll let you know what I find out, though."

"It sounds good." Bungees turned to him. "Now, I don't

want to be crass, but I do need to know about the money situation you have going. Obviously, I assume you have a good amount of seed money from your eighty or so trips into the Zoo."

"Eighty-three," he corrected him.

"Right. But I do need to know what I'd leave my current employment for. I know you won't have any specifics, but do you have anything basic to give me?"

Taylor nodded, retrieved his phone, and studied the numbers he had come up with while trying to determine if he could afford this kind of venture. "Well, these are some rough numbers, you know that. I won't pay you hourly, so we're looking at a solid hundred thousand annual base salary to start. Since I do want you here working and not mooching off my good fortune, there will be performance bonuses based on the jobs we finish. We won't have any of that fucking one and a half overtime pay. It sucks troll balls."

"Damn right," Bobby said and chuckled. "You know, I think we'll be able to do business. I'm still tied to the auto-shop with my contract, but I've disputed it with them for a while, mostly over severance pay. Now that I have leverage on my side, I'll be able to get them to pull back."

"That sounds good to me."

"Unfortunately, it means I'll need to keep working for them until my contract is up in a couple of weeks or so," the man continued. "I'll still be able to come here and work but it'll be on a part-time basis, so keep that in mind when you cut me my first couple of checks."

"Will do." The chances were he wouldn't be too picky about paying Bobby for his services. Good help was hard to come by, especially in this economy, and the man was taking a chance on this little venture as well.

"I think we can do business," Taylor offered his hand. It would have to be what they worked with for the moment until he could work up some actual contracts.

His friend took it and shook firmly.

"I'm looking to build something here," he continued as they called a cab to take Bobby home or to the auto-shop or wherever the fuck he wanted to go.

"And I'm looking forward to building it with you," Bungees replied.

CHAPTER NINE

He had sold the premises well to Bobby, mostly because he was sold on the location himself.

There was considerable work to put into it, but when was that ever not the case? It was miles cheaper than anything else he had looked at during his time with the realtor, and he would be able to lower the renovation costs by doing most of the repair work himself.

With that said, of course, he couldn't ignore the fact that there was one hell of a lot of work to go into the place. It was run down and wires stuck out all over like it had been destroyed by those who wanted the wiring inside but hadn't realized that prefab couldn't take copper. They would have had little use for the much cheaper CCA and fiber optic hybrid cabling that had a considerably lower price in the market.

He would need to look into replacing most of the wiring, although from the looks of the lights and the outlets, almost everything was still functioning.

It definitely would take considerable work but it would be worth it. Taylor returned to his truck and retrieved the tools that would enable him to start on it right away.

No time like the present.

His efforts started in the parking lot, of all places. All the talk about how this would be a dangerous location told him that security had to be his first concern, and honestly, it was the quickest thing to accomplish.

He had set up scores of night camps in the Zoo and the basics of it didn't change, even in this location. Obviously, he couldn't set up any turrets that would shoot people on sight. That was illegal, but it would be nice to know if he could expect to have company, which would give him time to prepare for it appropriately.

Seismic sensors wouldn't do in this location since cars and trucks were likely to set them off by driving across the road, but the basics of setting up camp remained the same. The motion sensors would be rigged to not trigger if something smaller than the average stray cat crossed their lines. He planned to set these up all around the property to give him a solid view of the surrounding area to a distance of about fifty yards.

It was quick work to rig the system up to one of his laptops to provide a second by second feed of the area as well as send updates to his phone should anyone breach the perimeter. He would need to find some way for it to recognize him and Bungees. It would be a pain to constantly receive notifications every time he and his employee moved around.

Either that or they would have to set it up only when

they weren't there or once Taylor had settled in for the night.

Still, it was better than nothing and more advanced than the average security system in this neighborhood, or so he assumed. There would be time to set cameras up that would give him a comprehensive view of the premises without needing to leave the shop.

That was the dream, really. He wouldn't have to interact with anyone unless he really, really wanted to.

He stepped out to where he'd parked the truck, started it, and moved it farther into the parking lot and closer to the grocery store section of the building. His phone buzzed before he had enough time to even start unloading his belongings.

A quick check told him that someone had already breached the perimeter. Not him, although there was a register of that too, but three figures that moved across the parking lot toward him.

Taylor sighed, pushed himself away from the vehicle, and turned to face the newcomers. All were dressed in what they might have thought was classy clothing. The reality was that no one would be brave enough to tell them it was way too shiny to be considered anything other than compensating for something.

No one needed to warn him that he was about to meet the local branch of organized crime in the neighborhood. Taylor couldn't see any distinctive gang affiliation, but there were enough cheap prison tats to confirm that they weren't there for a pleasant chat.

"Good afternoon, sir," one of the three—the apparent

leader—said and gave Liz an appreciative look before he turned to face him. His pleasant smile revealed a line of silver and gold grills that could hardly be considered reassuring. "We heard someone was moving into these here premises and thought we would welcome you to the neighborhood."

"Well, it's always nice to meet the neighbors," Taylor answered and made a careful study of the area to make sure it was only the three of them. All the men were armed but they kept their weapons hidden for the moment. "How long have you guys been around here?"

"Oh, we've been in and out of the area over the past few years, yeah," one of the others told him. "What brings you to our lovely neighborhood?"

"Business," he replied. "As in mine and the kind I don't appreciate talking about."

"Hey, we appreciate that a man's business is his own business," the first man said, raised his hands, and smiled. "We don't want to make you feel unwelcome around here in any way."

"I appreciate that." There were no prizes for anticipating the pitch that would inevitably follow.

"With that said, we do feel that in the spirit of neighborly appreciation, you should be worried that working around here will be a little dangerous," the leader said with a meaningful glance at both their surroundings and the neighborhood in general. "There's a fair amount of trouble with a local...uh, criminal element."

"You don't say?" Taylor raised an eyebrow.

"I know, it's a terrible situation," the grilled man continued. "Which is why we are here to present you with a fantastic opportunity—the kind that would be impossible to pass up. It's insurance, see, the kind that would allow your business to run smoothly without having to worry about *any* kind of unpleasantness."

"I don't suppose you guys are connected to any of the national insurance agencies, huh?"

"We're a small, local business, sure, but we get results," the third man said. He definitely seemed to be the bad mobster to the others' more pleasant roles.

"Yeah, no offense, but I wouldn't trust you with a... uh," Taylor scratched his cheek. "Damn it, I had something for this," he muttered. "The point is, I don't trust you. I know they say to not judge a book by its cover, but when three dumbasses straight out of a fucking *Breaking Bad* episode try to run their shitty racketeering gig past me... Well, some books *can* be judged by their covers, am I right?"

The leader maintained a fake smile through his tirade and shook his head at the end of it. "I merely don't want anyone to get hurt, but if you feel confident enough to risk everything you have, I don't think we can do anything to change your mind. I'll tell you what. We'll come by tomorrow and see if you still feel the same way."

"I can guarantee that I will," Taylor replied.

"Have a nice day, sir." The man motioned for the other two to follow him to the low-riding Cadillac they had arrived in.

Well, he had expected to have a little more time before he needed to take care of the local criminal element, but it would simply have to factor into his plans of setting the shop up. He intended to do it anyway and there was no time like the present to make sure the locals knew he was not to be fucked with.

He watched them pull out of the parking lot.

Once he was on his own again, Taylor worked on positioning the cameras around the building, then hauled the mech suits out of the back of the truck and used some mechanized help to guide them inside. They were easily the most expensive pieces he owned and would need special care once he was settled in.

There were other items, thankfully—the kind that would allow him to settle in immediately without having to spend another night at the hotel. He had already checked out that morning, so all that remained was to find a space that would offer some degree of comfort.

He intended to live there anyway—that was the plan, after all—so there was no point in delaying the shit.

It couldn't have been more than two hours, just as the sun began to drift into the western skyline, when his phone buzzed in his pocket again.

"Fucking dumbasses." He hissed in irritation, picked it up, and studied the camera feeds.

The thugs had returned. Well, he realized, not the three he had met since they were probably supposed to be the front men. That was obviously their ploy to avoid arrest when they arrived the next day to see if the unfortunate they had tried to force into their racket was ready to be dragged in now that they had been robbed and roughed up.

Taylor didn't appreciate their business strategy, nor the fact that having to deal with them interfered with his work. He wasn't particularly worried about them doing any damage, but he would need to call the police and watch and wait for them to arrive.

That really wasn't fair, especially for a guy who was only starting off in a recently purchased property.

He considered the possibility of simply paying the assholes off, but he didn't have enough hard cash on him to make the payment even if he could persuade himself to do it.

Besides, there was the small matter that he did not want to have to continue to pay them to not rob him blind. That scenario was still robbery but essentially with the consent of the victim, willing or otherwise.

After a deep breath, he shook his head and double-stepped it to the truck. He had to rummage through his belongings but finally located and retrieved his aluminum bat.

It had been a gift from his father when the man had tried to get him to enroll in the local little league team. The dream hadn't lasted long since it very soon became clear that he absolutely sucked at baseball.

The bat had proven useful in other situations, though. He had held onto the piece of aluminum like it was his friend and introduced the bullies in his high school to it— as well as a couple of car thieves before he joined the Marines.

Of course, he'd long since graduated to weapons that didn't need to be swung around, but the bat had always held a special place in his heart. He kept it with him almost everywhere and always close enough for him to use in an emergency.

And if this wasn't an emergency, he didn't know what

was. He patted it into his palm a few times as he circled to the rear where the men attempted to break in through the back door.

He was undecided whether he wanted to wait for them to actually accomplish that or not since there had been no keys for that particular door. He would have to take it down at some point, but it would be easier if the door was open.

"Come on, Jay, we don't have time for this," one of the criminals said. "Beeker wants us back before nightfall."

"I've needed to practice my lock-picking skills," the man who knelt in front of the door protested.

"What skills?" one of the others asked. "I'm with Drew. We should break a window and get in that way."

And that was where he drew the line. He would let them get in through the door, but if their shenanigans would add to his work he needed to do to bring this place into working condition, he would stop them right there and then.

He grasped the bat a little tighter. "I thought you guys were supposed to pull this shit at night?"

The five men paused in their efforts and spun to look at him. They were obviously surprised to see him and more importantly, surprised by how calm he was as he stood there with his baseball bat which he used to point at them.

"Seriously, you'd think you people would do this when there's as little chance as possible for you to be caught by the people who run the place, have them call the police, and have you arrested," Taylor continued. "Think about it. If you are arrested, all this needs to be done all over again.

You're simply *not* that intimidating when I stand here and watch you guys do it."

"I—wait," one of the goons said with a hasty glance at his cronies. He recalled that he'd been referred to as Drew. "There are five of us and you're not intimidated?"

"What do I have to be intimidated by?" Taylor asked. "You guys have been stumped for the past five minutes by a fucking door."

"I need to practice, man," Jay complained, looking between Taylor and the door. "Don't be shitty."

"Don't be shitty to the dumbasses trying to break into and trash my property?" He adopted an incredulous expression. "Yeah, that's a huge stretch to ask me to do."

"Fuck you," the first man retorted and drew a pistol that had been tucked into his pants.

Taylor was already on the move before he even pulled the weapon clear. He stepped closer as he raised the bat, and swung it hard in an underhanded arc.

The man's knee cracked audibly. He tried to scream in pain, but it was cut off as the bat hooked around and hammered him on the side of the head.

Drew fell without so much as a sound and flurried a cloud of dust around him. Taylor had already moved toward the others. They were used to the kind of people who would avoid conflict at all costs, even if it was directed at them.

Their arrogance and bravado were based on bullying simple business folk who merely wanted to make a living.

It was painfully clear they really hadn't anticipated that someone would retaliate. And given that none of the others made any effort to draw weapons when he attacked them, he could tell they hadn't come very prepared for any resistance.

No one else had a pistol.

Well, that was their loss. He was used to staying on the move and always delivering pain whenever he could. His survival instincts had been honed for optimum damage in the shortest possible time. It was how he had lived as long as he had in the Zoo.

Well, that and his fair share of luck.

He was in the midst of them before they could fully comprehend what he intended. The man who tried to pick the lock took a blow to the head and sagged. His comrades immediately tried to go to his aid. The first caught the knob of the bat in his gut and again in his ribs. The crunch of bones breaking could be heard even above his shriek of pain.

By now, the two men left had realized that they were horribly, horribly outmatched. They spun away, dropped the knife and tire iron they carried, and rushed to the car they had parked down the street. He wasn't sure if they were not used to running or if the whole shitting their pants in terror reality made them a little uncoordinated. Neither one would have surprised him, in fact, but he was able to catch up before they had crossed half the distance.

One collapsed and clutched his knee after Taylor's crushing blow. The second tripped over his own two feet and sprawled in his distraction.

"Hey, man, I'm cool here," the thug said and raised his hands. "I'm on the ground and I surrender. There's no need to bash my face in. If you have to do some bashing, maybe stick around the torso area or maybe the legs. Not the face, please."

"Do you think I want to beat you clowns?" he demanded and waved his bat. The man flinched. "I'm defending my property. You know what's a good way to avoid having your face bashed in? Don't break into other people's place of business."

"Not the face, man, please."

He shook his head. "Get the fuck up. I won't hit you with the bat. But you will help me to handle your friends."

"Anything you say, man."

Taylor eyed him. "Hard of hearing? I said get the fuck up."

The goon clambered quickly to his feet and looked like he considered running again before Taylor tapped him on the shoulder with the bat.

"Don't even think about it," he warned when he anticipated where his mind was going, caught him by the shoulders, and shoved him over to where his comrades had begun to recover. The leader, Drew, was conscious again but after a few seconds, he pulled himself to his knees and threw up.

"Fucking— Damn it. Now I'll have to clean that shit up." He yanked his phone out of his pocket and dialed nine-one-one.

"Nine-one-one, what's your emergency?" said a calm, feminine voice.

"Yeah, I have five dumbasses who tried to break into my place of business," he told her belligerently. "You have my address already, right? I need someone with a badge to come and take them off my hands."

The woman hesitated for a moment while he began to collect the weapons the thugs had dropped.

"Of course, sir. We have cruisers in your area and the officers should arrive in a few minutes," she said. The pause had clearly been so she could check. "Please find someplace safe to stay and they should be right with you."

"Yeah." He growled his annoyance as he hung up. "I don't think that'll be a problem."

CHAPTER TEN

She'd said a few minutes but it ended up being closer to ten. That meant enough time for Taylor, with the help of his new friend, to drag the characters into the delivery entrance at the back and find wire to tie them all up with. It was a nasty business, but the upside was that it seemed they would prefer to deal with the cops than whatever he might have in mind for them.

If the truth be told, it was the smartest decision they had made all day. They would simply wait quietly until the cops arrived and they wouldn't have to face the angry man with the bat anymore.

Some of them nursed injuries that would require medical attention, but he really didn't care. He was pissed to the point where they needed to consider themselves lucky that he hadn't locked them in the meat freezer in the back of what had once been a grocery store.

The ten minutes passed before he finally saw the red, white, and blue lights flashing as the sun began to set. They were probably looking around for something that would give them a pass to head out and say the call was a hoax when he moved over to open the larger gate that would allow them to drive in.

Or maybe Taylor was merely feeling particularly cynical.

"They're in there ready for you," he told them as one lowered his window and directed them to drive inside where the five goons waited in silence to be taken away—or rescued if their expressions were any indication.

He didn't want to tell them how to do their jobs, but only two officers in a single cruiser were not enough to take five perps to jail. In fairness, if they had found it was only a prank call, they would only have to arrest the caller so maybe that was why they had come alone.

"You guys took your sweet damn time," he stated and shook his head. "Do you think it's my job to hold the guys who were breaking into my place of business for you?"

"I...I'll ask you to mind your tone, sir," one of the officers said and narrowed his eyes. "Now, would you like to explain the situation?"

"I did to the nine-one-one operator but sure, I have nothing else to do today so I'll explain it again. These five guys were breaking into my place of business—in which you stand—and I stopped them."

The cop raised an eyebrow and Taylor closed his eyes and forced himself to take a deep breath.

"I apologize for my tone, sergeant," he said when he felt a little calmer. "It's...been a long day, and these guys got on my last fucking nerve."

"No problem, sir," the man said. "I'm Sergeant Smith, and this is Officer Smith." He indicated his partner, who tipped his cap. "No relation."

"Fantastic. I'm Taylor McFadden." He waved a finger around in a circle. "I own this whole lot and I was working on some repairs when a trio of toughs came up and asked me to pay them off for protection. I refused and not two hours later, this cavalcade of fuck-ups tried to break in through the back."

"Wait, you own this property?" the sergeant asked.

"You took all five of them down?" the officer said. Clearly, he was the one who asked the real questions.

"In order," Taylor said, "yes, I own this place. I bought it yesterday and started working on it today. And, yeah, I took all five of them down."

"On your own?" the man asked in disbelief. The sergeant rolled his eyes but kept his mouth shut like he wanted to hear the answer to that as well.

"Well, me and Betsy," he replied.

"Betsy?" the sergeant asked.

"Betsy the Baseball Bat." He tugged the bat in question up from where it rested next to him. "They were armed too if you were wondering. I collected all the weapons and put them in that trash bag in case you guys wanted them. I didn't actually touch them, so fingerprints shouldn't be an issue."

"Don't worry, we're fully aware that you were well within your rights of self-defense," the sergeant said. "Besides, being from the area, we know a thing or two about these five."

"Yeah?" Taylor looked over at the glum group. "They don't seem the type who would be too memorable as criminals. Goons, from the looks of them, and not up for much more than the dirty work."

"Hey, fuck you, man," Drew shouted.

"Sit tight, Drew, or I'll let you have another long talk with Betsy," Taylor called in response.

"I can't condone any further use of violence sir," Sergeant Smith said, shook his head, and chuckled. "Between you, me, and Officer Smith here, though, I don't really shed any tears about you treating them roughly. These five have been in and out of jail their whole lives—racketeering, aggravated assault with a deadly weapon, you name it. Some have even done time in the past, although it was always for lesser charges. All five are on the last of their three strikes."

"Fun times," Taylor quipped. "Wait, Nevada has a three-strikes law?"

"We do," Officer Smith confirmed and retrieved handcuffs from his belt. "It's not quite like the Cali law, but these quote, *habitual criminals*, unquote, will face between five and twenty years in the slammer depending on how good their lawyers are and how busy the prosecutor is."

"Yeah, he's had a ton of work from the gang activity around here," Sergeant Smith said morosely. "The chances are they'll be given the opportunity to roll over on some of their compadres for reduced jail time since we know these ass-munchers won't last long in the maximum-security jails—right, Jay?"

No answer issued from the five. Taylor recalled Jay as

being the inept lockpicker and could guess that hard time would be akin to hell for someone as young as he was.

"Anyway, we don't want to take up any more of your time, Mr. McFadden," the sergeant said and gestured for the officer to start rounding the group up. "Suffice it to say I don't think any of these hoods will bother you in the future. We appreciate your efforts."

His partner began to handcuff the group as a second police vehicle turned slowly into the lot and approached the group.

Maybe they weren't that lackadaisical after all as it seemed they'd already had backup on the way. It most likely had something to do with the neighborhood, which meant his earlier assessment of their attitude had been a little skewed. The thugs were shoved none too gently toward the cruisers—a few complaining about their pain.

"I appreciate that," Taylor said and took the sergeant's proffered hand. "And again, sorry for my attitude before. It's been something of a day."

"Hey, I completely understand," the Smith said with a laugh. "I'm glad you held back on taking them down too hard. With self-defense laws being what they are, you wouldn't have any charges pressed against you, but they would have still made us bring you in to make a statement at the station."

"As is, though?" he asked.

"Oh, I'll use the statement you gave us here and put that into the report," the sergeant said. "A detective might come over to get extra details for the DA, but it shouldn't be more than that."

"Well, I appreciate that, sergeant, officer." He nodded

briskly to the two of them. "If you don't mind, I think I'll get back to work. There are still a couple of hours of work I can fit in before it gets too dark."

"Everyone likes an industrious man," Officer Smith said as he moved to keep an eye on Drew who stood beside the cruiser and seemed to have regained a little of his belligerence now that he was safely tucked beside a police vehicle. "By the way, I noticed you had some cameras outside. Would you mind—"

Taylor already had a memory stick ready. He pulled it out of his pocket and handed it to the sergeant. "I thought you guys might like video evidence of what happened. There should be markers on the footage that says it's tamper-proof too."

"Much appreciated, Mr. McFadden."

"You'll regret this, man," Drew yelled although he made no effort to move closer. "Do you think this shit will simply go away? Nah. My peeps will tear into you and make sure you don't live long enough to see an officer of the law to talk to. You'll be silenced for fucking ever, *asshole*."

The officer looked like he was about to tell the man to shut the fuck up but Taylor felt something a little more emphatic was needed. He closed the distance in a few long strides, grasped the thug by the collar of his knockoff brand shirt, and dragged him in close so their eyes were barely five inches apart.

"Listen up, bubba, because I'll only say this once." He deliberately kept his voice calm and measured as he stared directly into Drew's eyes. "Folk have tried to silence me for a long time. Well, not folk, strictly speaking, but they were a hell of a lot more intimidating than you five incompetent, dumb shits."

The man tried to turn away, but he caught his chin and twisted him to make sure he paid attention. "Eighty-three times they tried, and eighty-three times, I was the one who walked away alive. There's nothing *you* and your gang of Crips impersonators can do that will make me flinch. When the screams of your dying comrades are the noises that keep you up at night, hell isn't your biggest worry anymore. Staying alive is. Try me, punk, and next time, it won't be Betsy that bashes your fucking skull in. I'll do it with my own two hands."

He released Drew's collar, shoved him back into Officer Smith, and turned away. While the thug tried to put on a brave face, his knees shook visibly and he had to almost be lifted into the car.

Neither police officer had much to say about what he had said, but the sergeant had apparently looked away as if he didn't want to be a witness if any of this came to trial. His gaze landed on the trio of mech suits that were inside.

"What the fuck are those?" he asked, not too well-versed in the suits and what they were used for. "What, are you trying to be Iron Man or something?"

"Fuck no," Taylor retorted. "Iron Man never fought in the Zoo."

Sergeant Smith nodded. "Thanks for your time, Mr. McFadden. You have a nice night."

He and his partner gestured for the first cruiser to pull away and slid into their vehicle.

"Did he say the fucking Zoo?" Officer Smith asked once

they were out on the road again and on the way to the station.

"Yep," the sergeant said as he watched the footage Taylor had given him on the cruiser's computer. "But looking at this shit... Well, let's say I wouldn't want to be the one to call him a liar."

Neither the officer nor the sergeant looked forward to the sheer amount of paperwork it would take to book all five men. While it was mostly an open and shut case, four of them required at least some kind of medical attention and it would therefore take a while until they were all processed.

Three were still talking to paramedics while two were in the holding cells, waiting for the arrival of their lawyers. None of the five were the sharpest knives in any selection of drawers, but they had been around law enforcement for long enough to know how to shut the fuck up before their legal advisors arrived.

Normally, Sergeant Smith would have been annoyed by their knowledge since it would have been easier to get a confession from them if they didn't have their lawyers around, but not tonight. Drew Haskins would be a tough nut to crack, but all the others would rather have a chat with the DA and take deals to avoid hard time.

It wouldn't make them too popular with the people who sent them to try to rob McFadden, but everyone in their type of situation did it. The whole "snitches get stitches" threat was only uttered by those who never faced hard time themselves. Finding honor among low-level hoods was like hunting for diamonds in sewer sludge.

Thankfully, he wasn't the one who had to look through that sludge. He was literally looking for everything else.

A woman stepped into the station, glanced around like she was a little lost, and drew the sergeant's attention away from the pile of paperwork he was working on.

In fairness, she didn't look like she belonged in a police station. All five foot six of her—helped a little by the heels she wore—looked like she would be a little more at home at a marketing firm. Or maybe in LA, trying to make it as the next strong woman Latina typecast.

She flicked stray brown hairs from her face and tucked them behind her ear before she walked over to where he had begun to stand.

"Excuse me, miss?" he asked and moved out from behind his desk. "Are you here to file a police report? Because you can do that with the desk sergeant at the front. As you can see," he waved a hand around. "We're a little swamped here."

"Actually, the desk sergeant told me I would be able to talk to you about an arrest you made," she stated. "Five arrests, actually."

Oh shit. "I'm sorry, who are you?"

She withdrew a badge from her jacket pocket. Not simply a badge, he noted—a golden shield with an eagle at the top and three letters emblazoned on the front. The FBI had arrived.

"I'm Special Agent Niki Banks," she said by way of introduction. "I understand that you, Sergeant Avery Smith and Officer Case Smith, no relation, brought in five local toughs for an attempted robbery?"

He didn't like where this was going. These conversations usually ended with the agents claiming that one of his perps was a federal witness or something like that and needed to be released immediately. It would fuck with all his paperwork.

"Yes," he said, nodded, and tried not to let his displeasure show. "I'm not sure what the FBI wants with a bunch of low-level thugs, though."

"Oh, I'm not here for the five," Banks said with a firm shake of her head. "I'm here about the man they tried to rob. A…Mr. McFadden?" She checked a notepad to be sure.

"Oh, right," he said and recovered from his surprise in only a few seconds. "I'm not sure what you want with him either…although yeah, considering the way he beat the poor bastards, I'm not surprised he's some kind of special forces dude. He said something about being in the Zoo, but I'm not sure I believe him."

"It would be best if you put him out of your mind, Sergeant," the agent said and consulted her notepad again. "In fact, I wondered if I could talk you into removing any mention of his name from your reports. His location should be considered…well, sensitive information."

Smith nodded. Was the guy a witness in protective custody? It sounded about right. McFadden had seemed like the kind of man who had a dark past.

"I'll keep him out of my future reports but I've already filed a couple on the arrests and sent them to the DA's office," the sergeant said, genuinely apologetic.

"The office that only opens tomorrow morning," she

nodded. "Shit. Well, I guess I'll need to talk the DA into making the necessary redactions. Anyway, thanks for your time, Sergeant, and I appreciate your cooperation."

"Of course, us folks in law enforcement need to stick together," Smith said, chuckled, and proffered his hand. "Fuck all the jurisdiction crap, am I right?"

"Correct." Banks gave him a small smile and shook his hand briskly.

CHAPTER ELEVEN

Taylor did spend a fair amount of time after the cops left working on the building to spruce it up a little, even though the last hour had to be done with the help of Liz's headlights. He had enough time to finish what was required for the electricity so he could work with the building's lights for the next few days.

It wasn't the most elegant situation, but he didn't mind spending the night at the location. It would give him a better feel for what it would be like when he actually moved in. Besides, he didn't want to be out of the picture if or when those goons decided to turn up again.

He moved a portable bed inside and set up the Wi-Fi to be used for security and personal access. After ordering something out for dinner, he ate quickly, went to bed, and slept better than he had at the hotel. There was something about staying in a place he owned and had a right to be in that was relaxing.

Which was weird since it had been difficult to get any sleep in the truck when he had been traveling. He assumed

that having an actual bed—even a portable military one
—helped.

The sun had barely begun to rise when he woke with
the realization that there would be no hot water for a
while.

Maybe there was a boiler or something in one in one of
the basement rooms he hadn't checked thoroughly yet. If
not, he'd have to install one sooner rather than later. Still, it
meant an icy cold shower in the staff ablutions behind the
grocery store—a lucky find, in his book, as he hadn't
expected to find one in that kind of property. He was more
than used to cold showers from his time in the corps.

As always, it was as unpleasant as fuck but endurable.

With that done, he ate leftovers from the night before
as a hasty breakfast before he set to work again. His first
priority was to resolve the hot water situation. Priorities
became flexible when faced with real need.

Hours later, his phone rang.

"It's all day with these people," he grumbled as he
yanked the phone out. He thought it was probably the cops
trying to get another interview with him over what had
transpired the night before. When he looked at the number
that was calling, however, he realized that it was not even
in the States.

There were one or two people who wanted to talk to
him outside the US, but none of them were in law enforcement. Taylor answered the call and put it on speakerphone.

"Hi, I'm calling the number that was left in the men's
room?" said a rough and familiar voice through the
speaker.

"Was that number for a good fucking time, emphasis on

fucking?" he asked. "Because if so, I think you might want to talk to someone else, Trevor."

"*Tayloorrr!* It's nice to hear your voice again," the man said and laughed. "How are things going back Stateside? Are you enjoying all the peace and quiet?"

"I was until there wasn't any peace and quiet to be had around here," he replied. "There was, and the ladies in Vegas are fucking insane, but I had trouble with a few of the local criminals. Nothing like the bounty hunters you're probably still dealing with in the Zoo but annoying enough."

"I can see how it would piss you off," Trevor commiserated. "Around here, we have suits with big fucking guns and rocket launchers and the like. I guess walking around in a full suit of mech armor and armed to the teeth isn't something folks around there are too willing to accept?"

"Well no, but that merely means I don't have to deal with a horde of alien monsters and equally well-armed bounty hunters," Taylor pointed out. "Seriously, the guys I had to deal with had difficulty getting through my back door."

"Now that's a low bar to miss." The man chuckled again.

"You're about as hilarious as a nine-year-old who discovered an old book of dirty mad libs," he rolled his eyes. "In the end, all I needed was a baseball bat. The last one tripped over his own feet and begged me not to beat his face. I guess that settles into the world of disappointments that defines leaving the Zoo."

"Well, I would enjoy a little more boring out here, even if it means we make less money. Wait, no—yeah, I'd still want the money. Last I heard, you came away from here with enough cash to buy your own island."

"Not an island, per se," Taylor corrected. "But a good enough start. I'm almost to the point where I can buy an island and declare it McFaddenland. That might work as an eventual idea, but for now, I'm focused on getting a business off the ground."

"Oh, right, speaking of which," the man said. "I heard you were setting up a location to start fixing suits. Is that intelligence correct?"

"Well, yes, but it's still in the setup phase right now. I asked my boys who are still there to spread the word that I'll have a shop that would undercut the repair costs of the assholes there, but I didn't expect it to happen so quickly."

"Well, sure, when word comes out that we might be able to get cheaper prices on suit repairs, it tends to get around. So, lay it on me—what kind of prices are we looking at? Depending on the cost and the quality of the work, I know you'll have one hell of a niche market with the smaller merc groups out here that don't want to deal with what those corporations charge."

"Well, give me a sec to look into my market research, one minute." He pulled the phone away and checked the files on it quickly before sticking it back on his ear. "Okay, from the prices I looked at, it should take you about twelve grand to airfreight your suits here. You'd find a better price in bulk, so send all the suits you need repaired at the same time. I'll fix them, add a couple of modifications on my own, and ship them back. If you're not a fan of the repairs or the modifications, I'll refund you for the things you're not happy with."

"What kind of mods can you put into them?" Trevor's curiosity was evident in his voice. "And more importantly, what kind of charges would you put on them?"

"I'll have to see what you give me and I'll quote you for what I can do, then you'll be able to choose what you want," Taylor replied. "There won't be any price negotiation, though, but I can assure you it will be cheaper than the quotes you'll get over there."

"Yeah, that's still not putting the bar too high, is it?"

"Well, yeah, it's how I made it out," Taylor explained. "It was me, some kind of Military R&D, and a FYOTON Manufacturing heavy mech suit."

"Yeah, you're a regular kickass."

"Hey, remember eighty-three trips into the Zoo?" Taylor pointed out smugly.

"You'll hold that over everyone forever, won't you?" The merc sounded both amused and irritated.

"Damn right I will until someone goes in there eighty-four times." That drew a laugh from the other man.

"Fun times," Trevor replied. "Anyway, I'll look into the shipping to get you the suits we need worked on. Shipping should only take a day or two for that kind of pricing. If the work is satisfactory, I'll make sure the word continues to spread. We need to keep guys like you in business."

"Works. I'm looking forward to it, Trevor. Stay alive in there."

"No promises," he replied cheerfully. "Have a good day. It is day there, right?"

"Yep, mid-morning."

"Well, have a nice day." The line clicked into silence.

"What do you know? I have my first client," Taylor told

himself and savored the feelings of satisfaction and excitement the knowledge brought. "I need to get the business all set up without delay." He looked around the large, cavernous, empty space. "And I need someone to talk to. I feel like I'm going crazy."

He took another shower—this one as cold as the last—and washed the couple of hours of work off before he pulled on a clean shirt.

Business needs now took precedence.

Banking hours were bullshit. Taylor was annoyed.

The fact that these people seemed to think the world revolved around their schedule was a problem, one that was usually exacerbated by the fact that there were countries elsewhere in the world that abided by the same rules. Inevitably, given that they were in different time zones, it meant that every country had different banking times.

Yep, still bullshit.

But it was the kind of crap everyone needed to live with since the world did, in fact, revolve around their schedule.

Which meant that even though Taylor had scheduled an appointment with the bank's loan office and he had arrived precisely on time, they still directed him to a waiting area with no Wi-Fi where he had to kick his heels until one of the loan officers was available.

Taylor sighed, shook his head, and leaned back in his seat while he toyed with the phone in his hand. There was only so much he could do on the device while he waited but he had enough time to sift through all his financial statements until he was bored to tears.

With that said, he actually did find the whole mathematics of the situation interesting. He'd never given it much attention while in school, but once he realized that money did make the world go around, metaphorically speaking, it suddenly became one hell of a lot more interesting.

"Mr. McFadden?" A tall, lean man with an aquiline nose and straight, short black hair walked up to him, adjusting his mid-range black suit.

"That's me," Taylor stood up, and up, and up. He smiled down at him as he

shook the man's proffered hand. "It's nice to meet you..."

"Jason Lewis. Nice to meet you too," he replied. "I'm sorry for the delay. We've been a little swamped around here over the past couple of days. Nothing interesting, of course, but still time-consuming."

"Not a problem It's not like we had a scheduled appointment or anything," he responded and managed to restrain most of the sarcasm that edged the words. "Oh... Wait."

"Hah, very funny, Mr. McFadden," Lewis said and had the grace to chuckle. He couldn't tell if that response was sarcastic or not, but it didn't really matter as he guided him toward his desk in the back of the open area of the bank's local headquarters.

"So, I've been led to understand that you've come here in search of a business loan," the man said. "I would like you to know that we work extensively with current and former military members and that should definitely improve your loan qualifications with us."

"Well...that's great."

"We looked at your history in the Marine Corps, but I'm afraid we didn't see much in the way of...well, notes of what you were doing." Lewis checked his phone.

"Wait, you guys have access to my military records?" he asked, a little offended.

"Well, yes. That is a part of how we would be able to use your time with the military to improve your credit suitability with us."

"Yeah, well, I'm not surprised, I guess. Most of what I did would have been redacted."

"Anyway," Lewis continued cheerfully. "What kind of financial support do you think you will need?"

"Well," Taylor said and retrieved the sheets of paper that contained the market research he had put into his business. "I'm not sure what my company's name will be as yet, so you can call it...McFadden's Mechs for now. Anyway, I already have the research done into the sales market, which has clearly established that I would have a viable and fairly constant demand, all while being able to undercut standard market prices in the area."

"And you're trained to repair and modify the...ah, mech suits?" Lewis asked and sounded a little uncertain as he tried to grasp the variety of makes and models Taylor had established as his starting point.

"I have a degree in engineering plus experience in both modifying and repairing them in the Zoo," he said with a firm nod. "Both in the jungle itself on missions and in the shop. Actually, I spent considerable time with the mechanics who did the job on a daily basis, and I plan to bring one of those mechanics in as an employee."

After a few minutes of going through the paperwork, Lewis looked up. "You've...put considerable thought and effort into this," the man said, leaned forward, and paid more attention to the papers set out for him.

"People keep saying that like they're surprised." Taylor scratched idly at his beard, a little irritated. "It's my life, so of course I'll put thought and effort into it."

"Well, you don't usually expect this kind of thing from —" the banker started to say and looked up hastily from the papers as if he suddenly recalled who he was talking to.

"From?"

"Never mind." Lewis shook his head quickly. "Well, this all looks to be in order, Mr. McFadden. Indeed, we don't often get business proposals this well-organized and laid out."

"Well, I do my best." He knew the man had intended to make some mention of his appearance—or maybe the fact that he was big and burly and it meant he was supposed to somehow lack in the brains department.

Taylor wouldn't have said he was anything close to a genius, of course, but he did know his way around a financial statement. Not only that, logic had demanded that he put time and thought into studying the economy he would work and live in. That wasn't only about being smart.

It was simply common sense.

"Well, I still need to submit it for approval, but I would say the chances are very good that you'll receive the approval for your loan." Lewis gathered the papers on his desk. "Do you mind if I make a copy of these?"

"You can print from here." He handed the man a USB drive and leaned back while he waited.

"There is one more small detail regarding the loan, however," the banker said a few minutes later when the printer whirred to life. "We do need some kind of collateral —you know, to insure it and make sure the bank has some security."

"I know what collateral is, Mr. Lewis." Taylor gave him a tight smile. "In the paperwork, you'll see that I own the property where I intend to run the business from and in fact purchased it outright, but I don't want it encumbered so choose not put that up as security. You'll also find Certificates of Deposit totaling around two million dollars."

Lewis raised an eyebrow and flipped through the documents as he took a sip of his coffee. The banker seemed distracted while he perused the paperwork and the silence dragged on a little.

"That should be enough to cover the collateral, right?" Taylor asked when his patience wore thin.

"Yes…absolutely, yes, Mr. McFadden. But it would have to be a personal rather than a business loan." The man frowned, his demeanor still professional but a little curious. A moment later, he looked up at Taylor. "I…if you don't mind me asking, if you have this much invested, why bother taking out a loan in the first place?"

"You're a banker and should know you *never* start a business with your own money." He chuckled to soften his somewhat abrupt tone.

"Well… yes, but not many people… Never mind," Lewis gathered himself again before he cleared his throat and stacked the papers he'd printed into a neat pile, removed the disc, and handed it back. "Well, Mr. McFadden, I think you should hear from us really soon. The prospects look good."

"Fantastic," he responded with a smile, pushed from his seat, and shook Lewis' hand firmly. "I look forward to working with you."

"Yes…indeed." The man rubbed his hand surreptitiously as Taylor left the building and strode out to the parking lot.

He narrowed his eyes as he approached Liz. The vehicle stood out like a sore thumb in the parking lot. He liked driving her, no question about that, but he would need something a little more fuel-efficient and that would be more maneuverable in the city. Maybe a lease, although he did want to have some return on any vehicular investment so it might make more sense to buy used.

But that was an issue for later, he decided, swung into the truck and started her, and eased out of the parking lot to return to his place of business.

CHAPTER TWELVE

S he had hoped to have already left Vegas by now. She didn't like the desert. People talked about the dry heat like it somehow mitigated the reality that it was as hot as balls all the live-long day.

Why anyone had elected to settle there and establish a large city that revolved mostly around gambling was beyond her.

Maybe some people simply liked the heat or even thrived in it. Niki knew some who hated the cold with the same kind of passion she felt for the heat.

In her defense, though, if you were in a cold location, there were all kinds of things you could do to counteract it. All were relatively simple—stay indoors, crank the heat up, and wrap yourself in a blanket while you sipped hot tea and you were golden.

Even if you needed to go outdoors, you could always bundle yourself up in a dozen or so layers and that would work too until you were back in the warm confines of the glorious indoors.

On the flip side, there was only so much you could do to counter the heat. There were air-conditioning for the inside and cold as fuck drinks to try to cool off, but once you were outside, there were only so many clothes you could remove before you were arrested for indecent exposure.

Besides, it wasn't like removing clothes really helped at all.

Unfortunately, she had matters she needed to attend to in the glorious city of Las Vegas and for some reason, people insisted on being annoying, which in turn kept her there.

The worst part was the unavoidable reality that the most annoying part of her job was still to come. McFadden had something of a reputation, apparently, based on statements from the people she had spoken to about his gigantic red ass.

By all accounts, he was stubborn, smarter than he let on, and insisted on acting like the barely tamed beast-man he appeared to be. He could have been on wall street based on his SATs and IQ score, but he'd chosen to join the military instead. True, it had ultimately paid dividends for him and he was proving that he knew how to invest the money he'd made in the Zoo, which simply confirmed her first assessment.

If he had elected to work at an investment firm in New York, she wouldn't have to track him to the literal ends of the earth.

That would have been the absolute definition of a win-win scenario, but she was stuck with the hard slog that resulted from his choices. Desk was fucking good at what she did, but when someone seemed to literally drop off the map overnight, even she needed something to work a miracle with.

"I'm sorry, ma'am," a secretary said and placed a hand on Niki's arm. "You can't go in there. District Attorney Goodman is not speaking to the press today."

Niki stared at the hand. "Do I look like press?" she asked and raised an eyebrow.

"I...well..."

The agent shook her head and raised a hand to stop the young assistant from saying anything else before she yanked the badge from her coat pocket. "I need to talk to Goodman about a case he should have on his desk."

"What case?" the woman asked and narrowed her eyes.

"I'm not at liberty to discuss that. Tell him Special Agent Niki Banks is here to see him rather urgently."

"Oh...right." The secretary looked a little put out as she pushed through one of the nearby doors. The office did seem to be in the middle of something significant and most of the assistants and aides rushed about while they talked on phones and seemed to get papers in order. They looked like they were preparing for a large case that was coming up.

Niki didn't know what they were involved with and honestly, she didn't care. DAs dealt with state cases, which the FBI usually had no jurisdiction over. She had no need and no time to stick her nose into their business.

The young woman returned from the office and closed the door behind her. "Mr. Goodman will see you now."

"I appreciate it," she responded and faked a smile as she

skirted her to enter the office before she could do something silly like announce her arrival.

There was a literal mountain of paperwork on the desk when she entered. Given that they were in an age when almost everything was done online, she couldn't for the life of her understand why people insisted on keeping their legal business on paper. It was a damn waste of time. So much would be avoided if they simply kept their files digital.

While there obviously were problems with hackers and the like, there were ways to keep that from being a problem too. No, the transition into the new age was hampered by laziness and people who were stuck in the old ways of doing things.

"Special Agent Banks?" the short, stout man with a receding hairline said from behind the desk.

"Thanks for taking the time, Goodman," Niki said. "I don't think I'll take too much of it."

"We're always happy to help our pals in the FBI," he said and gestured for her to take a seat. "With that said, we are in a rush in this office as you've no doubt noticed, so I'm sure you can appreciate why I'd want this meeting to be brief as possible."

"Then I'll keep it short. A file would have come across your desk last night or maybe early this morning regarding an attempted robbery and an arrest involving five... Well, I guess the term 'the usual suspects' applies in this case."

"Oh, right." The DA turned, attacked a stack, and sifted through some of the documents before he drew out a file near the bottom of the pile. "Okay, yes, an arrest last night.

Five hoods were beaten by the owner of a property and were brought in by the cops. Open and shut." He looked up. "What does the FBI want with it?"

"No interest whatsoever in the five criminals you want to prosecute. My issue is with the man who was involved."

"Is he...well, what about him?"

"I'm afraid I'm not at liberty to discuss the details of it," Niki said firmly. "But the long and the short of it is that the man in question, Taylor McFadden, is something of a critical player in a federal operation. The kind of player who can't be involved in the arrest of local toughs."

"I understand." He leaned forward. "How can I help?"

"I merely need his name removed from the record—redacted, cut, or simply not mentioned."

"We...uh, well, we need him for the case against those men," Goodman protested.

"All but one of them have already contacted their lawyers and filed for some kind of deal that involves confessions and lesser jail time," she pointed out. "The other... Well, he's either loyal or afraid. Either way, the video footage involved should be enough to encourage his lawyer to cut a deal too. I don't want to tell you how to do your job but I *need* you to keep Taylor McFadden's name off the file."

The man nodded. "Understood."

"I'll owe you a favor, Goodman," Niki said. "Having a federal agent owe you a favor is no small thing."

"I understand that, Special Agent, and I appreciate your consideration," he replied smoothly. "Anything to help a fellow law enforcement officer, right?"

"Correct," she agreed with another fake smile.

She left his office, ignored the assistant who hovered in the hallway, and strode out toward the elevator. That had gone swimmingly, she thought smugly.

Maybe her people skills were improving after all? Now, all she had to do was make one final call to McFadden and all would be right with her world.

Her phone vibrated with a message as she stepped into the elevator and she pulled it out with a frown, almost tempted to simply ignore it. Fortunately, she didn't.

Her boss did not like to be ignored. Her frown became a scowl when she realized that yet again, she had to put her potential new recruit on hold while she dealt with the latest clusterfuck long-distance. It would take hours to resolve too and she'd have to go back to her hotel to do so.

So much for finally seeing the end of her frustrating quest and fucking going home.

It was another long, productive day for Taylor.

The approval for the loan had come through about half an hour after he had left the bank and they'd sent him the number for the account in which the money would be deposited. There would be credit available in the bank as well, and credit cards would be sent in the mail in two or three business days.

The bank appeared happy to have him as a client. Initially, he'd wondered if Lewis had perhaps viewed him as a charity case—a military man they would assist with finance as part of a PR campaign.

He chuckled at the idea of him in the bank's national

commercials about how they supported the military or something along those lines.

Once it was clear that he wasn't there for a handout and could prove to be a valuable client, things moved swiftly. In the meantime, he did eventually find the boiler room in the basement of the grocery store. He fixed what he could but parts were missing and would arrive the next day via mail order.

For the moment, though, he was not in the mood for takeout food. He made a quick trip in the truck to Jackson's. This time, hopefully, things wouldn't turn out the way they had the last time.

Well, the drinking and the food had been damn good but being the replacement bouncer had intruded—although, he admitted to himself with a grin, that had also been fun.

He pulled the truck into the parking lot and activated the alarm and security before he wandered toward the entrance. He could see a powerful, six-foot-eight man standing in what looked like a uniform suit with the Jackson's logo on the front.

"Evening." Taylor nodded. "Marcus, right?"

"And you must be Taylor McFadden," the linebacker said with a small grin.

"I...did we ever actually meet?" he asked and wondered how he could have forgotten it.

"Nah, but Alex told me about how you filled in for me when I was out with family issues."

"Right, but how did you—"

"How many big fucking redheads do you think come to this bar?" Marcus interjected.

"Uh...yeah, good point. I hope the family issues have since been resolved."

"Well, it'll be a while, but she's on the road to recovery." He gestured towards to the door with his head. "Have a great evening."

"I appreciate it, Marcus, you too." He patted the giant of a man on his shoulder before he stepped inside to be greeted by the comfortable sight of the green and gold everywhere.

It looked a little fuller than it had been the last time he was there. Closer to the weekend, people tended to spend more time getting shitfaced, he assumed.

"Hey, Taylor!" Alex called from behind the bar. "Take a seat, hon. I'll be right with you."

He did as he was told and chose one of the bar stools while she refilled glasses for some of the other customers who were too busy playing video poker to look up and thank her. For a moment, he had to resist the urge to make a caustic comment that he hoped they would leave a sizable tip for their bartender.

Once she was finished, she turned to face him.

"How are you doing?" she asked. "Beer and whiskey sour, right?"

"I think I'll start with a beer and see where the night goes. Thanks, Alex. How the hell have you been?"

"It's all busy shifts and working on my studies so I haven't had much in the way of any time off," she said. "Not that I really do much with that time anyway, so it's all for the best I suppose."

"I'll take your word for it," he said and reached for his wallet as she placed a glass in front of him.

"Don't worry about this one," she told him. "Marcus said he would cover your first drink for helping me out the other day."

"You guys need to stop giving me free shit. Otherwise, I might not even bring my wallet here the next time around." He grinned and took a sip of his beer.

"Oh, you still owe me for the tip, mister man," she retorted warningly. "Don't think you can pull any of that cheapskate bullshit on me, even if you do get some free drinks."

"And food," he reminded her.

"Don't think you'll get any freebies. Well, aside from the drink, I guess, but no more free food."

"Well, that's fair enough. You guys do run a for-profit place here, I suppose."

"Imagine that."

"Well, I think I'll have something to eat anyway, the fact that I need to pay for it notwithstanding." He looked around. "I don't suppose you have a menu around here."

She ducked under the bar and retrieved one for him, then moved quickly to where one of the customers asked for another refill on her soda.

"So, what will you have?" she asked when she returned.

"I guess I'll have your chicken fried steak dinner and a side of fries." He closed the menu and pushed it toward her.

"You know we can replace the veggies or the mashed potatoes with the fries?"

"Yeah, but you know me. I have to stay healthy and shit. I have to eat my vegetables."

"Coming right up." She punched the order into the

computer to her left. "So, have you found a place to stay yet or are you still hanging out at that hotel?"

"No. I have a place now."

"So, are you settling into the town?"

"You know me, I'm a rambling man." He took another long sip of his beer. "I'll find me a place of business—which is what I did, by the way—but I don't think I'll ever settle down."

"Everyone says that," she pointed out.

"What?"

"Everyone says they don't think they'll ever settle down," she explained. "They love their freedom and will always be a packed suitcase away from hitting the open road to see where the winds take them. Then, they find a place they like, get comfortable, and soon, the idea of an open road simply seems exhausting."

"You sound like you speak from experience." He took a sip of his beer.

"Well, yeah, sure. My folks moved around a ton when I was a kid. They were a musical duo and had to get to gigs and the like all over the damn place and dragged me along with them and even wanted me to make them a trio. They eventually found a place and settled down."

"Fuck me, that sounds like it must have been tough. Especially for your education."

"And yet I still managed to get me a solid slice of that scholarship pie." Her grin was a little smug as one of the wait staff came out with his order. "What does that tell you about how smart I am?"

"In fairness, I never really doubted that you weren't as

smart as a whip." He nodded his thanks to the kid as he placed the two plates on the counter.

She raised an eyebrow. "How smart is a whip?"

"Ask me again when you've been lashed across the face with a bullwhip," he said. "My folks were fairly well-settled and my dad owned a tiny car shop, but my mom's folks had a ranch and she liked to take me and my siblings out there for the weekend."

"Ouch."

"Yeah, I was caught across the cheek when my brother was messing around." He showed her a small yet thick scar across his cheek. "People assume it was from a punch which, in fairness, is a good assumption."

"Well, yeah, I can understand that. A guy who fights like you do probably has scars that have a story or two behind them."

"And you just heard one," he quipped with a nod.

She turned to help one of the customers and his gaze drifted to the TV. They were taking a break from sports for national news. The story in question was happening near Washington DC, indicated by the text at the bottom of the screen.

"Police are looking into a series of deaths in the area about twenty miles from the Pentagon," the cute blonde reporter said. "There has been no comment from the local authorities on what might have been responsible for these deaths and whether it is natural, an animal attack, or maybe perpetrated by a human."

"Do you believe this crap?" Alex asked and scowled at the screen.

"Let's say that my standard for what is believable and

what isn't is a little skewed." He narrowed his eyes and focused on the anchorwoman.

"There has been no mention of the condition the bodies are in, but the word from one of the family members who claimed the bodies indicates that they will have a closed casket funeral," the reporter continued.

"And that's simply in bad taste." He growled annoyance and shook his head. "I swear to God they'll do almost anything to get people to watch these days. They've really subscribed to the 'all press is good press' philosophy."

"Agreed," she said and shuddered. "So…do you mind if I ask you a question?"

He shook his head. "Go ahead. I might not answer, though."

"Fair enough. So…what is your problem?"

Taylor narrowed his eyes. "Your question makes sense but the genuinely inquisitive tone doesn't."

"Come on, guys like you don't grow on trees some-where," she retorted. "They're made—generally in the most fucked-up ways, but still. Take it from someone who's heard enough sob stories that I might as well charge fees as a therapist as well as a bartender."

"Take it from me, you'd make one hell of a lot more money that way," he pointed out, finished his meal, and started on the fries.

"See what I mean? Regular dudes don't need therapy like that."

"Well, maybe if their parents were rich, fucked-up people," he quipped. "But I'll tell you what. I'm coming in tomorrow and I'll give you another story then. How about that?"

"That seems fair. You already gave me one, even if it was a shitty one."

He grinned, took enough out of his wallet to cover the meal and a generous tip, and placed it on the counter. "I don't know, I might feel a little more talkative tomorrow."

"I'll look forward to it."

Alex watched him leave as she collected the empty plates and glass. He fist-bumped Marcus on the way out.

"What the fuck is *wrong* with me?" she asked under her breath and forced her focus back to work.

CHAPTER THIRTEEN

A quick drive later in the evening was exactly what he needed to get his mind off Alex.

She was nice enough and hot as hell. He wanted to talk to her more, to get to know her and hear about what made her tick, which was fairly unusual for him. Most of his time with women who weren't in the military was spent trying to get into their pants.

He would need to rethink his approach, decide what he wanted and what he could offer in return, and get back to her about it.

Things were a little more comfortable in his new living space, and he fell asleep rather quickly. The combination of good food and booze was enough to put him out like a light.

What annoyed him was the fact that something buzzed demandingly beside his little bed and woke him at around two in the morning. Given that his phone was the irritant, he muttered an imprecation and pushed himself high enough to snag it from the table it rested on.

"Fuck it." He pushed upward on the bed and turned the device on. The notification wasn't anyone trying to reach him—not intentionally, at least. Someone had triggered the security measures around the building and buzzing was to alert him.

Taylor had a sinking feeling that it would turn out to be a pack of stray dogs. In his half-awake state, he wondered if they actually had stray dogs in the US and if they did, whether they were in packs like they had in Casablanca when he'd gone there to experience some semblance of civilization.

But no, they weren't dogs. Three dots on the motion sensors told him that they moved very deliberately toward the front entrance.

"Fucking assholes." He heaved himself off the bed and resisted the urge to fling the phone across the room. "It's two in the fucking morning and now, I have to deal with these ogre pricks. *Again.*"

It had to be the same gang that had sent Drew and his cronies to try to intimidate him. This time, he knew, it was no longer a matter of intimidation.

An example needed to be set or they would have problems with the locals in the area they extorted from.

Theirs was a business that relied on intimidation more than anything, and if word got out that one man had avoided having to pay them by beating the shit out of their people, very few others would continue to pay them for protection.

He could understand that, but damned if he would pay them now or ever. The asshats had made it personal.

Now wide awake, he dragged his laptop closer and called up the footage of the cameras around the building to give him a view of the men who approached.

This time, there were only three. Despite the lower number, though, these goons looked better prepared for a fight than Drew's people had been. They were each armed with pistols and knives.

Their weapons were probably not what he needed to focus on, he realized after a moment, but rather the jerrycans of what he could only assume were gasoline.

"Oh, *hell* no." Taylor hissed with quiet fury, pushed off the bed, and pulled a pair of pants on. "If anyone burns this place to the ground, it'll be me for the insurance money."

They clearly wouldn't leave him much time to prepare for it either.

He would have to give a little thought to traps he could set up and shit like in *Home Alone*. His would be considerably more deadly, obviously, but the concept remained.

The idea in his head was that his defenses would simply handle all intrusions without him and would-be arsonists would be killed in the maze of traps he would leave for them so he could get a decent amount of sleep.

"Fucking assholes." He shook his head. "Interrupting a businessman's sleep is not good for the economy. Seriously, do these guys want us all in some kind of gasoline-induced recession because no one lets us get any fucking sleep?"

He picked Betsy up from where she leaned on one of the nearby walls and hefted the bat in his hands. The intruders approached the front entrance of the former grocery store which did provide a small window of time for him to prepare. But they would still be between him and the weapons he stored near the back entrance.

From the looks of it, they were miles above what the previous crew could achieve given that they had already picked the lock and were on their way inside—to where he didn't have any cameras set up yet.

"Damn it," he whispered as he crept down the steps while he stowed his phone in his pocket. He took slow, deep breaths as he moved through the hallway toward the abandoned aisles of the grocery store.

Their conversation was audible before he was even close enough to see them.

"Did we have to do this at night?" one demanded. "And this late? The guy leaves at the end of business hours. If we'd given it an hour, maybe two, and then headed in, we'd still have been home in time for bed."

"The boss doesn't want any mistakes this time, which is why he chose the three of us," a second grumbled and sounded like he would have preferred to be in bed at this late hour as well. "The last guys fucked up, so we need to set an example. We only have to set the whole place on fire to make sure the guy knows he needs to pay up if he wants to work in this area."

Taylor smiled grimly. These guys thought he was gone for the day.

It was a reasonable assumption but if they had bothered to scout a little, they would have seen his truck parked at the back. He assumed the idea was apparently not to burn the place to the ground with him in it, but they really needed to up their criminal skills or countless people would be unintentionally crisped during their careers.

That was just unprofessional, and annoying for those crisped.

Then again, if they had any skills, they wouldn't be criminals in the first place. Or, at least, not the kind who visited someone else's place of business at two in the morning with arson in mind.

If not for the very real seriousness of the situation, he'd have found it funny. Instead, he focused and moved silently around the aisles they currently discussed using as a starting point for their fire.

They at least seemed a little more professional now that they had their whining over with and would be ready for a fight. They even lowered their voices somewhat. While still not the best in the business, they wouldn't be as easy to deal with singlehandedly as the others had been.

It was all for the best. Having been rudely awakened at this ungodly hour, he wanted a real fight.

He'd fucking earned it.

"Hey!" one of them shouted as he approached and stayed low while he advanced quickly. They reacted in seconds and brandished their weapons while they searched for a target in the darkness, but he reached them before they could identify him.

The first fell back into one of his comrades and dropped his revolver when Taylor pounded his chest with the bat. Both intruders fell to the ground and he turned his attention to the man who was still on his feet with a Beretta in his hands. Thankfully, he seemed unable to find the safety and generally seemed unfamiliar with the weapon.

What the hell?

Taylor pushed forward, drove his shoulder into the man's midsection, and pounded him into the aisle wall to knock the breath out of him. Before the thug could recover, he pivoted in place, thumped the gun out of his hands with the knob of the bat, and smacked the other side into his throat.

The man gasped for breath as Taylor took a step back and stayed low as he swung the bat hard into his left knee. He continued the movement to bring it up and deliver a forceful blow to the left side of his head. The attack felled him without so much as a whisper except for the clatter when his head impacted with the floor.

Some might call it harsh but when it came to survival, it was necessary.

The other two realized how deep in shit they were but unlike the previous team that had tried to run from their imminent doom, they tried to scramble to retrieve their weapons instead.

Taylor didn't care which was the smarter of the two choices. It wasn't like they would end differently either way, and he intended to deliver an even stronger message to whoever had sent them. Their response to his attack was irrelevant. They had started this, and he would finish it in the best way he could—*with extreme prejudice.*

A small part of him whispered that he was no longer in the Zoo and that extreme measures were no longer necessary for survival. It was easy enough to shrug it aside and respond to the instinctive drive that pushed him to do what he knew best. He had some issues to work out. Even he could admit that.

But in that moment, he considered it irrelevant.

The first man fumbled with the revolver he'd dropped and Taylor attempted to use a baseball bat as the world's most useless hockey stick. It worked well enough to skitter the weapon a few yards out of reach.

He stepped on the intruder's hand, stamped hard enough to hear a crunch in the wrist, and brought the knob of his weapon to bear on his back.

The third man had retrieved his pistol and leveled it at his adversary's head, but he simply swung the bat up and around and hammered his hand upward so the gun fired harmlessly into the ceiling. Another strike knocked the weapon out of his hand entirely and was quickly followed up by a third blow to the man's shoulder. He sprawled awkwardly and cried out in pain.

"You dumb fucks simply don't get it." Taylor glared at his opponent, who writhed and clutched his broken shoulder.

"What?" the thug asked.

"Well, not you precisely. I've already deduced that you three weren't told who would be waiting for you here if you tried to attack it. You're only the low-level foot soldiers, grunts really, who were told where to show up and what was expected of you."

"I'll have you know—"

"Yeah, yeah, I know you are the best guys that could be called on short notice, and yes, you make more than the average worker does in a year," he continued as he gathered the fallen weapons while they watched him warily. "I was talking about your bosses. You know, the guys who know what happened to the last team they sent here and decided to go ahead and send in another. You should really think about finding another place of employment. Provided you get the chance, that is."

"Oh, God, you love the sound of your own voice, don't you?" the man asked and pushed into a seated position. "Why don't you save us the torture of another monologue from you and call the cops already?"

"No, I don't think you understand." Taylor shook his head. "You guys came here in the middle of the fucking night with every intention of burning my place to the ground with me in it."

"We didn't know you were here."

"And that makes it all better, right?" He snorted derisively. "I have a thing against fire. Shoot me, knife me, punch or hit me with a blunt object...cool. It's kind of expected in my position. But when you set me on fire is where I see it as personal."

"So...you're not going to—"

"No." Taylor hefted the bat and swung it at the man's head. The impact could be felt all the way into his hands and the ring of the aluminum was all he could hear for a few long seconds. "I won't call the cops."

He would have to move them himself, which sucked. His grin became smug and feral. But not as much as the amount of suck that would be waiting for these dumbasses when they woke up.

If they woke up.

Something smelled like ammonia—a really strong smell that seemed to claw into his nostrils with such intensity that he recoiled from it instinctively in an effort to escape from the stench.

Bruce wasn't entirely sure it would improve, but it couldn't get any worse.

When he opened his eyes, though, he realized exactly how wrong his assumption was. They hadn't really thought this whole thing through.

They had been sent in to deal with some dude who was being problematic with his protection payments. It was the kind of thing they were tasked with all the time and were paid rather well to do so, too.

Sure, Big G had other guys to do the actual intimidation and the occasional trashing of a place, but when a real message needed to be sent, Bruce, Con, and Cal were the ones he called in. They mostly dealt with rival gangs and the like with the occasional divergence into serious arson and assassination—usually when the targets were asleep.

He still thought they could have scheduled it a little earlier to allow them to get in and out of this place in time for them to head home before the sun began to rise. It was funny how the mind latched onto minor resentments even when faced with much bigger issues.

Either way, it seemed like they wouldn't make it anywhere. He looked around the room they were in and it gradually dawned on him that things would definitely become far worse.

Already, they were well on the way to what he might call seriously in the shit.

It looked like they were in something like a walk-in

freezer but it wasn't on. There was no sign of the meat that used to be stored in the room, thankfully, but the poles and hooks they used to hang from remained. Bruce, Con, and Cal were now suspended on these, bound by what looked like old wiring.

Memories of what had happened previously began to seep in slowly. He recalled how confident they'd been when they had arrived and how they'd expected it to be empty. The guy with a bat had waded in unexpectedly and disabled them one by one to leave them each with their own personal and probably permanent injuries to remember him by.

Bruce could feel the pain in his wrist and head. Con looked like he nursed a broken knee and a concussion as well, while Cal had what appeared to be a broken wrist but not much else.

Had the guy simply given up?

It didn't really matter, though. They were strung up like three Christmas hams, ready to be carved by the man who put the smelling salts he'd used to wake them up with away.

"You can't hold us here like this," Bruce said. He knew it was a weak argument, but hey, the guy had turned the other team over to the cops. Maybe he could be persuaded to do so again.

"You can't break into my place of business like this," their captor responded, picked up the baseball bat he had used against them from a nearby table, and rested it against his shoulder. "We appear to be at something a legal impasse that I'm…ninety percent sure will be decided in my favor.

Although I doubt those odds will remain the same if they ever find your remains and realize what I did to you."

"What you—"

"Self-defense is one thing," Taylor spoke over him. "Obviously, but the kind of fucked up shit I have in mind supersedes that," he continued and moved to where Con had a little difficulty staying awake to pat his cheek lightly. "A line has to be drawn somewhere." Taylor turned to Bruce. "Wait, does Nevada have any duty to retreat laws?"

Bruce looked hastily at his cronies while his brain wrestled for a way out of this murder dungeon.

"That's what I thought," the man said. "It's all a moot point anyway, given that no one will actually find your bodies, but it's always good to know. See, the nice realtor who sold me this place never really thought about how easy it is to hide bodies around here. There's a furnace in the back that needs a few bits and pieces fixed but is still functional. It's like these people didn't even look into the possibilities a place like this presents."

A chill shivered down his spine. The guy was talking like a serial killer would and rambled on about terrifying topics as if he discussed sports or the weather.

It wasn't helped by the fact that he reached into a duffel bag and withdrew what looked like a ten-inch-long scimitar knife, thin and wickedly curved, as well as a knife sharpener. He began to work the blade to an even sharper edge than it had already while he paced at the opposite end of the room.

"Honestly," Taylor called over his shoulder. "I didn't think I would do this much blood-letting now that I am in what is supposed to be the civilized US. But, as it turns out, you irredeemable dumbasses simply can't take a hint."

"We were only here to give you a message," Bruce said and tried not to let the tremor he could feel in his legs seep into his voice. "To get you to pay like everyone else in the neighborhood."

"I have no intention to pay anything," he said and shook his head vehemently. "And, you know, I happen to believe in killing the messenger..."

"Bruce."

"Bruce, I do believe in killing the messenger," he continued. "You know why? Because it *sends a fucking message.*"

He tried to inch away as his tormentor pressed the now razor-sharp blade to his neck. Most people tried to look intense when they wanted to be intimidating and waved a weapon around to show the people they didn't give a fuck.

It worked—sometimes, anyway—but this guy's deadpan delivery was far more terrifying. He wasn't trying to intimidate. It was exactly like he said. He wanted to send a message.

The blade dug a little deeper into his neck and even drew a little blood until something buzzed nearby and broke his captor's concentration.

"Oh, for fuck's sake," the man exclaimed, pulled away from him, and returned to the table where his phone was. "Goddammit," He looked at Bruce. "Did you guys bring friends? What's with all this traffic? This ain't fucking Halloween and I don't have any candy."

He shoved the phone into his pocket and walked toward the only entryway—a door, Bruce realized, that couldn't be opened from the inside—and gathered everything that might be used as a weapon on the way.

"Hang tight there, little buddies. I'll be right back." The man closed the door behind him.

The silence that settled over them was palpable as their captor walked away.

"Don't hurry back," Con said softly in the darkness.

"We're in no rush."

CHAPTER FOURTEEN

"All these fucking people, all fucking night," Taylor muttered belligerently and put the knife away where he could retrieve it quickly later if he needed to. The meat freezer was entirely secure, especially considering that the trio inside would have trouble standing at all, but it was better to be safe than sorry.

And he hadn't lied, not entirely. The building did have a furnace and it was mostly functional. The parts were expected the next day along with those he needed for the boiler, but he had no idea what he could use it for as yet. Maybe if they really needed to forge and cut metal?

Either way, it would be complicated—if not totally impossible—to use it for body disposal. It wouldn't work for full corpses at all.

Besides, he wasn't sure if he actually did want to kill them and dispose of the bodies like that. He was seriously pissed, so it wasn't off the table, but it would be best to simply scare the absolute shit out of the dumbasses and drag them back to their boss in person to make sure he didn't try this bullshit ever again.

It wasn't like he was unreasonable.

Yet people constantly arrived to piss him off even further.

The failed raids aside, he doubted the disturbance outside was backup for his three prisoners.

They would have sent more than one person to get them out, for one thing, and based on the looks of the woman who approached his front door, he didn't see her as a member of whatever the fuck gang the three were a part of.

He moved toward the door and peered at the camera feed that showed him who it was. She was dressed in what looked like a grey pantsuit—though he couldn't be sure in the lighting—and heels, her long hair pulled into a rigid ponytail.

She looked tired, bored, and definitely not in a good mood, which coincidentally reflected his own emotional state at the moment. He was simply in no fucking mood to deal with much of anything at this point. All he wanted was to go to bed.

Was that so fucking wrong?

Taylor still didn't think she was a member of the gang, but there was no real point in making assumptions. He chose one of the guns the goons had involuntarily surrendered to him and checked the magazine before he chambered a round in the Beretta and flicked the safety off. After a quick moment to think, he cocked the hammer back as well as he moved toward the front door.

Given recent events, he decided he couldn't be too

careful and pressed the barrel to the door so it aimed at the woman in question when he pulled it open.

It creaked softly and drew her attention to him.

"Hi," she said with what he immediately recognized as a fake smile. "I'm looking for Taylor McFadden?"

He narrowed his eyes, tilted his head in query, and gave himself a moment to study her. She was armed judging by the gentle bulge under her left shoulder, although her hand position and body language told him she didn't expect to have to use the weapon. Maybe she didn't realize that he had a gun of his own aimed at her.

Or she didn't care.

Either way, he had little inclination to give her the opportunity to explain the reason why.

"Hi," Taylor said with deliberate rudeness. "We're actually closed for business for tonight. Well, this morning anyway. There are issues with the labor force that, quite frankly, don't involve you, so you could come back at about...well, *never* would be just fantastic."

Her eyes widened and her mouth fell open before he shut the door in her face. He really, really hoped this would be the end of it. Or that she would at least take the hint and come back in the morning.

For some reason, though, he really doubted that would be the case.

She stepped in closer and pounded her fist against the door. It wasn't the sturdiest, to begin with, and still needed work to be a viable security barrier against people who wanted to enter.

He had actually thought about getting steel bars to reinforce the door itself as well as the frames. That way, even a battering ram would have difficulty gaining entry.

Unfortunately, the current, weak frame shuddered with each and every blow. He expected her to stop at some point, either because she ran out of steam or maybe because her hand would hurt.

But no, this was definitely not his lucky night.

"Listen to her," he grumbled irritably. "Seventeen, eighteen, nineteen… Goddammit, *fine!*"

He returned to the door—although he didn't bother with the gun this time—and yanked it open. "What the fuck is the matter with you? Don't you have…like, sleep to get to?"

"I'll go ahead and assume you're Taylor McFadden," she said and shook her head as if to try to control her annoyance. He simply stared at her while she rubbed her hand meaningfully before she slid it into her coat pocket to withdraw a badge. "My name is Special Agent Niki Banks, and I'm—"

"A fed?" he demanded incredulously. "Now I want to talk to you even less."

Another shocked expression crossed her face as he slammed the door shut again. It was gratifying to see but he doubted that would be the end of it.

As if on cue, she began to pound on the door again.

"Seriously, if this is how the FBI runs things, I wouldn't be surprised if you have a thousand noise complaints on your hands!" he shouted from the other side of the door, took a deep breath, and headed toward the freezer.

He had to assume his prisoners had been left alone long enough to consider a way to escape and he didn't want them thinking that way. He wasn't done with them by a damn mile and hope in their minds would poison whatever punishment he finally decided to subject them to.

It took effort to ignore the furious assault on his front door as he pulled the lever to open the freezer and peered in at the three assholes he had strung up on the meat hooks. He had managed to secure them in such a way that kept their feet on the ground, but only barely, before he'd locked the hooks in place.

They wouldn't go anywhere without breaking the pipe that kept the three of them in place, which would make almost as much ruckus as the fed at his front door made.

"Hey, guys," Taylor said as he checked each one to make sure none of them had managed to loosen their bonds. "How are you all doing? Do you need something to drink... eat? I can whip something up in the kitchen...nah, that would be funnier if I actually had a whip to use, but anyway."

None of them responded and all avoided his gaze like they wanted to avoid attracting his attention to any one of them. It wasn't something he really cared for since it could mean they were, in fact, trying to find a way out of the restraints they were currently in and didn't want him to read it in their eyes.

"No?" he asked and checked the integrity of the pipe. "No comments about how I won't get away with this or how I'll suffer once your boss finds out? Maybe begging me to let the cops pick you up?"

Silence was the only response.

"Ugh, fine, be like that." His mockery aside, he hadn't expected them to be anything but less than helpful and maybe a little surly about being held against their will, but he really didn't give a shit.

If they wanted to piss him off further, he would simply kill them and most of his night would be wasted finding a way to get rid of the bodies.

Of course, the woman who continued to knock at the door now got on his last damn nerve. He could still hear her from the back, and from the sound of things, there was a real danger that she would simply break it down soon.

She had stamina, he had to admit, and her determination drew reluctant admiration although the sentiment behind it wasn't entirely complimentary. In other circumstances, he might be appreciative of it, but he wanted to get some fucking sleep and he had the feeling that she would be a serious obstacle to that.

More so than the trio inside, he acknowledged grimly.

"Hold on. It looks like I have a caller," Taylor said. "Don't move. I'll be right back."

"No!" Bruce called. "Leave the door open."

"I can't hear you over the sound of..." He paused and shook his head. "Some...joke about you three having vaginas. Let your imagination fill in the rest. I'm too tired for this shit."

"Please, do—" they started to say but he cut them off when he closed the door behind him.

It was comforting to know that the room was at least soundproofed. He didn't know when that might come in handy, but he was sure he could be creative enough to find a way to make it useful. When he'd had a full night of sleep. Preferably in this lifetime.

The woman was still beating the door to within an inch of its life when he reached it and yanked it open.

"For fuck's sake, what?" he roared and forced her to take a step back. She looked surprised and more than a little pissed.

Still, she showed more self-control than he was capable of at the moment and took a deep breath before she spoke. "Taylor, is it? Do you mind if we talk?"

"If we do, will you continue to break your hand on my fucking door?" he demanded.

"Well, I think I was closer to breaking the door than my hand."

"Yeah and considering that I'm in the middle of remodeling this whole fucking place, I'd rather not have that charge added to everything else," he retorted. "Say your fucking piece and get the hell off my property."

"Well, I think I should preface this with the fact that I know you have a trio of criminals strung up in there somewhere—assuming they are still alive, of course," Banks said and folded her arms over her chest. "With that and the fact that I am a federal agent in mind, are you sure you can't invite me in?"

Taylor scowled. He didn't want to let her in but he also didn't want to have a horde of other federal agents trampling over his business either. He assumed that she wanted more than merely to talk but at this point, he really didn't give a shit. He only wanted to get some fucking sleep.

"Fine." He finally stepped aside and let her enter.

"Thank you," she replied, her voice still calm. "You should also know that I'm not the kind of agent who wants to be embroiled in the paperwork of arresting you for killing the three men, so assuming they're still alive—"

"They are."

"I'll be able to take them off your hands without too much trouble," she continued. "In doing so, we'll also save you the trouble of doing something you probably wouldn't lose any sleep over."

"Not a wink," he admitted.

"Right. Not a wink. That said, would you consider keeping your mind open to what I have to say? I have the feeling you have a habit of tuning out anything and everything any authority figure might say."

"You're not wrong." He folded his arms and regarded her warily. "And you only want to talk?"

"Well, I want much more than that but talking is how we'll get there," she replied.

"So, you take the three stooges in there off my hands," he said. "And I get six hours—"

"Four hours," she said.

"Four more hours of sleep," he continued and scowled at her. "And we'll talk then?" She simply stared at him and he sighed. "Sure, what the fuck ever. I am curious to know about how you plan to take them off my hands, though. It's not like you can write them up after what I did to them."

"What did you do to them?" she asked as he guided her through the empty grocery store toward the back where he had them bound in the freezer.

"I worked them over with a baseball bat," he said. "I was rougher than I needed to be, but given that they arrived with gas and the intention to burn this place down, I thought it was warranted."

She shook her head. "Of course you did."

He snipped, "What's that supposed to mean?"

"Nothing," she replied quickly. "Let's get this over with."

Taylor yanked the lever and pulled the door open. He was greeted by the surprised and even a little hopeful eyes of the three men when the light filled the space again. They weren't happy to see him obviously, and no discernible emotion crossed their faces when Banks stepped in behind him.

After a moment, their stoic expressions gave way to a little surprise, but they said nothing. They didn't really want to know what his friend would want to do with them.

"Well, boys, it looks like today is your lucky day." Taylor checked to make sure their restraints were still in place. "Special Agent Banks here is willing to take you dumbasses off my hands as long as you are really, really sorry and promise to mend your ways."

"Actually, all I really need is a confession from you three and we should be good," the woman said, retrieved her phone, and set it to record. "I only need to hear how the three of you broke into this man's property with the intention to burn it down with him inside and all that."

"We didn't know he was in here," Bruce said and shook his head vigorously.

"Yeah, because that shit somehow makes it all better?" Taylor snorted.

"I don't need any interference from you," Banks said and focused her full attention on the three men who were still strung up on meat hooks. "So, continue. Why did you come here?"

"We had word from our employer that there was a

certain character who didn't want to pay his protection money in this area," Bruce said. "We didn't know who he was or why he didn't pay. We were sent here to torch his place of business since apparently, he gave the first guys our employer sent a hard time."

"I beat them up and let the cops arrest them," Taylor explained.

"I know," the woman snapped. "I spent all day getting your name off that particular police report, dumbass. Sorry gentleman," she said to the hoods. "Continue."

"Anyway, the three of us filled up with gas and came here to do our business," Bruce continued. "We were trying to decide where to start the fire when this guy showed up out of fucking nowhere and beat the shit out of us with a baseball bat. I have a concussion and a broken hand. Con looks like he has a broken knee and a cracked skull too, and Cal...well, he's in a bad way too."

"With a bat, huh?" Banks said. "Well, I think that's all I need for the moment, really. Thank you, gentlemen."

"What—you know none of what I said it admissible in court, right?"

"Court?" She raised an eyebrow. "This is enough for me to send your sorry asses to the Zoo. Do you think you guys could handle that?"

"Not to be overly judgmental, but my money's on them getting shit out of a monster before the end of the week," Taylor said and grinned. "In fairness, though, that's still paradise compared to what I had in mind for them."

"Shut up McFadden and help me get them to my car," the agent said as she rescued the first one from the hook.

Any worries he might have had that they would try to

make their escape were quickly allayed. None of them wanted to risk their unexpected way out of there, and once he released the other two from the hooks, they put up no resistance to being walked—or in Con's case, carried —outside.

When they reached the vehicle, however, Bruce seemed to suddenly grow a spine as he shoved himself away from Taylor's hands, yanked hard, and writhed out of his grasp before he attempted to make his way to where they had apparently parked their own car.

The man's fear of what might have occurred in the walk-in freezer had apparently dissipated and he thought he had a chance at freedom.

In fairness, with his captor still mostly carrying his comrade, he might have had a chance if Banks hadn't been there.

The man had apparently forgotten her and he stumbled into a run. She released Cal and rapidly gained on the runaway.

Taylor's eyebrows raised when she caught up with him. He stopped and spun to lash out at her but she planted her feet, caught him by his collar, and flipped him expertly over her hip to land with a loud groan.

"You are almost more trouble than you are worth," she muttered and hauled him up again. "Do you want to stay here? I really don't care. I only need two of you to cooperate so he will meet with me later."

Bruce made no objection to being shoved into the back of her SUV, followed quickly by his comrades.

"Are we good?" Taylor asked, anxious for the whole thing to end.

"Sure," she replied and wiped her hands clean on her pantsuit. "I'll see you in four hours."

"Yeah, don't fucking remind me," he retorted. "I need to get some sleep. See you on the flipside, Banks."

"Yeah, whatever." She slid into the driver's seat and headed off without a backward glance.

CHAPTER FIFTEEN

Four hours went by all too rapidly, and the persistent and now appallingly familiar buzz dragged him from sleep yet again. He felt for the bat he had hidden under his bed with one hand while the other fumbled for his phone.

Instinct told him that more invaders tried to break into his property and recommended that he prepare himself to deliver the next round of pain.

As his eyes focused and his fingers finally unlocked the phone, he realized he was both right and wrong in this instance. The motion sensors told him that someone had moved through the perimeter and parked a car in front of the entrance.

The buzzing wasn't only the alert from his security system but also an unknown number that now made a third attempt to reach him.

He answered when the caller tried again and pressed it to his ear as he pushed himself into a seated position.

"What?" he mumbled.

"What? That's not very nice." Banks sounded inordinately chirpy on the other side of the line. "How are you doing, McFadden? Are you ready to have that talk we agreed to have?"

"Fuck off. You wouldn't believe the night I had."

"Get dressed, maybe take a shower, and get out here," she replied. "I assume you smell like the south end of a northbound cow. I'll wait for you here in my car—and I have coffee."

Well, that was one way to get on his better side, he decided, pushed from the bed, and did as he was told. He was a little whiffy, he had to admit, and so it took him about ten minutes before he headed down to where she was parked outside the entrance in the same SUV she had been driving the night before.

Hell, she looked like she hadn't had any sleep but still looked rested—or active, anyway—as she pushed the passenger door open for him.

The aroma of coffee greeted him as he joined her in the car, shifted to get comfortable, and scowled when she handed him one of the disposable cups.

"How the fuck are you so cheery this early in the morning?" he asked and sniffed the coffee suspiciously before he took a sip. It wasn't great but it would do for now.

"I've learned to keep myself up and alert for as long as possible without rest, then sleep for twelve to fourteen hours to recover all the hours I lost," Banks said, started the SUV, and pulled out of the parking lot. "That and I do a shit-ton of cocaine. Whichever you prefer."

He shrugged. "I'm no fed so I don't give a shit what kind

of chemicals you need to use to keep yourself in the business."

"I tend to think the same way." She kept her eyes on the road. "But I guess that kind of thinking would have to stop if I were ever to work on a drug task force."

"Right. Speaking of which, what the hell do you want from me? It's enough for you to be willing to take those hoods off my hands, so it must be good."

"If you only knew how much work went into finding you and getting you to this point. But that can wait. I'm in the mood for breakfast. Do you know any diners around here where we can get food?"

"Sure." He leaned closer to the touchpad between them and added the name of the diner he had gone to the day before. The food had been good, even if the service had been a little iffy, and it was the only place outside of Jackson's he knew and liked.

They pulled into the parking lot, entered, and selected one of the booths in the corner.

"So," Taylor said. "Here's the part where you tell me what the hell it is you want from me."

She nodded and raised a finger. "Just a sec," she said and turned her attention to the waitress who approached their table with coffee mugs and a full pot. "Hi...yeah, black coffee, thanks. And I saw you guys have a special on waffles?"

"Yes, ma'am." The waitress was the same woman who had waited on Taylor on his last visit. "And for you?" she asked him.

"Black coffee works for me." He rubbed his temples.

The day would need an endless supply of the brew so he'd give it a kick-start.

"Should I give you two a moment to think about food?"

"Sure," Banks said and the woman backed away quickly once she'd poured their coffees.

"I hate repeating myself and don't want to ask again," he said and took a sip. "So maybe I'll throw in a joke about you not having a dick and yet still being one."

"Classy," she retorted. "Anyway, to the issue, then. I'm Special Agent in Charge of a task force in the FBI that's been given the fun opportunity to locate and dispose of cryptids."

"Cryptids?"

"Animals of a...shall we say, non-terrestrial origin?"

"So, Zoo creatures," he said immediately. "But wait, the FBI only has jurisdiction on operations inside the US."

"Exactly. Issues have arisen ever since the arrival of the damn goop. We have gathered the kinds of people who would be able to hunt these cryptids and use them to deal with the monsters."

"Okay. What kind of setup do you work from?"

"Are you guys ready to order?" the waitress interrupted. "We didn't have much time to talk the last time you came by, handsome. I didn't know you had a girlfriend."

Taylor opened his mouth, tilted his head in confusion, and looked at the woman. Was she really trying to get them involved in small talk?

"I...I'll take one those waffles," he said and ignored her attempt. "With bacon, eggs, and toast. Get me the works, if you don't mind. Oh, and apple juice."

"I'll have the same," the agent said. "It's been a long night."

"You can say that again."

"Long night, huh?" The woman sounded less than happy to hear it.

Taylor fixed her with a scowl. "Do you need anything else?"

"Nope. I'll...uh, get your orders in. Back in a jiff," she said, turned quickly, and headed to the kitchen.

"So, what was it you liked about this place again?" Banks asked.

"I wish I could say it was the service but it's actually the food. The special on waffles they've had for the past five years or so means they are actually really good."

"Anyway." She shook her head and her expression grew serious again. "Regarding our setup, we mostly work with freelancers and bring them in on a bounty payment system to deal with the issues that have arisen. They're not always Zoo monsters, mind you. Sometimes, they can be regular animals going on a rampage, *The Ghost and The Darkness* style. At other times, it can be a human with a fucked-up head. We don't really mind one way or another, as long as it doesn't get too much press."

"That makes sense. At least you don't have these people on an official salary with the FBI."

"Quite. In your case, though, I will be your handler, which basically means I oversee you and make sure you get anything you need to get the job done."

She paused and narrowed her eyes at him when the waitress returned with their plates, topped their coffee up again, and moved away. At least she didn't try to talk to them this time.

"What?" she asked after a moment. "No lewd remarks about that? Something about handling or how I'll take care of you?"

"Nah, I thought you would do a better job of it than I ever could," he replied. "Besides, I'm only after empty relationships that have no meaning and where we both go away happy, so there's no need for any handling like that. From you, anyway."

"So, what does that make me?"

Taylor paused to take a mouthful of food, which consisted of bacon and syrup-covered waffles. "A toxic attitude with delusions of awesomeness in high heels and a need to feel dominant all wrapped up in an attractive gift package that smells like a body that's been left to rot for a week."

Her eyebrows all but reached her hairline. "Excuse you."

Another mouthful of food meant a short silence before he continued. "I'm sorry, do you need me to make it more specific? Here, try this one then. You look like Eva Longoria except with more brawn than brains, you probably can't spell Latina, and obviously, you don't care about showers. Which is okay. The government only wants you for your brawn anyway."

Banks narrowed her eyes. "Yeah, I smell like the three cretins you needed me to get rid of for you. Between the stench of fear and gasoline? Yeah, I guess that does make for a foul smell."

He shrugged. "I showered, at least."

She scowled at him. "You're a jackass."

"Correction," he said with a grin. "I'm a jackass who can kill—what did you call them?—cryptids. A jackass who can kill cryptids who's living here in the US, no less. The kind of jackass who has the experience you need to kill something that couldn't be handled by your average cop or SWAT officer."

"Oh, great," the woman grumbled. "And here I am, stuck with a Jason Momoa wannabe Cro-Magnon Neanderthal with slightly better dental hygiene and a god-complex. I don't get paid enough for this shit."

"What was that?" he asked.

"Nothing." She sighed, the sound long-suffering. "So, are you onboard? Will you help us?"

"Who is us?"

"Well, there's me, obviously." She toyed with the food on her plate. "And there will be the Cryptid Research and Elimination Task Force, which is what you'll work as, by the by. I'll be your field agent, but your operations contact will be Desk."

That caught his attention and he paused his loaded fork halfway to his mouth. "Desk?"

"It's a code name since not all our operators in the office or who work from the desk, as it were, are comfortable having their names given out freely to the kinds of field operatives we use." She finished her waffle and focused on the bacon. "Think of them like the Moneypenny to your James Bond."

"And that makes you..."

"M, obviously," she snarked around the food in her mouth. "The one who runs the whole show. Desk will manage your day-to-day, get you any equipment you need, and generally keep you apprised of anything you need to know while in the field."

"Wait, wouldn't that make Desk Q to my James Bond?"

"Huh…I guess it would. I, in the meantime, have a group of other overly-testosteroned operatives who like to play with bombs I need to manage."

"Boobs," Taylor corrected her.

"Excuse me?"

"You know…tits. Tatas. Feminine Fun bags."

"I know what boobs are, moron," she retorted through clenched teeth.

"Well, yeah. The thing is, I tinkered with bombs in the Zoo," he explained. "As fun as they were, I came all the shit-fucking way out here to get away from the explosives and dying and shit that are usually associated with them. I want to play with building things that save people and boobs. I have a company. You came to me, so let's lay this out straight. I don't care if you call me names, I find it funny. I want to be very clear that I'm not politically correct and will say what's on my mind. I'm a contractor, not an employee, so feel free to fire me any time you feel like it and I can get back to the two things I want most—building things and boobs. Not always in that order."

"So, you really don't care about lo—"

Taylor shook his head. "Don't go there. Don't be that person. I know enough women who are adult enough to admit that all they want is fun, frolicking and f—"

"Don't fucking say it," Banks warned.

"I intended to say fornicating but fine, be a prude," he responded with a chuckle. "But it's good that we under-stand each other. I'm not politically correct as I've already pointed out. I'm here to help by killing shit that needs to be killed. I don't push myself on anyone but if she wants me, I have no reservations or regrets. I've almost died twice—horribly, I might add—and I've been around friends who have died horribly. Call me whatever names you want—"

"On that topic," she said, drew a manila folder out of her briefcase, and put it on the table.

He wiped his hands and lips on a napkin and pulled the folder closer to see the title written in marker at the top.

"The Cryptid Assassin?" he asked and raised an eyebrow. "What, was the Grim Alien Reaper not available?"

"As a matter of fact, it wasn't. Besides, the code names are given by people inside the Bureau. It would seem your reputation precedes you."

"Fun times." Taylor put the file down and focused on finishing his meal. "Well, you can color me on board, Longoria-Adjacent." The truth of that surprised him, as did his easy capitulation. Even a month ago, he'd have run like hell from only the idea of facing Zoo monsters again. But there was the fact that this wouldn't be massed attacks because this was the US. At worst, he would face one or maybe two of the mutants. Besides, he hated the Zoo and the idea that it might have a foothold in the States already. He had to do what he was trained and supremely qualified to do. It was part of keeping the Zoo Armageddon at bay.

With Bungees now working for him fulltime, he knew his business interests and the property renovations would be covered, and it wasn't like he would be away for weeks at a time. Days, maybe, but they could stay in touch unless he was actually on the mission itself. Besides, the man was more than capable of taking care of most things. That was one of the reasons he had hired him.

"I've always wanted to be a James Bond type," he added with a grin, "even if it is only for the FBI."

"Well, we all have to start somewhere," she retorted.

CHAPTER SIXTEEN

Breakfast was finished quickly once the discussion was concluded between them. It wasn't like they didn't like the food, after all. As Taylor had said, while the service was lacking but still passable, the food was close to fantastic and after the business part of their meal was finished, they could finally dig in.

When the bill arrived, Banks was quick to pick it up and told him she would be able to write it off as a business meeting anyway. That meant he was stuck with the tip. He went with the twenty percent he had last time because he didn't really have any complaints that would justify cutting it.

Once they were finished, they headed to the SUV and the agent drove him to the strip mall he now called home. The drive, like the tail-end of their breakfast, passed with little conversation between them. He didn't mind that, of course. There weren't many people in the world you could enjoy a nice long silence with.

Maybe Banks felt the same way. Or maybe she was

tired of talking to him and needed a break. She had what she wanted from him, after all, and since they clearly weren't cut out to be friends or anything like that, there wasn't much to say.

It seemed reasonable enough, and if he actually cared enough down the line, he would think about maybe being a little more civil to her in the future. They would now work together, although maybe not directly if this Desk person had anything to say about it. He could understand why someone in their position would want to keep their actual names a mystery to the people in the field. It was a matter of protecting oneself, and he couldn't blame anyone for that, especially when they were used to being safe and protected behind a...well, a desk.

With that in mind, Desk seemed appropriate as a name, but it wouldn't roll easily off the tongue. Calling someone a desk simply didn't feel natural to him.

They pulled up to the strip mall and Banks parked the SUV in the parking lot and stepped out.

"I still don't know why you bought this property," she said as she studied it with a definite look of distaste. "I understand the whole need to own a piece of land for oneself, but it looks worse during the day than it did at night and believe me, that's saying something. I'm telling you this whole place looks like shit, by the way."

"You don't have a lick of imagination," Taylor said and shook his head. "While I suppose that's essentially mandatory for all government employees, it means that all you see is what it is and not what it can be with a little work and remodeling."

"Fuck you," she replied. "How will this be anything but a

heaping pile of shit, no matter how much work you put into it?"

"It is difficult to make prefab look good," he admitted. "But the looks aren't what this is about. There's room for development here, work can be done, and improvements can be made—all while working on some of the highest-tech mech suits in the business. There are people in the world who have settled for less."

"Okay, fair enough...I guess that makes sense." She still shook her head as though she might like to continue the debate. "Anyway, if you're interested in getting to work right away, I have one or two files on me you can look at—see if you can start getting a feel for the business."

He nodded and they went inside and climbed the stairs to the area he had sectioned off for his living quarters, which had a desk and chairs for them to use.

"These files are highly classified, so maybe keep that in mind when you're talking to your drinking buddies." She placed a couple of manila envelopes on the desk for him to look at.

"How many drinking buddies do you think I have?" He picked one of the envelopes up, withdrew the files, and studied them. "I've literally just moved into town."

"I know that you have already employed someone," she said. "Robert Zhang, one of your buddies from the Zoo. We actually worked up a file on him, but he didn't qualify for the program since he didn't actually spend enough time in the Zoo."

"It's one of those things," he said. "Heading into the Zoo is a traumatizing event that either breaks you or makes you, and it broke Zhang. He even had the courage to head back in a couple more times, but…I'm glad he stayed out. And I'm glad he was able to pull himself away from the fucking allure of that place. Aliens are such a romantic idea until they try to devour you while you're shooting at them. People kind of forget about that. I did more than once. But heading in there eighty-three times tends to drill the point home in your head."

"I guess. But…do you see anything that you like in there? Something to start you off?"

Taylor focused and examined a variety of the files before he decided a couple were more interesting than others. "You really should be more trusting of the people I take on as my drinking buddies, you know, especially Bobby. He's one of the best when it comes to mech repair and building. I'll probably need help from him anyway, at least to cover for me here while I'm hunting monsters for you. Actually, he can tell you all about it since his truck just pulled up."

Banks narrowed her eyes, stood quickly, and walked over to the window through which she could see a truck had, in fact, pulled up outside.

"How did you—did you hear him?" she asked. "I didn't hear him. Do you—"

Taylor kept a straight face for as long as he could before he broke into laughter. "Hah, no, I wish. How cool would it be if my time in the Zoo had honed my senses to allow me to detect shit normal humans aren't even aware of? But no, my phone buzzed to tell me there was a breach in the perimeter. He told me last night he could come in around this time to help me get started on the place."

"You're an asshole, you know that?"

"I'm a jackass. Don't get your insults confused," he responded with a grin.

"You can be both." She followed him to the stairs and they both headed to the first floor and out into the parking lot where Bobby waited for them.

"This place looks even worse than I remembered it," the man said and slid a pair of sunglasses on. "We have our work cut out for us here, let me tell you something, Taylor."

"Right?" The agent shook her head with a smug expression. "I tried to tell him the same thing but he went on and on about potential or some shit."

"Yeah," Bobby said with a chuckle. "Hey, Tay-Tay, who's the broad?"

"The broad is standing right in front of you," she all but snarled.

"Sure. I can see that. I didn't know you would have girls over this early in the process of rebuilding. Do you think she should head out before we get started on the renovation, or does she want to stick around?"

"Actually, this is kind of a new client," Taylor said. "Our first. Show him, Banks."

She pulled her badge out. "Special Agent Niki Banks. It's nice to finally meet you in person, Mr. Zhang."

Bobby's eyes widened. "Holy shit. You're getting us involved with law enforcement already?"

"What? Fuck no. That's not what I wanted you to show him."

"What did you want me to show him then?" she asked. "My tits?"

"Yes," the other man said with a hopeful grin.

"No." He shook his head. "Just... goddammit, never

mind. Law enforcement won't be involved in the business itself. It's simply that apparently, my country will need my services here at home and are willing to pay top dollar for it, right?"

"Something like that, yeah," Banks said. "Do you really think I trust this guy?"

"I really don't give a shit," he retorted acidly. "But know that I trust him, and if you don't want him involved in any way with your little task force, you can go ahead and fire me too."

"Thanks for the vote of confidence," Bobby said.

"Sure. The vote actually came when I hired you to help me here but sure, whatever." He grinned at his friend.

The woman rolled her eyes and sighed. "Fine. He can look at the files if you really, really need him to. Otherwise, you can think about how much you want him to be involved—or not. I don't care. I'm running on eight hours of sleep over the last forty-eight, so…come on."

They all returned to his office area and Taylor showed his employee some of the files he had been given while she fumed silently in the corner.

"Fuck me," Robert said softly. "You guys want us to hunt for Zoo monsters here in the US?"

"Correction, we want him to hunt cryptids here in the US." Banks glowered at them. "It will mostly involve investigating a variety of suspicious deaths that occur. People don't want to believe there are monsters. Some suspect and like to post shit in conspiracy websites, and that's what the FBI thought they were until reports came from the Zoo and they realized there might be some truth to the so-called conspiracies. Similar…things have appeared in other parts of the world and their agencies are handling it. We needed to deal with it in the States so the FBI was selected for that task and I was appointed. I chose people who were willing to throw themselves at monsters, and there are those who want to get away from the Zoo but also want to continue to fight it."

"Fair enough," Taylor said softly. "The fact that there are monsters here…is that merely the goop being the goop or is that some kind of human error?"

"Honestly, I'd say it's probably a mixture of the two. But I don't know enough about the goop to provide a definitive answer although there's apparently enough evidence to support it."

"Human error will do all kinds of shit for you," Bobby said with a shrug. "There's no need to add anything mystical to it."

"I'm not saying there's anything mystical about it," Banks responded a little acerbically. "But…well, there's something about the goop that seems like it's not here by accident. Like what it's doing isn't by mistake or natural occurrence and all the shit it's trying to do is intentional and we simply haven't found the truth yet. It's only my own personal theory, of course."

The man grimaced, his face a little haunted for a moment. "Honestly, I saw shit in there that I can't really explain, so I'm not about to try to tell you that you're wrong. But anyway, Taylor, are you okay with all this?"

Taylor looked up from where he had slid into silence when the two had begun to talk about the Zoo. He had zoned out while reading one of the files and had honestly not even paid attention.

"Say what now?" he asked.

"Will you be okay with all this?" His friend repeated his question.

"Why the fuck wouldn't I be?" he snapped.

"Oh, right," Banks grumbled. "I did see there might be some psychological issues regarding your return to the hunting of Zoo monsters and the like."

"I'll be fine," he insisted. "Christ, you two sound like my mother, hovering over me like a fucking Apache helicopter."

"I'm simply covering all my bases," the agent said. "Protecting the bureau from any and all possibilities that you might sue us for something no one has even thought of yet."

"Fucking hell. Give me a paper to sign and we'll be fine," he said. "Of course, it would have to include the kind of paycheck I'll receive for this. And moving on, am I supposed to simply choose one of these and get to work on it? How does this kind of shit actually work?"

"Well, eventually, yes, that's how it'll work." She gathered the files. "For the moment, though, I only shared those so you would have an idea of what the work will be like. As of right now, I still need to prove to my superiors that you're a necessary asset to the task force. In fact, they have already selected a mission for you to prove exactly that."

She placed a single file in front of him. There was no title on it but when he opened it, he realized he'd seen these pictures before. Or, at least, something similar enough. And the location was the same one the news report from the night before had highlighted.

"I've seen news on this," he said. "Bodies were discovered near DC and the cops are completely lost as to what it might have been."

"You can think about it as an audition of sorts," the agent said. "If you're ready. There is a time factor, so I need a yes or no now or we'll send one of our other operatives in to deal with it."

He nodded and picked the file up. "I'm in."

CHAPTER SEVENTEEN

"Fantastic," Banks said as she glanced quickly at the papers Taylor had signed and slid them into her briefcase. "I'll be back in a short while with the details of the mission."

"Don't hurry on my account," he said with a grin and waved as she headed away to file the papers with her superior before the window closed.

It seemed logical to assume a window of some kind was closing because it also explained why she had been unexpectedly pleasant. He had the feeling that she harbored less than civil feelings for him and held them in check because she needed him.

That was the part he didn't fully understand. On one hand, there weren't that many people coming out of the Zoo who had the experience he did, so for something like this, he was a prime candidate. He didn't need a genius IQ to grasp why she'd want him on her team.

With that said, though, if she had a strong antipathy toward him and especially if it was of the professional variety, there were enough Zoo survivors out there who could probably do the job too. Not as well as he could, of course, but that was the kind of shit that went without saying.

Which meant that whatever she had against him was personal and she kept her own feelings in check for the good of the task force. He could respect that, although he did want to know the nature of the personal feelings and what had caused them.

It could simply be that she had met him and he'd rubbed her the wrong way. That would have some part in it if it was the case, but from what he had been able to pick up about her, the bad feelings had started long before they had met. That made him wonder where they came from.

But it wasn't like he intended to dig into her past and he wasn't curious enough to ask her about it. Especially since she probably wouldn't tell him given that she likely hated him already.

Ultimately, he didn't really give enough of a shit to worry about it. If her personal feelings overrode her professional opinions, she could fire him and he would be back where he started, opening a business and living life the way he had planned.

There really wasn't anything remotely negative in that worst-case scenario at all.

Bobby stood and stretched with a groan before he turned to face him. "Are you sure you're okay with this?"

"Jesus fucking Christ, you're worse than my mother," Taylor said and leaned back in his seat. "Seriously, I'm fine. Better than fine since now, we have a new source of income that will help us get off the ground even faster."

"Well, you say that. Everyone says that, actually." His

friend folded his arms. "But if you're bullshitting on this, no kidding, I will beat some sense into you."

"You'll fucking try." He laughed and pushed to his feet. "But that's enough shooting the breeze for now. We have work to do. I have to work on the boiler room in the basement but since I'm still waiting for the parts to be delivered, we can start on the security grid."

"Okay." They turned and descended the stairs together. "Is there any reason why we're focusing on security for today?"

"Well, I guess you would find out eventually, but I didn't want you to find out like this," he said, tried to inject a little fake emotion into his voice, and failed. "Twice now, some dumbasses tried to break into the place. Both times, I caught them on the motion sensors I set up and beat the shit out of them. I called the cops the first time and the second time, also known as last night or this morning, Special Agent Banks took the criminals off my hands."

"What did she do with them?" his companion asked.

"Well, it was a 'don't ask don't tell' kind of situation. But she might have insinuated that she killed them and burned the bodies to a crisp."

"Do you believe her?"

"Fuck if I know. I don't know her well enough to decide if she's full of shit or not. All I know is that if a federal agent talks about burning bodies for me, even if she's full of shit, I'll maybe let her have her say."

"Do you think she'll try to do the same to you?" Bobby asked.

"I'll tell you what I do know. I won't turn my back on her for a fucking second." Taylor opened the door and let his companion out before he joined him. "I guess one of the things I need to have installed here first is some kind of HVAC system to make working in Vegas somewhat doable."

"Have you talked to some of the contractors who can do it?"

"Not yet. There's kind of a whole list of shit we need to do here, and if we work through the priorities, the first thing on the list is security."

"Sure it is." The other man nodded. "And it's a good thing you didn't get started on any of the small stuff yet because I have connections who should be able to come in and do most of the renovations in bulk for a quarter of the price you would get."

"Yeah, I guess I reek of a tourist they can peddle their shit to for twice the regular price."

"Right. I'll call a few of them and I'll get you quotes later. Now, what do you have in terms of security?"

"Well, I set it up basically like how we would set a camp up in the Zoo." He pointed out the devices he had spent most of the past couple of days installing. "Motion sensors give me a full view of the property for about fifty yards out. When triggered, they bring the whole camera system up, which alerts my laptop and my phone about the distur-bance and gives me the option to look at who it is on the camera feed should I want to."

"There seem to be too many possible holes," Bobby noted. "Like...what if someone knows about the motion sensors and decides to trigger it with an animal, get you to deactivate it, and then move in."

"Well, I do have it set to not be triggered for anything

smaller than a big dog," he explained. "And the programming is set so I don't have to turn it all off simply to ignore any particularly large dogs that might wander in, intentionally or otherwise. But yeah, there are holes I'd like to fix."

"Most secure installations that use this type of equipment are military and are set up with turrets to be triggered by the security and motion sensors. What do you have set up for when someone does come in with the intention to kill you? Aside from...wait, are you still using Black Betsy?"

"It's Bat Betsy and she's silver aluminum. And yeah, I put her through her paces to beat the shit out of the guys who tried to break in here. Besides, it's not legal to set up defense turrets on US soil. I don't think they even have them in the military bases they have here."

"Well, I think they definitely do have turrets defending the higher security bases like around Area Fifty-One since people still keep trying to break in every year," his friend argued. "Fucking dumbasses. But yeah, I don't think they allow civilians to have turrets to defend their personal property."

"So, do you have any suggestions on what we could put there instead of them?" They began to inspect the motion sensors with a critical eye. "There are non-lethal options we can use, right?"

"The best I can think is some kind of turret you control manually from inside the safety of your property that shoots non-lethal ammunition," Bobby said thoughtfully. "Like...tasers or beanbags or something."

"Wait—beanbags?"

"Yeah, haven't you seen shotguns that shoot beanbags? Riot police use them all the time."

"Uh...you hear beanbags and you think fun for the family, not broken ribs."

"Yeah, I guess, although those can be painful and are even potentially lethal. I don't know, maybe a water cannon instead? Possibly with an option to deploy tear gas and smoke grenades if crowd control ever needs to be an option."

"That's...actually not a bad idea," Taylor said. "Having those bad boys to cover each entrance would definitely be good. Of course, we'd need to see if that shit's legal before we deploy it."

"Or maybe you can ask your new girlfriend to get clearance for all of it," his friend suggested slyly.

"She's not my girlfriend. Seriously, the best I could probably hope for—if I had any desire to hope, which I don't—is a little angry sex between the two of us later down the line to get some of the tension out of the way. Aside from that, she's really not girlfriend material, at least not for me. Frivolous fun is all I'm looking for at the moment."

"I really don't want to talk about your sex life."

Which was a good thing, he decided. It would be a short conversation given the distinct lack of it.

Most of the day was spent working through the security system, and when the parts arrived for the boiler room, they took the time to install them. The work proceeded quickly with two of them involved and the hot water flowed by the time Banks called again.

"The light is green on the mission, McFadden," she said

in the message she left when he didn't take her call. "I'll come over to discuss the details in person shortly."

"Don't you think you should take that call?" Bobby asked. "She is your boss now, right?"

"Nah. Just because I'm taking money from her doesn't make her my boss."

"I think it does, by definition."

He shook his head firmly. "Nope. She pays me for something she needs but I don't actually need her money. It's simple. When the supply is limited and you control it, you can basically do whatever the hell you want to the people who make the demand."

"Thanks, John Maynard Keynes," his friend responded with a laugh.

"Who?"

"He was a famous British economist."

"Oh... Fuck, whatever." He shook his head to clear it and refocus. "Do you have any word from those insurance guys yet?"

"I had word from them saying they'll be able to come for an inspection this week. They couldn't be too specific about date or time, though."

"And since I'll travel to DC sometime in the near future, I think you'll have to cover on that for me." Taylor frowned as he considered plan B, which was to delay the inspection. "Will you be able to do that around your schedule?"

"Sure. I have already been cut from the crew in the auto-shop, so I'm clear to start here full-time. I don't think my boss liked the fact that I already had other options. Thanks to his shitty treatment, though, I do have some savings to support me if you couldn't pay a salary—because it's earlier than we discussed, I mean."

"Which I can, no problem there."

"Right. Anyway, the whole thing will go forward swimmingly. Besides, I'll save you tons of money anyway when I get the folks working on the repair and refurbishing of this whole fucking strip mall."

"Okay, I'm happy if you are."

"So, the only question that remains is whether you can do this?"

"Seriously? Do you ever quit? Besides, there's nothing more terrifying than the Zoo other than having it in a populated area," Taylor said. "I can and have killed these critters on eighty-three different occasions. As long as I'm paid for it, I'll be the hero they want me to be."

"That's really not what I asked," his friend pointed out with infuriating persistence.

"And I really don't give a shit, Mom." He grinned despite his irritation.

"Right," the man said dryly and obviously decided that was all the answer he'd get. "Although if they don't give you enough work, we could always rent out some of the spaces here, especially when people find out it's the most secure building in the fucking state."

"I don't like the idea of renting it out. There should be enough business for us not to have to rely on that."

"It's still a valid option."

"Agreed. And we should definitely keep it in mind, but for now… Let's focus on getting this off the ground…and the monsters out of the US."

"Fair enough." Bobby suddenly looked animated. "Do

you think we should start talking about working on your truck, though?"

"Why, what did you have in mind?"

"Well, as a thank you, I thought of installing a few upgrades. While working for the parts shop, I pulled some parts for myself over the months. I could install improvements for the fuel pump, the suspension, and more importantly, for the auto-driving options."

"Go on."

"So this guy who won a shit-ton from the craps tables bought himself one of those top-of-the-line Teslas—you know, the ones that work off of an AI—and they sold it to the shop for metaphorical bananas after it was involved in an accident," Bobby said as they made their way to the garage where Liz was parked. "Without my boss knowing, I pulled the AI's computer from the wreck and it was still intact, and I've saved it for something special. I think Liz would be something special."

"Do you really think it's a good idea to give my truck a personality?" Taylor asked and stopped at the truck in question.

"Hell yeah." The man laughed. "And I can get her to respond to the name Liz too. How many guys have dreamed about being able to talk to their cars?"

"That's weird, and we should talk about that." He shook his head to clear the less than appealing thoughts. "But... damn it, I'm interested. Get the parts and we can work on it this afternoon."

CHAPTER EIGHTEEN

The afternoon was one of the best Taylor had ever spent. Bobby had brought most of the parts they would need to work on his truck and thus allowed them to spend the next few hours on Liz to improve the suspension and fuel pump as the man had suggested.

With beers in a cooler and a lunch ordered to share, the time passed amicably with them shooting the breeze while they tinkered. It reminded him of the times he worked with his friend at the base near the Zoo to build and repair the suits they used on the trips into the jungle.

Well, that he used, for the most part. Bobby had elected to withdraw his name from the list of those mechanics who were available to work in the Zoo itself.

It was a smart move and most of the mechanics thought so, which really only left a handful who were brave or crazy enough—or desperate for the money—to venture in. It wasn't that they tried to be overly cautious. Some things simply weren't worth the risk for some people, especially since they were mechanics and not trained fighters.

Either way, whatever had happened there was in the past and they both had a rare opportunity to do something they really enjoyed. The afternoon was certainly one that he didn't think of as work, even though some people might. There were enough good times to be had while working on Liz's engine.

It was as the sun began to descend toward the western horizon and painted the desert sky a vibrant shade of red that an SUV turned into the parking lot. He'd already noticed its arrival when Banks called his phone.

For the first time that afternoon, he picked up. "Pull the SUV into the back. We're in the garage."

She did as she was told and parked close to where they worked on the truck.

"It looks like you guys had a productive day," she said as she stepped out of the SUV. "Working on a car?"

"Truck," he corrected and she rolled her eyes. "Why are you here? And did you get any sleep?"

"In order, I'm here to tell you the mission is a go and we'll head to DC as soon as possible. And yeah, I had a power blackout—about six hours' worth—and I feel much better, thanks for asking."

"Well, you know there's nothing I care about more than your well-being, Banks," he said with a grin. "Anyway, since we're good to go, I will start packing for a road trip."

"Are you insane?" she asked incredulously.

"What do you mean"

"What the hell do you mean with a road trip? I have plane tickets that will get us there later tonight."

"Fuck no," he said and shook his head vehemently. "Being stored like fucking tuna in a giant flying can—in coach, I assume—along with fifty or sixty other people, of which there will be three people with tuberculosis and at least one baby who will definitely cry for the duration of the flight? Thanks, I'd rather drive."

"But—"

"Did I fucking stutter?" he demanded and raised an eyebrow.

"It'll take you a week to get to DC, you dumb shit," she pointed out sharply. "Do you think I have the kind of clout to delay the local law enforcement for that much time until you get there to start investigating the area to see if it's a Zoo monster?"

"No, it won't." He turned to pat Liz's hood. "With this baby on full roar, I bet I could get there in two, three days tops. Especially with the new upgrades we put in."

"Yep, she's way over what you would expect from a huge beast like that," Bobby confirmed. "Besides, assuming you want to go in with a full suit of Zoo-tested armor—which yes, you definitely do—it's easier to transport it in Liz."

"I'll admit I hadn't thought about getting your armor there." She grimaced. "Most of our operatives work with the suits and weapons we provide for them—nothing special, obviously, but enough to get the job done for the most part."

"That's because they're mostly idiots," Taylor stated dismissively. "Well, I assume so, anyway. The kind who relied on the suits the government handed out while they were in the real Zoo. Because those who are smart know well enough that you don't head into the Danger Zone—

thanks, Kenny Loggins—with a suit you haven't used at least two or three times before."

"Okay, fine." The woman gritted her teeth and rubbed her temples as if it was all a little too much to deal with. "Because I intend to take some Ambien for the flight and would appreciate having an empty seat next to me, I'll say fine, drive your shitty truck across the country in mere days. I'm sure there are probably downsides to that, but at this point, I honestly couldn't give a shit. I'll see what I can do to keep the local law enforcement out of the area until you get there."

"It's for their own good," he pointed out cheerfully. "Seriously, if there actually is a Zoo beast in those woods killing hikers and shit, regular cops won't stand a fucking chance."

"I think the biggest problem will be to keep the park rangers out of the area," she said and grimaced. "Or—and I'm not kidding here—the National Guard. Send about fifty guys up into the woods and carpet bomb the bastard."

"You're still looking at a seventy-five percent kill rate, at the very least. Besides, if they really do head up there to kill anything they happen to come across, it'll simply be a disaster for the local flora and fauna like what happened in Yellowstone Park in the 1930s when they killed all the gray wolves in the area."

"Thanks for the history lesson, Mr. Peabody," Bobby said and cackled.

"Well, with that in mind, maybe don't take the scenic routes while driving across the damn country," Banks snarked. "I'll have enough trouble containing the situation as it is. I don't want to think about what will happen if a few campers decide to head into those woods despite the warnings."

"I'll go ahead and assume there'll be a few bodies to deal with," Taylor said.

"Yes, bodies that will be on your hands," she retorted acidly. "So, get packing and move. Every second counts here."

"Given that I won't be able to sleep on the trip thanks to us not having time to install Bobby's AI and that I am working off of a very short night of sleep—as you no doubt recall—don't you think it would be better if I left in the morning?"

"I really don't give a shit." She fixed him with what he was beginning to think of as her Bitch look. "I'm not your fucking mother."

"That makes one of you." He nudged Bobby in the ribs.

"Fuck you," the man retorted.

"In the meantime, I think what all of us need is a drink. Mostly because none of us will drive anytime in the near future."

"Yeah, I could actually use a drink," Banks admitted, her expression a little hopeful. "Although if you delay the trip because you're fucking hungover, I swear I'll fucking lose it."

"Look, if I'm not there in four days, you can call one of your other operatives to work on it. Take me off the fucking case, and if you want to still keep me on and give me another mission elsewhere or simply fire me and let me get back to opening my business, you let me know on the phone or something."

"What would be the point?" she asked. "You don't even answer your phone."

"I don't answer when it's not really relevant to me," he corrected. "Which essentially describes you keeping me updated on every little detail of the bureaucratic bullshit that keeps the FBI running."

"Fine." She threw her hands in the air in a gesture of exasperation. "Where do I meet you guys for this drink?"

"Well, I assume that since you need to turn that SUV in before you leave and we'll be drinking, we'll take a taxi. You can meet us at this great place called Jackson's Bar and Grill." He looked the address up online as he spoke.

The woman sighed and looked more tired than she had that morning. "Fine, I'll meet you two there."

Bobby couldn't help a small chuckle as she drove away.

"What?" Taylor asked, already working on ordering an Uber for the two of them.

"Okay, you say she's not your girlfriend but in the process of a five-minute conversation, you already have her agreeing to drinks," the stout mechanic pointed out.

"Drinks don't mean anything. She's taking a flight sometime in the next two or three hours, so there's not really that much time for anything anyway."

"Not with that attitude, there isn't. Seriously, do you not even think about that?"

He shrugged. "She's really not my type."

"Leggy and with an ass that will not, for all intents and purposes, quit isn't your type?" The man sounded genuinely astonished.

"She's the kind of woman who needs to be emotionally attracted to someone to be sexually attracted to them," he explained. "And while I don't judge—it's great for her that she can do that—I have no desire to up my emotional game to her level. Ergo, she isn't my type."

"Do you mind if I take a pass?"

"Be my guest but keep in mind what I told you. Make an emotional connection."

"I know you're fucking with me," Bobby accused.

"Oh, am I?" he asked in an overly dramatic voice. "Tune in next time to find out. In the meantime, we have a fucking car waiting for us, so let's fucking go."

The young man in the Prius that arrived was wisely a little cautious about giving the two larger men a ride, but after a few minutes into the trip, he appeared to calm. His attitude improved even further when both men left him a generous tip in cash once they arrived at Jackson's Grill and Bar, where Banks joined them moments later.

"Hey, Marcus, how are you doing?" Taylor asked and bumped the man's fist. "This is my friend Bungees, and I'll be responsible for his ass. And this is my...um, this is Niki Banks. She won't be here long enough to be any trouble."

The massive bouncer laughed and waved them in. The place was a little more crowded than usual since a baseball game was showing and they needed to sit in one of the back booths. Alex wasn't on duty either, and while he did think he would miss her, he probably wouldn't stay for too long either.

He could always come again once he was back from DC. Assuming he came back, of course. He didn't like that he needed to think like that again but hopefully, the odds would be in his favor against a smaller number of the beasts. They couldn't come in the same hordes he'd started to expect from the Zoo, right?

The beers were delivered together with a basket of fries for the table and they stared at the drinks in silence for a moment.

"To...new business partners, I guess," Taylor said with a laugh and raised his glass.

"I guess so," Banks replied but shook her head.

"To new business ventures on my part since I won't have anything to do with whatever the fuck kind of deal you two have struck," Bobby said as they clinked glasses.

"Are you sure?" she asked.

"I actually insist on it from the outset," the man replied quickly and took a sip of his beer. "Unlike Mr. I-Went-In-Eighty-Three-Times over here, I've had enough of that fucking place to last me a lifetime. I'll be happy if my life is as boring as me heading to my apartment for a shower and a long, long night's sleep."

"I'll fucking drink to that," Taylor said.

"Okay, I never went into the Zoo so I don't actually know anything about it and can't really talk about what's happening in there," Banks said. "But from what I can tell, the place is a shitstorm. Which begs the question, why the hell did you go in that many times?"

Taylor shrugged and looked thoughtful. "Honestly? I'm not really sure. My first time ended with me dragging a fucking scientist out of there with only one of my team. The three of us were the only survivors of what they ended up calling the Battle of the Armageddon Gulch or something like that. Almost seventy good people died that day, and only me, one other guy, and the scientist made it out.

Now, I don't even remember their names. I guess it felt like a waste to take what I learned that day and walk away, so I kept going in."

"You don't need to talk about it if you don't want to, man," Bobby said and patted his shoulder.

"It's behind me, that's all that really matters," he said with a grin and downed most of his drink.

"Look at that." Banks cackled. "The big guy thinks he can pound a beer?"

She lifted her glass, tilted it, chugged the remainder, and thumped the empty glass down once it was empty.

"Jesus H Fucking Christ," Taylor said, his eyes wide. "Do they teach you that shit at Quantico?"

"Nope, a bar just outside of Quantico," she corrected and belched loudly. "Unfortunately, I have a plane to catch, so I'll see you bitches—"

"That bitch," Bobby said and pointed at his friend.

"That bitch," she said without a pause, "later."

Both men stared at the woman as she left.

"You're right," Taylor admitted. "Her ass will seriously not quit."

"And you still think she's not your type?"

"Yep." He rolled his neck to ease the sudden tension that had crept in. "What do you think—one more for the road?"

Bobby leaned back in the booth. "Sure, why the hell not?"

CHAPTER NINETEEN

Taylor had assumed that Bungees would not see him off, given that he planned to leave at the crack of dawn. It was a good assumption and meant that handing the spare keys to the man the night before as he suggested was as good an idea as he'd ever had. It would allow him to work there without having to break in, which really was a good thing.

Bobby suggesting that they name it something other than "the strip mall" came in a close second. Even so, he still couldn't think of a better name than McFadden's Mechs, so he told his partner in business, who was also his employee, to start thinking about what they could name it once they had it all set up.

They had a long road ahead of them, but he was confident that they were bound to settle on the right idea eventually.

With that all said and done, he returned from the bar, packed what few clothes and items he would need for the journey, and loaded them all into the back of the truck along with the suit he intended to take with him.

It wasn't that he didn't trust the FBI to provide him with a suit and weapons, he told himself while only slightly buzzed from the two or three drinks he'd had with Bungees. His real motivation was that he didn't really trust them to supply him with equipment that would work the way he wanted it to.

Given that he had worked and tinkered on the mech suits for the past few years, he knew his standards were much, much higher than the people around there were willing to rise to.

Once his packing was done, all that was left to do was to set his alarm and get an early start on what promised to be a very, very long drive. His route would take him over the same roads he had traveled on the way to Vegas, with only a few alterations.

One of the more serious deviations, of course, was the fact that he planned to make what had been a leisurely drive that lasted almost a week into one that only lasted less than half the time. It would not be relaxing, but he had the feeling he could do it with a little help from Liz herself.

With that in mind, he had no hesitation when the alarm rang. Instead, he pushed out of bed, took a warm shower thanks to the repaired boiler, and set out. After a quick stop to buy breakfast he could eat on the road later, he turned Liz loose on the open highway.

There weren't many things that made his heart tingle more than looking out onto a road that stretched on as far as the eye could see and pressing down on the accelerator like it owed him money.

Liz's new parts already showed their worth to provide more efficient mileage and better control of the truck as she hurtled down the highway. There was always the chance that something would burn out or break if he pushed her too far, although it wasn't likely, of course. He trusted his own work and more importantly, he trusted Bobby to double-check what he had done.

It was always possible, of course, in which case it would be a simple situation of calling the nearest Triple-A, get a rental, and drive to the nearest airport where he would do what Banks had wanted him to do all along and take the next plane to DC. He didn't like the notion, but that kind of shit came with the territory. Sometimes, you needed to do shit that you weren't comfortable with for the greater good.

For now, though, he stuck to the plan and played the part of a lead foot to push Liz as fast as she would go toward the capital of the country he had put so much effort into serving.

This time, however, it would actually serve him. He had made the assholes who turned the wheels around there enough money and it was about time he got some of that shit back.

Something vibrated in the cabin and startled him out of his thoughts. It couldn't be the security for the building since he had transferred all that to Bobby's system. He would connect to it again when he got back but for now, he needed to focus on the mission and on that alone. He had a feeling it would take a great deal of focus to get into that dark little part of his mind that allowed him to fight the Zoo monsters.

It wasn't a part of himself that he particularly liked but it was the part that got him out alive when so many others had died. Too many others had died. He wasn't sure what it was that had pushed him to survive, but it had been there. Maybe a little luck, maybe some instinct. His experiences had forged him into something he hadn't quite come to terms with. He was grateful for it because it kept him alive. At the same time, he resented it because it seemed to be a driving force that compelled him to enter a place from which he might not be able to step away from one day. The thought of being trapped in that space was chilling.

Shit, his phone was still ringing.

He connected it to the Bluetooth in his vehicle and answered with a touch of the button on the steering wheel.

"McFadden speaking," he said and kept his eyes off the road.

"Hi, McFadden, it's nice to finally meet you," said an unfamiliar voice. "Well, not really meet, per se, but this is about as close to meeting as we'll ever get."

"Who…is this?" he asked and glanced quickly at the phone screen. The number was blocked but there were only so many people who would contact him at this point in his life. Random women didn't simply call him and talk to him about meeting like this.

His luck wasn't that good.

"I'll go out on a limb here and guess that I'm supposed to call you Desk?" he asked and fixed his gaze on the road ahead of him again. The car did most of the driving at this point and the motion sensors kept him a safe distance from the cars ahead and centered in his lane. It would be a while before he needed to stop so he felt comfortable to simply follow the road for now.

"That is a good assumption," she said. "I'll work with you out in the field now that you're a part of the team, albeit on a temporary basis. You still need to prove yourself useful to the task force, although I'm sure you'll go above and beyond expectations."

"It's good to know Banks' opinion of me hasn't spread to the rest of the FBI." He grinned and leaned back in his seat.

"I wouldn't say that," she replied. "She has a personal reason to dislike you. And since it is personal, I don't think it's my place to discuss it."

"What isn't your place to discuss?" Banks asked as she entered the call.

"Your personal life," Desk answered honestly.

"Right. I'd appreciate it if you steered away from that topic while talking," the agent said but showed no emotional response one way or the other.

"You should have let me know you were turning this into a three-way," Taylor said. "How can I help you, Banks?'

There was a pause, which he had expected. He was in a playful mood and maybe his two handlers weren't quite in the same mindset. They weren't looking at a long drive ahead of them—something he enjoyed despite the time constraints.

"I believe he means that he didn't expect you to turn it into a three-way call," Desk explained. "Although I guess there was supposed to be an undertone of sexual innuendo."

"Thanks, Desk," Banks said. "I think I understood.

Anyway, McFadden, this is Desk. She'll deal with your day-to-day operations as well as the money-handling and getting you anything you need when you need it like we discussed."

"And here I was hoping that you'd changed your mind about handling me," he responded with a small grin.

"I know you were looking forward to working with me." Sarcasm dripped from her voice. "Unfortunately, I have a number of other assholes I need to handle in this task force so I have to delegate the handling duties."

"Well, I can certainly understand you wanting to have as many assholes in your hands as possible," he said with a soft chuckle and more silence followed over the line.

"I believe he is attempting more humor through sexual innuendo," Desk explained again helpfully.

"Yes, I think I caught a whiff of that." The agent definitely sounded a little more annoyed now. "If we can all be adults, why don't you break the news you called me for?"

"No and yes," Taylor replied in response to her requests.

"Right," Desk said. "I was alerted to a ticket that was issued by the local road authorities regarding a vehicle I was supposed to keep an eye out for. It would appear that you have been speeding somewhat on your way to DC, Mr. McFadden."

"That sounds like the kind of thing you should handle from now on, Desk," Banks said.

"Well, yes, but I was merely alerting you to it."

"And if I have complaints about Desk, should I bring them up with you too, Banks?" Taylor asked.

Another moment of silence followed although this one didn't require an explanation from Desk.

"Let me know if you have any trouble handling the ticket, Desk," Banks said without addressing his question. "Banks out."

She hung up her side of the line.

"Do you think it's wise to antagonize her like that?" Desk asked.

"Hell, I don't know," he replied. "I kind of antagonize everyone and those few who see through it and recognize the humor behind it are the ones I'm proud to call my friends."

"So, your abrasive style is something of a barrier you put up," she concluded. "It protects you against those you fear will hurt you and only lets in those who have similar barriers and so can understand."

"Well, it sounds like you should be a therapist," he quipped with a nod. "Hell, you sound like my therapist."

"You're not currently undergoing any kind of therapy," she pointed out.

"Well, yeah, but the therapist I used to have before they finished my honorable discharge. Doctor…I want to say Bedford?"

"Jane Bedford, yes."

"Well, it seems like you've read my file. Is there anything you don't know about me?"

"Only what hasn't been made a part of your official military record," she said. "As well as what hasn't been posted online in some form or another. It's an egregious gap in my knowledge, I know, but I hope to close it while we work together."

"What, so you think you're the kind of person who can handle my abrasive nature?" A small smile touched his face.

"I think I can handle it," she assured him. "It was my job to study every inch of your available file and I was the one who asked to be assigned to you, so I think we should be able to work swimmingly together."

"I think you should know that I don't do much in the way of long-term relationships," he said, prompted by a vague suspicion where the conversation might be leading.

"Well, you should know that I don't do relationships at all," Desk replied without so much as a beat between their sentences. "But that shouldn't keep us from working well together. Those were the only parameters I took into account when I selected your file from thirty-four others."

"I have to say, that warms this long-dead heart of mine. Seriously, though, you have to know I'm not easy to work with, right? If you have my file, that is."

"I know," she said. "But I still think that despite our difficulties, we would achieve the best results."

Taylor nodded. "That sounds fair. I like having a little give and take with the people I charge into the fray with. Well, technically, you don't actually go into it with me, but it's about as close as I can ask for."

"Indeed it is, and indeed I do not," Desk said emphatically. "Call me a coward, but I've seen footage of what happens in the Zoo and I'll choose virtually anything else any day of the week, thanks."

"You'll get no judgment from me."

"Excellent." She sounded like she was smiling. "Judgement is one of the most annoying human characteristics. While I'm sure there will be judgment from you, I will be happy as long as you keep it to yourself."

"Don't forget, I'll still be an abrasive asshole," he reminded her. "Banks said so."

"And she was right, too. In more pressing news, the ticket has been handled. You should note that this was only because you are on the job—or on the way to the job, at least. Your regular speeding will not be taken care of in a similar fashion."

"I can't argue with that and I'm only speeding because I want to get there as quickly as possible."

"Which is why it was handled. I will keep you apprised of any new developments."

"Have a great day," he said but she had already hung up. It took a moment before he realized he was talking to himself. "I like her."

CHAPTER TWENTY

I t was a long drive, but he was finally there.

Well, technically, it had been a shorter drive than his trip to Vegas, but that was only because he hadn't been in a rush on that trip. It wasn't that he didn't think Banks would wait for him. She had expended enough effort to get him on board that she would have been willing to wait a few days more. Of course, she would complain about it ad nauseam.

Still, she wasn't his greatest motivation. What spurred him to hurry was the very real truth that he didn't like the idea of there being Zoo monsters in the US. He didn't approve of them being as close as the Sahara. Alien critters that killed anything and everything on sight were welcome only on the alien planet they had come from, thank you very much.

Having them in the US when he planned to retire as far away as he could from what he was sure was the coming apocalypse was not acceptable. He knew he was being a little selfish about it, but what was the point of doing everything he had and not being selfish about it when he was out?

His own feelings aside, there were people to help and save and folks who needed to be protected from the jaws of the crazed monsters. While that was important too and he could at least recognize it, he also couldn't pretend that his primary focus wasn't on solidifying his retirement situation. That would simply be a lie.

And his mother didn't raise a liar. An asshole, maybe, but not a liar.

All that notwithstanding, an endless supply of coffee interspersed with less than healthy meals from roadside diners had helped him through the drive across the country and he made it in two days. Liz had been put through her paces, no question about that, and the improvements he and Bobby had put into her had certainly proven their worth. It wasn't something he wanted to do often, of course, especially when he faced a fight on the other side of it, but it was something to keep in mind for later trips.

Assuming there were later trips—which, of course, he did. Somehow, the notion that this was something he was supposed to do had settled in. He didn't quite know where it came from or what it meant, exactly, and decided not to explore it too deeply. There were monsters to be annihilated, after all, and that took precedence over weird flights of fancy.

When he drew up at the office Desk had directed him to, Banks stepped out of the building and narrowed her eyes like she didn't quite believe what she was seeing.

"So, you drove across the country?" she asked, raised an eyebrow, and scrutinized the dust-covered vehicle.

"That, or you're one hell of a convincing hallucination," he retorted. "I mean, like, top-notch."

"You look like you're sleep-deprived," she snarked and stated the obvious. "Did you get any rest on the drive over here?"

"I took power naps here and there when I needed them."

"Power naps?"

"You know, the naps where you drink a double espresso before you take a fifteen-minute nap which gives you the power of a nap and the kick of coffee all in one? Come on. Someone in your position has to have at least heard of power naps. It's what most people in law enforcement live off. Also doctors, I've heard. The medical kind, anyway."

"I know what a power nap is." She scowled at him and shook her head. "I merely think it's a temporary solution at best and incredibly unhealthy for you, especially considering what you drove all the way here for."

"That is a good point," he agreed.

"Do you think you should get some sleep before we get started?" she asked but he could read the impatience on her face.

"I came here to drink a literal gallon of coffee and kick ass," Taylor said firmly. "And I'm all out of coffee, so we might as well get started on this shit before I crash."

"What happens if you crash while you're out in the field?"

"Well, if that happens, you will at least be able to describe what you're hunting for the next guy who takes the job." He grinned. "And you don't have to work with me. It sounds like a huge win-win for you if we're honest."

"True," she admitted. "Come on in. I have new files for you to look at. Some park rangers went out in their free time, thinking it was a bear or something like that. Their bodies were found a few hours ago and in a pretty foul condition too."

"Well, if there's anything in the world I want to see, it's pictures of bodies in a foul condition." He grimaced and gestured toward the building behind her. "Show me the way."

"Only a gallon of coffee? Nothing else?"

"I plead the fifth," he replied and followed her inside.

They moved through the small building to an office on the third floor where she had apparently been set up. The Cryptid Task Force or whatever the name of it was apparently didn't have much in the way of a budget—or, at least, not enough of a budget to justify having its own office in the actual FBI headquarters in the city. Most of the money probably went into paying the hunters who were called in.

He could see how that was both possible and logical. They would give the task force a budget but there would also be priorities. Those obviously didn't include having a nice comfortable office for the handler to work from.

With that said, it was really all that was needed. They moved to the desk where the pictures were apparently still in a courier pouch, waiting for them.

"See if you can figure out what we're looking at here," Banks said and dropped into the chair on the other side of the desk.

Taylor took a seat as well, removed the pictures from the file, and narrowed his eyes as he tried to make some sense of what he was looking at. There really wasn't any preparation for the horrifying things that could be done to a human body when someone or something was willing to do it.

The sterile pictures depicting the bodies were a little sickening to look at, even for him.

"If I remember the files correctly, there were reported sightings of strange beasts in the area," he said and studied the images one by one. It helped if he stepped into a kind of clinical detachment. "They were routinely ignored until the bodies began to appear, right?"

"Correct," Banks said. "Even then, we didn't realize it could be our kind of case until classified documents of tests run on the goop coming out of the Zoo were made available to us from labs that worked directly with the Pentagon. Honestly, we're still not sure since there aren't any solid sightings of what might be doing this. Be ready for that since there will be considerable hearsay and sifting through to find the truth."

"That sounds about right. I'll bet that there are more than enough reports of the fucking Bigfoot out there to make your people take most of the eyewitness reports with the proverbial grain of salt."

"A grain? Make that a fucking bag," Banks retorted. "But for every hundred Bigfoot or Yeti sightings, there can be one or two who actually see monsters out there. We tend to gravitate toward the sightings where bodies have appeared in the area."

"That makes sense." He narrowed his eyes and leaned in

closer to the picture in his hands. "I don't suppose you have the coroner reports too?"

"In the bag," she said, and he pulled out the reports from the medical officers who had examined the bodies.

"Okay, that's interesting." He retrieved the reports on the other two bodies.

"What?"

"Look at this. Most animals, when they hunt something, tend to make more of a mess of it. They eat all the muscle tissue as well as the organs and usually only leave skin, hair, and bones out, right?"

"Gross." She shuddered. "But continue."

"Gross maybe, but that's how most animals hunt. In this case, though, the bodies were savaged almost like an animal would, but most of the muscle tissue is left untouched with a focus on the internal organs. Two of the cases have the heart missing. In all the park rangers, their livers were gone."

"What makes the liver special?"

"It's the most nutritious body part, for one thing. Hunters like to call it nature's multivitamin."

"Would animals know about that?"

"I don't see how they would." He shook his head. "It's why they usually go for everything they can eat, although they tend to gravitate toward it since it has the most taste of all the organs. But they still take everything else. With these, though, it looks like the livers are removed and everything else is left."

"So, are we looking at some kind of Hannibal Lecter wannabe?" Banks asked and leaned back in her seat, an expression of discomfort on her face.

"Well, if we are, it's some kind of crossover with Wolverine or something," Taylor said. "There are claw marks all over, mostly to tear into the body. Oh, and in park ranger number two, you can see the ribs were ripped open from the inside."

"How strong do you have to be to do that?"

He shrugged. "I have no fucking clue, but I would guess a little stronger than your average human."

"So it's probably not an animal and probably not a human," Banks said and nodded. "It sounds like our kind of case."

"It merits investigation, anyway," he agreed. "Although you probably already knew that since you wanted me all the fucking way out here, right?"

"No prizes for that one." She grinned, then sobered and her gaze flicked to the images. "How do you propose we go after this bastard?"

"When in the Zoo, you don't generally try to track the monsters," he said and shrugged. "It kind of works the other way around. With that said, something that big and that strong has to leave distinct tracks. With a little help from my suit, I think I should be able to find it."

"Finding it is only step one," she reminded him. "Steps two, three, and four involve killing it, making sure there aren't any more around, and getting the body back for us to identify and pay you for it."

"That seems reasonable enough. Although you have to understand that there are occasions where there won't be enough of a body to bring back and you'll have to settle for, like…a head or an arm or something. Those fuckers take a shit-ton of killing when they are worked up."

"I understand that and an actual body isn't always required," she said with a nod. "With that said, you will be expected to show some proof of death before you get paid. I'm sure you understand that people can be...uh, a little untrustworthy at times."

"Hey, I worked with mercs in the Zoo before." He raised his arms as he stood from his seat. "I understand that you guys need to see results before you pay for any monster killed. So, shall we get started?"

"Whenever you're ready."

"I need to get into my suit. It's still in my truck."

"I had some people pull it out and have it ready for you in the garage downstairs," Banks said. "Apparently, you were too tired to lock your truck after leaving it."

He scowled. "Maybe. Or maybe I merely assumed it would be safe in the parking lot outside a building used by the FBI."

"And I'm sure I'll grow sick with anticipation to find out which is true. In the meantime, you should get into it, while I bring the SUV big and powerful enough to carry you and your suit around. Believe me, it's not easy to find fuckers like that."

"I'm sure that's the last time you'll complain about it." He rolled his shoulders to ease the stiffness of the long drive.

"I wouldn't be," she retorted.

Taylor headed into the basement where men in FBI-marked windbreakers used a forklift to carry his suit into the garage.

"Thanks for the assist, boys," he said as he began to take the pieces off and attach them. "I'll take it from here."

The preparation was a ritual he had performed eighty-three times before and he doubted he would ever forget how to do it. Putting your suit on was more than merely necessary. Getting into your armor was getting ready for battle, and no one could ever help you with that. It was something you needed to do for yourself, much like the decision to head into the Zoo in the first place.

It was quickly done and he was ready by the time the impressively large SUV pulled into the garage next to the forklift.

"You look like someone ready to head into the Zoo," Banks said as he mounted up and settled into the massive seat clearly designed to accommodate precisely what he wore.

"Groovy," he replied, quoted from his favorite movie of all time, and rolled his shoulders. The suit picked up on the small movement and exaggerated it. "I guess I still need to get into the zone."

"You'd better get that done before we arrive." Once again, she pointed out the obvious. She seemed to have a knack for that.

CHAPTER TWENTY-ONE

The drive wasn't long enough for him to experience any discomfort. They were already a fair distance away from the center of the city and within a few minutes, they were out in the boonies and driving on a two-lane road that wound up into the hills that grew steeper and steeper.

Before too long, they came to a stop in front of a striped police line that indicated it was still a crime scene. Taylor assumed that maybe the locals weren't fully convinced that it was a regular old animal doing all these killings. He could understand why they had a tough time with that concept. After all, he'd seen the bodies.

Animals didn't usually do that shit.

He stepped out of the SUV, settled the weight of his suit, and turned the HUD on. With night already starting to fall, the woods looked a little too dark and gloomy to head in without any help, which explained all the cops involved where the bodies had been found. He could see more police lines a little deeper into the woods, which he assumed was the actual crime scene.

The officers seemed confused to see them there. Many pointed and gaped at the mech suit he wore. The rest were merely surprised to see Banks and the golden shield she flashed to the officers in charge of keeping the area clear.

"What the hell does the FBI want with an animal killing scene?" one of them asked and looked around at his fellow officers. "Well, I assume it's still an animal killing? I saw the bodies and there's no way that it was human, right?"

Once again, their attention focused on the suit. If that was needed to hunt a human, they didn't really want to know more or be involved with that particular human. Wariness and unease were written on every face

"We're a part of a special task force that's been assigned to this case," Banks said with the kind of laid-back cross between boredom and professionalism that people had come to expect from the FBI. "My guy will simply head on up there, look at the crime scenes, see what he can see, and get out. There's nothing to worry about and certainly nothing for you all to stick around for."

"Are you sending us away from our own crime scene?" one of the officers asked, his head tilted in what might have been a mixture of relief and challenge.

"Something like that, yes," she said. "Well, no, not really, this is still your crime scene. But it doesn't look like all of you are here to…well, protect it, so maybe send the redundant personnel home? Come on, man, this isn't a circus."

"For all you know," the officer retorted, "it could be a circus bear up there killing humans one by one as revenge."

"Or maybe a demon clown that's preparing itself for some kind of ritual sacrifice," another officer added.

"Or maybe you two have seen way too many horror movies and are trying to fill in what you don't know about the case with insane theories," the agent replied and shook her head. "And as fun as the theories and the movies are, I'm afraid we at the FBI have a slightly higher standard when it comes to proving our theories."

"Hey, fuck you," the officer said.

"Watch it, Serpico," Taylor snapped. "Or do you want to head into the fucking woods to see what you can discover yourself?"

"Nah, we're good," the man said and backed down hastily as the seven-and-a-half-foot mech suit stared at him. "Good luck out there."

"I'd normally say that I don't need luck, but I'm working on maybe half an hour of sleep in the last thirty, so maybe I will," he replied. "Anyway, do you guys have any theories on what might be up there? Aside from killer clowns and killer circus bears?"

"McFadden, what are you doing?" Banks demanded and narrowed her eyes.

"I'm merely trying to see if I can make a little money off this," he replied with a casual shrug.

"You're already making money off this, now get the fuck up there," she all but hissed through clenched teeth before she turned to the officers who still watched the exchange. "He's a freelancer and is experienced in these matters—tracking crazy shit and putting an end to man-hunting creatures. Hence the suit."

"The only place I've seen suits like that is in those video

games about the Zoo," the second officer said. That was Taylor's cue. He rolled his eyes and decided to simply get to work and head into the forest while Banks justified his being there to the people who still had no fucking clue what they were up against.

Honestly, if he were them and knew there was even the slightest possibility that a Zoo monster hung out in the woods, there wouldn't be enough money in the world to get him to stay anywhere near the forest without a whole shitload more backup than the officers currently had.

"And here I go, heading in there in a suit of armor to hunt the fucking critter." Surprisingly, he needed to get used to the movement of a suit again. He forgot how sensitive the motion detector was until he reached up to scratch his nose and played the world's most concussive game of stop-hitting-yourself.

"At least the trees aren't trying to kill me around here," he continued. "That's a plus."

"Are you talking to yourself?" Desk asked through the speakers in his helmet.

"Of course, I am," he replied without considering the implications of the unexpected company. "Everyone knows the best way to psych yourself up is to have a conversation with yourself. It helps to calm you and ease you into the zone. All soldiers and pro athletes know about it."

"Right," she said in a tone that clearly indicated amusement.

"I also didn't know you would be listening in," he continued. "Oh, yeah, quick question—why the hell are you listening in?"

"I'm supposed to keep tabs on you through your first

mission," Desk replied. "We don't usually tell the operatives when they are on a test mission, but I'm fairly sure the best idea is for us to work openly, given that we'll be a team in the future."

"There's one small problem with that logic."

"There is?" She sounded genuinely confused.

"You hacked my comms," he pointed out belligerently, irritated that he actually had to explain what was essentially Trust 101.

"Well...yes. How else was I supposed to keep tabs on you?"

"That's...fuck, that's not the point. For one thing, someone should have told me you would tag along as a fucking babysitter. And," he continued hastily as she made a noise of protest, "this is not an FBI suit. It's private fucking property. Mine. I think I should at least have some say in who is allowed in here with me—and when because you suddenly appearing out of nowhere could have cost me my fucking life if you did that at the wrong moment."

"As if I would," she retorted sharply. "I have enough experience to know better, I'll have you know. And besides, you're currently on an FBI mission. We've hired you and so we've hired your suit as well. For the duration of this operation, it's technically FBI property, so you might as well get off your little high horse before you fall off—although in that monstrosity, it's unlikely to hurt much, more's the pity."

He actually gaped for a moment, utterly taken aback, and wondered if she secretly copied Banks when the woman wasn't looking to learn her tricks.

"Be that as it may—and I'm not saying I agree with you,

only that it's up for discussion—I still think I should have been warned that you would tag along."

"And that is precisely what I did. In the interests of keeping our working relationship on the straight and narrow path of honesty, I felt it was advisable to make you aware of my presence."

"Right. So tell me, will that straight and narrow path of honesty extend to telling Banks that I like to talk to myself to get psyched up?"

"Oh indubitably," Desk replied. "I'm supposed to report on all behavior and responses."

"Fan-fucking-tastic." He didn't bother to hide the derision in his tone.

"That's all you have?" she challenged. "No begging me not to tell or talking about how we need to keep it between us? I expected you to either offer to bribe or threaten me, at the very least."

"I'm sorry to disappoint you," he said and turned his attention to the first crime scene. "But in case you've forgotten, I'm in the field and trying to stay focused at the moment. I could threaten you with all kinds of bodily harm, but I can tell you right now that my heart wouldn't be in it."

"Well, we could always do it later," she suggested.

"If there is a later," he snarked. "This is potentially life-threatening, remember, not a fucking picnic in the botanical gardens. I need to focus, not be continually distracted by the uninvited voice in my fucking head."

"Fine." She sounded sullen, but he didn't give a shit. "The other reason I came forward was because I thought I might be able to assist you."

He laughed. "Look, I made eighty-three trips into the Zoo without a...a handler. I think I can manage."

"Well clearly, we need to define the parameters of our interaction," she conceded stiffly. "However, I shall be here —you know, keeping tabs on you."

"Fine. Whatever floats your boat."

"But," she said quickly, and he rolled his eyes, "at least keep an open mind. For now, you are not yet in a life and death situation and I need to say I honestly believe I can be of assistance. While you're simply investigating, why not experiment a little? Perhaps we can find a way to work together that adds value rather than irritation. Unless, of course, you're afraid I'll crack the case before you do."

He didn't miss the sly edge to her tone but, dammit, the challenge did get through to him. "Look," he said brusquely, unwilling to admit that she'd struck an ego-nerve. "I don't really have time to debate this. So yeah, if you think you can add value, be my guest. But I reserve the right to tell you to fuck off when I need to."

"Of course." Now, she sounded smug and he wished he could see her face. He shook his head to settle himself. After all, the exercise would simply prove him right in the end. "I promise I'll respect it should it come to that."

Taylor grunted acknowledgment, his mind already tuned out to focus on the matter at hand, and activated the higher vision functions embedded into the suit. Heading into the Zoo required the night vision and motion sensor combo to be turned on almost immediately as the trees grew thick enough to blot out most of the sunlight. The forest was far less dense and he still had some light from the fading sun, but this high and this close to where the bodies had been found, he needed as much vision as he could possibly harness.

There wasn't much to see at first, but as he circled and gave the area closer scrutiny, all the hidden details gained clarity. First, he identified the numerous boot prints from the people who had found the body, examined it, and taken it away to the morgue.

He then broadened his search to exclude non-evidence he could safely ignore like cigarette butts and broken branches around the area. Finally, he located set of tracks that warranted a closer inspection.

They weren't boots and they weren't the kind that one might see from the animals in the area. They resembled bear tracks, although Taylor didn't know much about tracking them. The claws, however, seemed to leave too deep an imprint in the ground.

"Did you find something?" Desk asked as he crouched beside the clearest set of tracks.

"I think so." He pushed aside his irritation at the unexpected question. "Do you know if there are any species of bear that are native to these parts?"

"There are a number of species of black bear," Desk said and added a couple of images to his HUD. "But only one in this area. There aren't many of them around there, given that they tend to avoid heavily populated areas. They don't like having humans around and apparently, the feeling is mutual."

"Yeah, I can see that. Okay, I'm no tracker, but these look like a bear's tracks but are much larger than your average black bear."

"Do you think it's wise to follow the tracks on your own?"

"That is what I'm here for, right? If it ends up being merely an overly large and mutated black bear, it's my job to eliminate it and make it pay for killing all these humans."

"That is your job, yes," she said. "That was a test and you passed."

"Oh, yay, what do I win?" His sarcasm had clearly returned in full measure.

"It's a test, and you passed. The fact that you passed is what you win."

"Of course. Why didn't I think of that?" The prints were deep enough in the mud that they were easy to follow as they moved deeper into the woods. He didn't know why it had been so difficult for the local people to follow them, but maybe their focus had been more on the dead bodies and less on the wildlife. Besides, he wasn't even sure if the bear whose tracks he now followed was even involved.

It could have merely been the smell of blood and death that attracted it. The information in his HUD indicated that black bears were omnivores and when they lived this close to humans, they tended to be scavengers and fed off the garbage around campsites and the like. It could have simply moved in to see if there was any food left after whatever it was that had actually done the killing was finished. Except, of course, for the disconcerting fact that only the organs had been taken. He didn't think any self-respecting black bear would turn down a free buffet.

The tracks began to be spaced farther and farther apart as he followed them. While he didn't know much about tracking, he did know it meant that it had started to run.

The sounds of humans would cause that but it would stop running once it was clear, right? It would realize that it was safe and it needed to conserve its energy.

That seemed the logical deduction but for some reason, the animal seemed to run like something was in pursuit. There weren't any other tracks around it and it had moved in a relatively straight direction into the hills above.

"Have you found anything?" Desk asked.

"I might if you didn't keep interrupting me." Taylor looked around to make sure there weren't any other tracks before he resumed trailing the most obvious ones through the soft mud.

"Is that a yes or a no?"

"I'm…following something," he admitted. "I'm not one hundred percent sure what I'm even looking for, but I have the feeling I'll know it when I see it."

"That doesn't seem too hopeful," she observed.

"Well, yeah. Again, the monsters tended to hunt us in the Zoo," he grumbled. "When the roles are reversed, I'm a little out of my eleme—oh shit!"

He yanked his sidearm clear of the holster around the suit's hip and pulled the trigger three times at something big that suddenly stood over him. It looked like a regular fucking bear at first glance, and there wasn't much else to it.

His second glance, however, revealed something altogether different.

"What's the matter, Taylor?" Desk didn't sound even remotely worried.

"I…found the bear." He shook his head and moved closer cautiously. It was definitely the bear but it had been impaled on the branches of the tree, which was what held it up and gave him the impression that it stood over him.

More importantly, though, it looked like it had been savaged in a way that was reminiscent of the park rangers. He wasn't a gambling man, but he would have put good money on the liver and other internal organs being missing from the eviscerated body.

"I think I found something else too." He caught a glimpse of movement in the trees above him, drew his assault rifle clear of the holster on his back, and primed it for combat.

CHAPTER TWENTY-TWO

I t was difficult to tell what he was looking at, in all honesty. The motion sensors needed a little more calibration and even then, it seemed like there was all kinds of movement everywhere around him. Maybe it was the wind moving the branches, but the pine tree above the dead bear moved contrary to the wind as if something wound down the trunk and moved closer to him.

Something distinctively skin-crawling about the movements and the way it sent shivers down his spine told him that what he was looking at wasn't the kind of crazy shit he could expect to see around there on a daily basis.

Hell, he was sure this kind of shit hadn't been seen there in the past few million years, if ever. The way it crawled down the tree made him wonder if it was a kind of giant snake, but as it drew closer, he realized that dozens of tiny legs were responsible for movement. In that and the carapaces that covered the lower body, it resembled one of the big fuckers from the Zoo. What were they called again?

Oh, right, the killerpillars.

That fact was enough evidence on its own, but the top half of the beast definitively convinced him that it was a Zoo beast—or at least a product of the same goop that caused them in the first place. It looked like it had recently molted into a new form—like it had slid out of a cocoon and was still getting used to its body.

The top half, away from the killerpillar half, looked more like it was from a mammal or something like it. It had hind legs that appeared to have the same dimensions as a rat, although they were five or six times larger.

As if that wasn't weird enough, the front of the beast captured most of his attention. The arms might have been the last to come out of the molt as they were still covered in some kind of slime that coated the fur. They looked like fully-grown bear limbs. The neck was a little too long, although the sinewy movements told him there was some kind of advantage to it. The head itself looked like a cross between a rat and a bear, with the elongated snout and quivering nose of the rodent and the powerful jaws and long teeth of the larger animal.

It had almost made its final descent from the tree and was now close enough for him to see it properly. The bottom half of its jaw split down the middle to reveal a pair of dripping fangs that he could only assume were venomous.

It was like it had simply absorbed the DNA of any crea-ture it could get its jaws or paws on—which possibly explained taking the innards—but he couldn't see any human characteristics in the beast.

Except maybe the eyes, he thought, and a chill traveled down his spine. They possessed a kind of intelligence that he didn't remember ever seeing in the creatures he had encountered in the Zoo. It seemed to study him, evaluate him, and try to determine what the hell he was and what it could take from him. That fact alone was disconcerting enough without the inevitable outcome. He had little doubt that the freak of nature would follow up its appraisal with a vicious and single-minded DNA-snatch.

Taylor really, really didn't want to be around for that part.

"Holy shit, you're terrifying," he said and took slow steps away from the tree. It continued both its scrutiny and its descent and for the life of him, he wasn't even sure how it was doing it.

"I take it you've found the beastie we've been looking for?" Desk asked.

"Yep," he whispered, although he wasn't sure why. The helmet he wore was virtually sound-proof, and he could only be heard talking if he keyed the outside speakers. Still, it felt like the smart thing to do.

"Is there anything I should tell Niki?" she asked.

"Don't you have any of the footage from my HUD?"

"Oh…right, you have one of those newfangled suits with HUDs that broadcast images as well as sound," she said and he could see the feed going to her monitor. "Oh…wow, that is something straight out of a Lovecraft novel."

"Right?" He continued to back away. "They didn't have anything like that in the Zoo. There were vines that ate people and a horde of other weird and not so wonderful mutants, but this is a whole new genre of 'hell the fuck no.'"

"Why aren't you shooting at it?"

"Because…well, everything I've learned in the Zoo tells

me that I should never be the first one to attack something," he explained as the beast reached the place where the bear was still propped up and promptly knocked it over.

"Well, need I remind you that you're in this business to kill monsters like that and be paid for it?"

"Oh…right you are." Taylor took a deep breath. If he'd encountered a beast like this in the Zoo, he most definitely would have elected to simply walk the other way if that was an option. Getting into a firefight with something that big would attract everything else in a five-mile radius and there would still be no guarantee that he would get out of either fight alive.

In the continental US, though, he didn't have to worry about other monsters coming to this one's aid. It was only it and him, staring at each other, and maybe the voice in his head had a valid point. It would probably be the wisest choice to shoot the fucking mutant before it worked out where his liver resided.

He raised his weapons—both assault rifle and sidearm —and without so much as a second thought, began to pull the triggers. The powerful weapons lit up the forest up with the flashes of his barrage.

The beast moved faster than he could believe and curled into a ball around the tree. His opening salvo did nothing to pierce the carapace that protected the lower half of its body. It did more than enough damage to the tree, though, and the huge pine slowly creaked and cracked and started to plummet while the beast uncurled and rushed away from it and toward him.

"Oh shit." He gasped and flung himself to the left as it

charged and uttered a ground-shaking roar as it rushed past him. The massive, razor-sharp claws swiped through empty air that he had occupied not a second before.

It was fast and it was big—impossibly so on both counts—and he realized that he had underestimated it. With the carapaces covering most of its body and it moving too quickly for him to target it effectively, he would have difficulty killing it. Normally, he would have elected to simply fell it with grenades or rockets and then work it over in search of any weaknesses, but he needed help for that.

And explosives, of course. He had been allowed to bring the suits and the guns back, but rockets and grenades weren't exactly the kind of thing civilians were supposed to carry, and that included him now too.

He needed to get creative.

The suit had finished reloading both weapons, and Taylor opened fired again without delay and kept himself in motion while the creature once again hid its fleshy body behind the carapaces that were still impossibly and annoyingly immune to the bullets. He moved back and reloaded quickly as the creature attacked him again.

Taylor ducked behind another tree and felt the impact when the creature barreled into it. So, it was intelligent but not really that smart. Or maybe it had thought that it could knock the tree down on top of him?

He could really do with fresh ideas.

Cautiously, he circled the tree and opened fire but the creature now stood almost top of him. One of the insect-like limbs on the bottom half of its body swept his legs out from under him while the rest bore down on him. It tried to punch through his armor with both its claws and fangs. The claws failed but a fang more or less succeeded.

He could actually feel it penetrate the suit, and alarms immediately blared to warn him that the outer layer had been pierced. Thankfully, the inner layers—those that were supposed to provide most of the impact reduction—were still intact.

"Small miracles," Taylor muttered and powered his right arm down as rapidly as he could. The mutant jerked away and with an odd snap, the fang pulled loose and blood poured over his armor. It uttered another roar, this time in pain, and he positioned his sidearm and pulled the trigger as quickly as he could. In his prone position, he was able to watch the hollow-points drill through the soft tissue of the creature's upper body.

It was weakened but not dead, not even remotely so. He would need to find a way to actually kill it, and soon.

He gritted his teeth and took full advantage of its moment of weakness to maneuver his legs out from under where it had them pinned and managed to twist himself to position them for maximum leverage. He used them to push as hard as he could and added the power function of the suit to launch the beast at the already weakened tree.

The pine shuddered under the impact and the creature bounced off with a soft crunch. The sound reminded him of when he stepped on a cockroach. He grimaced at the thought, aimed his reloaded assault rifle at the tree, and held the trigger down until it was empty. The frag rounds ripped through the trunk and it groaned as it began to topple onto the wounded mutant.

It tried to move out of the way, but one of the branches

speared easily through the carapaces of its midsection and impaled it. Another branch caught it a little higher up and pinned it to the ground as the full weight of the tree thundered on top of it.

Another roar issued, still suffused with pain but less enraged, which told him he'd managed to wound it severely. Taylor pushed to his feet and brushed its blood from his arms and chest. Cautiously, he yanked the severed fang from where it had been buried in his suit.

He looked at it and made a face. Scientists would want to study the venom that still seeped from the tiny pore at the tip. Maybe someone could devise an antidote for it to use should anyone else be poisoned—although hopefully, there weren't more of the monsters around.

Then again, there was always the second fang that hadn't come loose, he thought but resisted the urge to attempt to crush the fang in his fingers. Instead, he dropped it and ground it under his heel.

"Is it dead?" Desk asked into a silence punctuated only by his heavy breathing.

"All but." Taylor waited while his suit reloaded his assault rifle with frag rounds before he strode to where the creature continued its death throes.

"I wish I had something wittier to say," he remarked gruffly and aimed the assault rifle at the abomination's face. "But...well, eat shit and die, I guess. I'm too tired for this crap."

He raised his weapon and unloaded the magazine into the creature's upper body until all movement ceased.

"Now it's dead," he told Desk and moved closer to the body. "You can go ahead and let Banks know."

"She'll want to see the body," she reminded him.

"Shit, right...hold on." He holstered his weapons again before he took the final paces toward the beast. Moving the tree was out of the question, of course, but he could always simply drag the mutant out from under it.

His attempt precipitated considerable cracking and splattering as the pieces still impaled by the tree tried to stay in place, but they were no match for the power of his mech suit. Before long, he dragged the long-ass beast behind him as he proceeded down the mountain.

"I don't suppose you've ever done anything like this?" Desk commented dryly.

"I never had to drag a body out of the Zoo, no," he conceded. "And never really had the opportunity to, either. Some of the scientists did cut into a few of the larger critters to get samples they wanted to study, and it was my job to cover for them while they did."

"Were you any good at it?"

"The— Well, I almost said the best, but that's not really true, no." He had always been better on the offensive than holding and defending a single position.

"I know it's a weird thing to say, but I think I actually missed this." He glanced over his shoulder at the creature he hauled unceremoniously over the rough terrain. "Having to evade and look for the opportunity to attack while I fight for my life against an alien monster. Well, what the hell do you know? You're dead."

"What was that?" Desk asked, clearly confused by the last statements.

"I'm having a talk with my new friend here." He patted

the disgusting and slightly destroyed head. "I think I'll call him Fluffy."

"You're weird." It was a simple statement rather than a direct insult and he decided to take it as a compliment. "That aside, I think I should remind you that you don't need to drag the whole body back."

He stopped, frowned, and studied the cumbersome and already smelly corpse. "I don't?"

"Obviously not. I'm in your head, remember? I have access to your feed, which means everything you see and do. As of right now, you're looking at one very dead monster. All I need to do is send that to Banks as proof of the kill."

"Right. That makes things easier. Thanks."

"So, how did our little field experiment go?"

He rolled his eyes. Unlike him—although he'd been sufficiently distracted—she clearly hadn't forgotten their agreement. Now that he thought about it, though, it hadn't been a complete waste of time. She had actually contributed valuable information that he would otherwise not have access too—and saved him the pain in the ass trek with the beast in tow. Still, it irked him that he had to concede the point.

"Well…" he said reluctantly, and she chuckled. "Okay, I admit that you might have added some value—you know, in the interest of straight and narrow honesty—but it's early days. One small mission isn't a total game-changer."

"Oh, so you'd want to continue the experiment?" Did she have to sound so fucking smug?

"Uh…maybe. But," he added hastily before she could put her triumph into words, "that doesn't excuse the whole hacking thing. No way. You still invaded my space without my permission."

"Well," she replied quickly, and he thought he detected a note of cunning in her tone. "It would seem I have much to make up for. Perhaps that can be addressed in our further experiments. It's only fair to give me the opportunity to redeem myself, even if technically—as I've already pointed out—your suit was under my jurisdiction at the time."

"I suppose we could discuss it," he said after a long pause during which his mind rather disloyally considered the potential advantages her redeeming herself might bring to future missions. Her participation had opened a window to all kinds of possibilities, although he sure as fuck wouldn't give her the satisfaction of telling her that. Not right now, anyway. It wouldn't hurt for her to stew a little, although she didn't seem to be doing much stewing, in all honesty. Still, he could hang onto a little of his pride. "Later, though. The boys in blue and Banks are waiting."

He finally pushed through the trees and into view of the road, the police cars, and the officers still huddled in a curious and wary group. They had likely heard the gunfire and the falling trees and decided to stay. They watched him approach in silence and he could only imagine their thoughts as he sauntered closer.

"Like I told you," Banks told them smugly. "He's a specialist. Did the critter give you any trouble, McFadden?"

Taylor raised his arm to reveal the hole it had made in his armor. "Nothing more than can be expected from the critters around here."

"Fair enough," she replied with a casual shrug. "Shall we get out of here?"

"Damn straight. I need to find someplace to sleep for about a week," he said, shaking his head.

"I can see that," she replied. "And you've earned it. The money should already be deposited in your bank account, minus taxes."

"Correct," Desk said and called up his bank statement, which confirmed a deposit of a little over ten thousand dollars despite the fact that it was already past banking hours.

"Not bad," he said as he clambered into the SUV with Banks. He chose not to protest the fact that she had accessed his bank account as well. He could maybe use that as ammunition down the line if he ever needed it.

"You'd be surprised what the government is willing to pay to avoid a civilian panic," she replied and started the engine.

"I still think I should be paid more for the job, though," he pointed out. "Seriously, did you see the size of that critter?"

"As a freelancer, you will be allowed to set your own rates," she explained. "For this job, though, the Bureau did have a say in it since it was basically an audition of your skills."

Taylor shook his head. "Whatever. For now, get me to the nearest motel so I can have something to eat and crash."

"I'm reasonably sure you need to peel that armor off," she pointed out. "And…sheesh, maybe wash it too. Is that blood?"

He glanced at the creature's blue blood that stained his breastplate. "Huh. I guess it is."

CHAPTER TWENTY-THREE

He desperately needed to crash. It had been a long couple of days, and Taylor literally collapsed in the four-star hotel where Banks had dropped him off and slept for a full fourteen hours. She had told him to bill them for the room and expenses, minus alcohol since he was technically still on the job.

It was, she had explained, a kind of job-well-done celebration. He had been too tired to argue that it should have included alcohol if that was the case. Besides, it didn't really matter. He didn't want to be in DC any longer than he had to be and wanted to return to Vegas to see what Bobby had achieved with the renovations. The guy had said the work would start the day he left.

After a day or so of rest and recovery, as well as restoring his suit to a functional condition—he had needed to put work into the hole the creature had made—he set off for Vegas. This time, he was in no hurry to get there. A four-day drive was all the time he needed to get there and also allowed him proper rest on the homeward journey.

One of the perks of the job, Desk told him, was that he could bill the FBI for traveling expenses too. Of course, Banks' superiors would probably try to cut down on those once they realized he would fly to and from some of the jobs he had to work on.

He was happy with that. While he could pay his own way if he had to, there was no harm in having it paid for him. He needed to make what he thought he was owed for eliminating a scary monster that would have laid waste to that area of the country if it had been allowed to roam free. Ten grand didn't cover it in his opinion.

After the overly long trip home, Taylor was ready to immerse himself in the business of opening his own shop, and it appeared that Bobby was happy to see him too. The man had driven out in his own truck to meet him as he entered the city, excited for him to see how the renovation work had progressed.

He had a few definite expectations, as evidenced by the money he'd left in his employee's care to use for the work, but he hadn't expected them to be met and surpassed after only a week.

It was immediately apparent that the contractors who had been called in were among the best and liked to work for or with Bobby. Most of the doors and windows had been redone and made to look new. Prefab was a difficult material to make appealing, but at least it didn't look quite the eyesore that he had left behind.

He could see his vision begin to take shape and said as much when he and his friend sat down for lunch inside the newly refurbished break room behind the grocery store.

"The place always had potential, and damned if the guys working on it didn't have a good idea of how to reach it," Bungees said with a laugh. He popped two beers open and handed one to Taylor. "Oh, and I got a carrier order from one of the delivery services that works to and from the Zoo. We already have suits on the way for us to start working on."

"Now that is music to my ears, my man," he said with a chuckle and tapped his bottle against his friend's. "Although I guess it needs to be said that the first suit we should work on is mine."

"I still get a bonus for that shit, right?" the other man asked and narrowed his eyes.

"Of course, you do, you greedy motherfucker." He laughed. "But yeah, it's only a little hole right under the arm." He patted at his ribs on the right side. "The beastie caught me there with a poisoned fang. I barely escaped from that shit with my life."

"How much did they pay you for the job?"

"Ten grand. Plus expenses."

"Ten grand for a week's work?" The man leaned back in his seat. "Folks around here would kill for that kind of opportunity."

"The chances are they would be killed for it, between you and me," he replied. "You should have seen this critter, Bungees. It was like it absorbed the DNA from the animals it killed—and maybe the humans too—and assimilated it all. I have pictures if you want to see."

"I don't, thanks." Bobby shook his head vehemently. "I'd like my lunch to stay where it is."

"It's your loss." He grinned and took a sip of his beer.

"So, how do you feel about choosing this over your other job?"

"Well, there was never really any kind of contest, you know that. That place was shit. Here's still shit, but it's shaping up to be something special."

"Yeah. I want to build something here—a business, sure, but something…that lasts, you know? Do you think it's a little too ambitious?"

"Probably," Bungees said with his usual realism. "But you're coming off the post-mission high so I'll forgive you without you even asking."

"How nice of you," he replied sarcastically.

"Yep, and I'll do you one better." His friend pulled his phone out of his pocket. "I've actually looked into making upgrades to your suits. Well, I actually already started working on the two you left behind. I played around with them and used new designs a friend of mine sent me."

"Who is this friend of yours?" Taylor asked as he studied the designs displayed on the phone's screen.

"I'm not sure if you ever heard of her, but it's Amanda Gutierrez. She's a freelancer mechanic who works out of the French Base. That woman is a bonafide genius."

"Yeah?" He scrolled through the designs. "I have heard of her and the interesting work she does, actually."

"Yep. She said she was working on developing a type of exo-suit that can be used in an urban environment without attracting too much attention. Well, less attention, anyway. It works with the same kind of reactor on the back and has a good portion of the same armor, but instead of using the hydraulics for power functions, it uses—get this—magnetic coils."

"Huh. I think I saw someone mention using magnets instead of hydraulics before, but they weren't functional for the larger suits."

"Not for the larger ones, no," the other man agreed. "But for the smaller hybrid and exo-suits, it should work fine since it would require less time to power the magnets from the reactor, which would improve the reaction times by a huge amount."

Taylor tilted his head and studied the specs. "It's actually kind of brilliant. Honestly, I'm pissed that I didn't think of it first."

"Well, thankfully, the designs haven't been copyrighted, so I've worked on turning the two suits here into something you can use like that," Bungees said. "It's something you have to get used to, obviously, but once you are, it'll be lighter, faster, and easier to use and put on in a hurry."

"How would you work the HUD, though? I don't see anything in the designs for anything like that. It seems like you'd have to work the suits by feel."

"Well, I thought about that and I think I have a solution. Come on. We can try it in the garage."

"Fine." He rolled his eyes. "But if I get my head blown off, you'll have to pay my bank loan, got it?"

"Understood." Bungees laughed, entirely unoffended. "Come on, don't you trust my designs?"

"Not even a little," he teased. "And don't think I'll forgive you for tinkering with my suits while I was gone."

"I thought you would probably die, but whatever. And you'll forgive me once you see what I've been able to do."

CHAPTER TWENTY-FOUR

"So," Bobby said as he watched his boss move around in the new suit, "what do you think?"

"Well…it's a little lighter than I'm used to," Taylor said and glanced down at the exo-suit he wore. "And with that, the slight lack of power function makes it a little heavier to move around in than I thought it would be. Not excessively so, obviously, but it's still something to get used to, you know?"

"This is a kind of hybrid of hydraulics and coils so either way, you can calibrate that shit. You can do it manually on the controls around your left hip, or you can have the suit do it on the HUD."

"What HUD? Because if you're thinking something like smart glasses, it's an elegant idea but it fails in the function since shit like that tends to be too easy to break to be functional in a combat scenario."

"Come on. I thought we had worked together long enough for you to give me more credit than that." Bobby smirked and moved over to where the suits were mounted for display and removed what looked like an overly bulky motorcycle helmet from one of the mounts.

"It has a wired connection to the rest of the suit," the man explained. "I tried to put in as much of a combination of mobility and neck protection around it as possible, but it's not a perfect system."

"Have you thought about maybe working it like the tank mech suits?" he asked. "Maybe anchor it to the shoulder and leave the head free to move around inside with external cameras to give a full three-sixty view outside?"

"That would make it a little bulkier than the rest of the suit so you'd be top-heavy," his friend replied thoughtfully. "It's not a bad idea, though. We could probably work in a hybrid of that idea to still give you some head mobility while protecting the neck."

Taylor nodded and looked at his reflection in the tinted windows of his truck. The suit looked slimmer than anything he had worn in the past but it felt solid. With the helmet added and maybe a coat that was two or three sizes too big for him without it, he would look like your average gym rat biker dude.

He would need to add the actual bike, of course. He decided to think about maybe settling for a bike instead of leasing or buying something that would be cheaper to run in the city. Bikes were supposed to be more economical and since he could use a full exo-suit to ride it, he didn't need to worry as much about personal safety.

But that would have to be a thought for another time, he mused as he rolled his shoulders. The action lowered the mechanical resistance and brought up the magnetic power functions until movement was a little more comfortable. The best percentage he found with his regular suit was closer to around seventy percent, which allowed him to carry some of the weight and gave him a feel for how the suit moved.

For one this light, though, he could even move it even without the hydraulics he usually relied on. With a little help, working at twenty-five percent capacity, he was able to move like it wasn't even there—much like a second skin.

He did have to admit that Bobby knew his shit. A couple of adjustments would make it perfect and they had time to do that.

"So, what do you think?" the man asked again as Taylor practiced the motions he would need to make while in the suit.

"I think we'll definitely make more of these. There has to be a market for urban-based suits, right?"

"Well, for one thing, we don't own any trademarks on it. If we started to make money on it, we wouldn't have the facilities to compete with the larger corporations so it wouldn't be a long-term thing. Besides, I feel kind of bad making money off someone else's idea—not without giving them some credit and cash for the effort."

"That's fair enough."

His friend was right, of course, and he should have thought of that himself. He decided to blame the fact that he was in full business mode since he wasn't usually the type to fuck someone out of their own idea. It was good for him that he had someone there to rein him in when he needed it.

Most of the day was spent on the suit to tweak the small

issues that came from converting a hydraulic power suit into an exo-suit. That had the benefit of giving him time to adjust to it more and get into the groove for natural movements before they could even think about starting weapons testing.

They were crazy but they weren't stupid. You didn't give the guy testing a new suit a gun to play with. That was how people had their legs shot off.

They finished the necessary adjustments about halfway through the afternoon and took a break to check how Liz had fared while she traveled across the country twice in the space of a week.

"How did the improvements work for you?" Bobby asked as he lifted the hood and examined the engine.

"I didn't feel any problems," Taylor said. "It was a hard push all the way on the trip to DC and a more relaxed pace on the way home. There weren't too many changes from the original—it maybe added a few numbers to the mileage and made it easier for the auto-pilot to hold it in the lane, but aside from that..." He shrugged.

"Well, what else do you really need for her? There's a limit to how fast you can reasonably drive a truck like that over longer distances. What kind of improvements do you want?"

"Well, there's the small matter of my having stayed awake for almost a full thirty-five hours on the drive there."

"That's because your dumb ass wanted to drive," his friend pointed out. "You could have taken the plane ticket and had a nap during the in-flight movie."

"I don't like flying."

"You flew to and from the Zoo."

"Sure, when I had to, because I know how to keep my phobias under control. But it doesn't mean I'll test them at every opportunity."

"So you think you'll want to work with the AI installed, then?"

"Yep," Taylor replied. "You don't need to give it a personality or anything like that but it would be nice to have something in there that can take over driving for the longer stretches to give me a nap here and there. They have lanes for that now, so it wouldn't be the worst thing in the world."

As with most things related to computers and cars, it took a fair amount of work to align the software to the larger vehicle it would now inhabit. Given that AIs were mass-produced to cover a wide variety of vehicles in the market, there wasn't anything to prevent them from applying the functionality to Liz.

There were bugs to work out but by Taylor's reckoning, it was a good day to be back. The building was mostly functional now and they had at least a day or so before their first client's suits arrived in need of repairs and the possible improvements he'd mentioned.

It was a good start to their little business and he allowed himself to enjoy the satisfaction that knowledge brought. Even if it didn't grow as rapidly as he hoped, he was still on top of his loan payments and if he needed to, he could always sell the property for a profit since it was in much better condition now than it had been when he bought it.

If that kind of worst-case scenario happened, maybe he would run into that delightful realtor again.

Once the work for the day was done, the two men locked up and headed off for drinks. It was partially a celebration over the condition of their business, the successful mission in DC, and Taylor's safe return. Surviving an encounter with Zoo critters was never something to be taken lightly and it was almost always best to celebrate if they had the time.

Marcus wasn't working the bouncer position, and while Alex did appear to be on duty, the bar was mobbed to the point that she hadn't even seen them come in. He decided not to bother her for attention. That seemed like the wrong kind of message to send and once again, the two men slid into one of the booths in the back of Jackson's.

"What are we drinking to?" Bobby asked.

"You ask that like we have a shortage of topics. First off, walking away from a goop monster is always a win in my book. I'm happy about that."

"Of course, you are." The man grinned and tapped his companion's beer glass with his own before he took a sip. He wiped the suds from his mustache. "And hey, I'm happy that my new employer didn't get himself dead before he paid me my first paycheck."

"I have to get payroll software running and I'll need your details," he reminded him. "Once that happens, you'll be swimming in cash like Scrooge McDuck or—well, it would have to be a shallow fucking pool and a ton of singles."

"I can dig that," They clinked glasses again.

"I really do appreciate you having my back with this,

Bungees," he said with a small smile. "I don't want this to be a chick-flick moment but I needed help and you were the support I needed so thanks for everything, man."

"No chick-flick moments, huh?" Bobby laughed. "Well, yeah, I owe you for getting me out of a shitty situation I was too comfortable with, so don't think I haven't taken anything away from this shit too. We're partners in this. Well, technically, I'm the employee and you're the boss, but we're still partners in everything but name. I have everything to gain in seeing McFadden's Mechs succeed."

"God, it sounds even worse when said aloud." He shook his head. "We really need to think of a new name for the business. Something like...oh, Cryptid Assassins."

"What kind of assassins now?" His companion raised an eyebrow.

"It's the code name the folks at the FBI assigned to me," he explained. "They called me the Cryptid Assassin."

"You have to understand that people will misinterpret that shit. I can only imagine the calls from the dumbasses who think you're some kind of assassin for hire."

"Eh, we're already working with the Feds so I don't see why we can't make a little extra money by passing on the names and numbers of the folks who do call us for that on the down-low," he responded and chuckled. "But you're right. I still like the idea of using something with Cryptid in it. Like...Cryptid Mechs or something."

"Now you're onto something."

Taylor was about to respond but paused when his phone rang in his pocket. Once again, it was a blocked number, which really said everything he needed to know about it.

He pressed the accept call and speakerphone buttons in quick succession and placed the device on the table between the two of them.

"This is McFadden," he said.

"McFadden," Banks said on the other side. "I hope I'm not interrupting anything?"

"Nothing important." He grinned when Bobby flipped him off for the comment. "How can I help you, Special Agent?"

"Another mission has become available and I thought you were the man for the job," she said, either not knowing or caring that she was on speakerphone. "Are you interested?"

"Have Desk send me the when and the where. She's already hacked my comms and everything else, so I might as well put it to use, right?"

CHAPTER TWENTY-FIVE

Desk messaged him with the details of the mission. He would have to head across the country again, it seemed, but it was a shorter trip and closer to the south of the country than he had been on the last one.

Taylor had never been to Georgia before, and while it seemed he would skim the edge of Florida too, he knew it would be far from an uneventful drive.

Thankfully, most of the heat was avoided since he kept the air-conditioning on full. Once night began to fall, he eased into the auto-driving lane on the interstate and leaned back in his seat. It wasn't the most comfortable night's sleep he'd had in his life but it was certainly a damn sight better than sitting there and driving and having to caffeinate every ten minutes or so merely to stay awake.

After he watched a short movie that played over the waves, Taylor actually snoozed through most of the night. It was light sleep but still restful and allowed him to pull in and park at a nearby truck stop to enjoy a proper breakfast before he continued on his journey. He actually made better time on this trip than he had on the other.

It wasn't too deep into his second day on the road before he turned off the highway and onto the smaller, lesser-traveled roads that would take him farther south toward Florida instead of Atlanta.

A huge swamp straddled the border between Georgia and Florida and comprised most of what he could see around him. While Taylor was all for different kinds of lifestyles, he honestly couldn't understand why people would choose to live in an area where they were outnumbered by mosquitoes to the tune of a million to one.

There were any number of different lifestyle preferences in the world, but that was one he couldn't understand. Living near or around a swamp was worse than living out in the desert, and for more reasons than that the Zoo would have an absolute orgy with the wealth of biomass it would find there.

His resident apocalyptic nightmare was never too far from the surface. He really didn't want to see what the goop could do if it got its metaphorical hands on the local alligator population. Aside from its insatiable hunger for the biomass it needed to feed its expansion, non-Zoo creatures also provided the DNA to create mutant monstrosities.

He definitely did not want to have to face alligator hybrids. If the beasts were capable of surviving the KT extinction, what they could do when infused with alien goop was truly the fuel for nightmares.

The GPS in his truck told him that he was now close to where Desk had told him to go. He realized that the location was nowhere near any real evidence of civilization. The largest building he had seen in the past ten miles had been a two-story gas station and convenience store, and from the looks of things, he couldn't expect anything even remotely like his previous experience.

At least the trip to DC had ended at an office that provided space in which to prepare. From what he could tell, there would be no such luxury there. Despite that, the SUV parked on the side of the road clearly indicated that he wouldn't actually run this operation on his own either.

Banks leaned against the side of her vehicle and watched as he brought his truck to a stop beside her.

"Another record-breaking trip," she said as he exited the vehicle and stretched with a loud groan. "If you cross the country any faster, you might almost be half as fast as your average airliner."

"Blow me," he retorted and rolled his shoulders against the inevitable stiffness. "What the fuck are you doing here?"

"Well, given that this is your first official bounty with the FBI, my supervisor wanted me to keep an eye on you," she explained. "I'm here to make sure you're getting with the program. That won't be a problem, will it?"

"What part of my earlier performance—or, to quote the exact terminology you and Desk used, audition—made you think I need someone to babysit me?" he demanded caustically. "It's killing monsters. The terms of engagement aren't exactly War and Peace."

"Be that as it may, my supervisor still wants an eye kept on you." She stated it in an off-hand tone like neither she nor he had any say in it, which he doubted was entirely the case. "Although I do admit that it's mostly because I don't trust you as far as I can throw you."

"I'm curious." He laughed despite the slightly offensive edge to the statement. "Exactly how far do you think you can throw me?"

"That depends. I'm fairly good with my Judo so I could probably throw you a short distance with a flip, but that's not the point. Or, rather, it is the point. I don't trust you to get the job done without any problems and I'm here to make sure that the problems are kept to a minimum. Understood?"

He stared at her for a moment, then shrugged. "Whatever the hell makes you feel better, Special Agent. So, why the hell am I out here?"

"Well, I take it you know a thing or two about the Okefenokee Swamp?" she asked and gestured widely with her arm.

"Well, call me Gator McKlusky and put me on an airboat and I think we might have a *Gator* sequel. With that said, I can't think of a single reason why Burt Reynolds would choose to return to this insect-infested shithole. I know I wouldn't."

"*Gator* was a sequel, dumbass." She rolled her eyes.

"I know, but it's the better known of the two films," he retorted.

"And there weren't any airboats in *Gator* anyway," she continued. "They used speedboats for the whole damn film. How did you miss that shit?"

"Thanks, Rain Woman." He snorted. "My point was that if I were to be Gator McKlusky in any possible sequels, we would use airboats because seriously, how kickass would that be?"

She rolled her eyes again. "You're impossible. Anyway, do you want to know why we are in the infamous swamp?"

"Well, on the outskirts is more accurate, which is better than in. Because I have to tell you, while the Zoo is the number one place I want to avoid, marshy swamps infested with insects and alligators is a not all that distant second."

"Well, I hate to break it to you, but the chances are that you will have to head into the swamp to find the monster we're looking for." The agent tried and failed to hide the glee in her voice. "But that's neither here nor there."

"What do you have? And why are we doing this out in the open instead of in an office, preferably with air-conditioning?"

"Well, unfortunately, there wasn't any time to establish any headquarters in the area. Not that it would be necessary since we don't expect to be here for too long. Should you die in the line of duty, though, be assured that the next man would be greeted in an air-conditioned office."

"The lucky bastard." He retrieved his sunglasses from his pocket and slid them on. "This heat is the fucking worst. Why do people live around here, anyway?"

"You got me there but we're not here to judge a civilization's choices," she responded dismissively. "As for what we have... Well, it's an interesting one, to say the least."

Taylor moved with her to look at the papers and pictures she laid out on the still-warm hood of the SUV. It seemed odd that she had elected to run this operation on paper instead of electronically. She didn't come across as the type who liked to waste time with piles of paper. It seemed out of character, but maybe she did it simply to irritate him. That wasn't impossible and it did make sense, at least to some degree, but he did have to admit that there was something settling and official about having the actual paperwork in his hands way out in the middle of nowhere when he once again prepared to put his life on the line.

That wasn't to say it wasn't an antiquated way of doing business, of course. It merely made him feel a little better in the present circumstances.

"Not too long ago, they originally ran tests on the goop that was pulled out of the Zoo in a couple of labs in this area," Banks explained. "They chose the swamp area mostly because of the lack of human inhabitants. As you can imagine, as more shit started going down in the Zoo itself, the people in charge realized that having goop tested in a dense biome like this one was inviting disaster, so the labs were closed and their test subjects moved out."

He picked up some of the paperwork on the transfers. It had been done quickly and all three labs were closed and moved out of the area in the space of three days. Obviously, they had taken the possibility of a threat very seriously and acted without delay. He didn't blame them, quite honestly.

"Anyway, since news began to spread—both about what was happening in the Zoo as well as the fact that there were labs in the area—people started to report sightings of monsters. There were even viral videos of the creatures seen and pursued," Banks continued. "They were all eventually proven to be fakes and that's where the task force closed the file."

"Let me guess," he interrupted and selected one of the

files that had a name attached. "That all changed when bodies appeared."

"Give the man a cookie," Banks said with a small grin. "Anyway, the whole problem started when bodies were found floating in the swamp by some trawlers. They pulled them out and called the cops. There was a ton of press around the discovery of the two dead girls, who were torn to pieces in a manner that indicated that it wasn't done by the local alligators."

"They don't leave the whole bodies like this," he concurred. "They like to tear their food up. You'd find pieces, if that."

"That's what the locals thought too. The assumption was that they were murdered and the killer dumped the bodies in the swamp, but that argument lost weight when more bodies were found."

"How many in total?" he asked as he sifted through the images.

"Including the first two, a total of seven. Those that were found, anyway. People were quick to remember the closed labs and more conspiracy theories came in hot and fast until my bosses decided it needed to come to my attention."

"And you decided it needed to come to my attention." He rubbed his temples to ease the first signs of pre-battle stress that always manifested before a mission. Thankfully, his mind, body, and emotions had long since learned to work in tandem to push him beyond that.

"The last body was found within the last two days— when I called you, actually. I know you might think I'm yanking your chain with a job like this but honestly, the folks upstairs simply want an end to the bodies. There's nothing too complicated about that."

Taylor nodded. "I get that. And you yanking my chain is kind of expected at this point."

She smirked but he was already too immersed in the information to challenge her.

"Anyway," he continued. "If the last body was found so recently, I assume there's still a crime scene for us to work with?"

"You bet." She nodded to indicate a dirt trail heading deeper into the swamp.

They both climbed into the SUV and proceeded down the trail until they reached an area that was still cordoned off with police tape.

"The best part about it is that the local cops were so terrified of being attacked by the monster that they left the crime scene almost completely intact," she said. "They brought the body out and left everything the way they found it."

"I guess that's why they didn't have too many pictures." He studied area with narrowed eyes. The ground was still more or less solid around them, which meant they were still far enough away from the swamp to rule out a water-dwelling creature like an alligator.

"Something like that."

Taylor shook his head. "Something's wrong."

"You mean aside from the fact that a woman was found dead here?"

"Yeah—I mean, no…there's something about this that doesn't add up." He scowled as he tried to access the instinct that pushed for clarity. "I need to look around more. Do you mind giving me a ride back? I'll feel more comfortable doing my investigation in the suit I brought along."

"Sure thing." At least, he acknowledged as they began the return trip to his vehicle, the woman didn't argue when it came to the actual live or die crap.

CHAPTER TWENTY-SIX

"Niki said you thought there was something wrong about all this," Desk said in his HUD. Her sudden appearance didn't startle him as much as it had done the first time, but it did remind him that he'd never actually tried to find out how she'd hacked his comms in the first place. Clearly, she had skills no one wanted to talk about, but it wasn't really surprising given who she worked for. Now, she'd done it again with a different suit and honestly, if he wasn't the victim, he'd have been impressed at her hacking abilities. That aside, it still rankled but he shelved it for a later argument, preferably when he wasn't potentially facing alligators at best and weird Zoo-mutated alligator-nightmares at worst. He merely scowled and ducked under the police line to examine the crime scene more closely.

"I also said I wasn't sure about what might be wrong. There's something lurking in the back of my brain that won't let go."

"Do you want to talk about it?" she asked. "I've heard

that simply talking about something in the back of one's mind could help to get to the bottom of it."

He shrugged. Banks had elected not to return to the crime scene herself and had simply said he could take it from there, although she would be nearby in case he needed her help, whether he knew it or not.

It obviously meant that Desk would let her know if he broke any rules and if he did, she would head in before too long, but he honestly didn't care. Desk did seem to have at least some of his best interests at heart and while he didn't trust her, there was the beginning of something he liked to think might be mutual respect between them that would at least allow them to work together—at least for one more mission until he decided whether she was a help or a hindrance. And found some kind of closure on the sense of invasion her uninvited participation stirred within him.

He tinkered with some of the manual controls on his new suit. Bobby had helped to load them when he realized Taylor had to go hunting again, and they had spent a couple more hours in the evening to hammer out the kinks. There was still a fair number of things that could go wrong, but they had managed to get to it work at a satisfactory capacity.

Eventually, they had decided that the reduced coordination meant an assault rifle probably wasn't a good idea, which led them to choose the automatic shotgun he had in his small arsenal instead. The sidearm was still the same, although he had one extra, and he'd also added a short machete that could be used if he ran out of ammo, thanks to the smaller storage space of the smaller suit. It occurred to him that he should look into melee weapons that included some kind of spike that might be useful for penetrating hardened carapaces.

"Like I said, I'm not sure." He continued to fiddle with the controls on his suit. "But…something's wrong. It doesn't fit. Like the beastie we ran into in DC—"

"Virginia, technically," Desk interrupted.

"In Virginia then." He pushed the surge of irritation aside in favor of mission focus. "That monster looked like it had assimilated the DNA of the creatures it had killed so it continued to grow and adapt. I didn't see evidence of human DNA, although the eyes were weird—like it could… uh, see with some degree of human appraisal, which might have been human DNA. That aside, it looked like it randomized its own DNA if that makes sense. There was a rhyme and a reason behind the killing and for some reason, it stayed away from where it could have found a group of humans it would have had no issue with killing."

"And you see something different here?"

"Right. And that's not necessarily all that weird. The goop has been anything but predictable but again, you kind of always feel like there's a reason behind what it does, even if the reason is only to tear you about three or four new ones."

"Gross, but go on," she muttered.

Taylor narrowed his eyes but shrugged the comment that sprang to his mind away for the moment. "The bodies from the pictures… I don't know how to explain it without sounding like a fucking psycho."

"Well, I'm well aware of your psychological issues, so why don't you simply go ahead and say it?"

"It's like the bodies were played with." He shook his

head, his mind rebelling about the possible implications even without voicing them. "Pieces were missing but never the same ones. It seemed random and...well, experimental or without reason. Merely...killing."

He moved around the crime scene, approached the place from which the body had been removed, and tilted his head to study it from different angles. "The blood splatter's wrong."

"What?" she asked, her tone bewildered.

"Take it from someone who's seen enough of it to know a thing or two about it." He dropped to his haunches near where the blood still stained the ground. "The blood splatter is wrong. It's off. The spray is random and in smaller amounts than it should be."

"What does that mean?"

"The blood was spilled over the body after the fact. And that means she was killed elsewhere and the body was dumped here and made to look like it had been savaged at this location, where it would be found."

"Do...Zoo animals do that?" Desk asked tentatively. She sounded more like she was giving him the benefit of the doubt than actually buying his explanation. Again, he suppressed his irritation.

"Okay, anything's possible when it comes to the Zoo." He shrugged and the suit overreacted to his movement and pushed him to his feet. "But no. No, they don't."

He focused his HUD's view on the area near where the body was found and sure enough, the signs of it being dragged through the mud and underbrush were there. Admittedly, they weren't too obvious, but they were definitely present. Someone knew how to cover their tracks, he thought, and the Zoo didn't do that. Not usually, anyway. It liked to clean up but never played hide the body. That was a very particular human trait.

He moved out from the cordoned-off area and deeper into the swamp, following the trail that had been carefully hidden. Eventually, whatever—or whoever—it had been would decide it was in the clear and stop hiding its trail. Or slip up and get lazy, which worked as well for his purposes.

Sure enough, as his surroundings transitioned into an area that had more clay, boot prints could be seen heading toward where a large amount of water had gathered.

"Fuck me," Taylor muttered and hissed a breath.

"What did you find?"

"Either Zoo animals now use boots, or there was a human involved in moving that body." He proceeded to move slowly through the marsh and needed to turn up the hydraulic help from his suit to be able to move through the slushy terrain and follow the tracks toward the body of water he'd noticed.

They disappeared at that point but there couldn't be too many places for the person to go. There was no place to park a boat. The marshes were too high to allow for an airboat to move through them and too thick for any other kind of vessel. Given that the body had been delivered on foot, there couldn't be too many options for a human to hide in the area.

Taylor moved around the marsh and pushed toward firmer ground. He scowled when two alligators eased from the water and began to trail him.

"Yeah, you see something packing this kind of hard outer shell and you think it makes for good eating?" He pulled the shotgun from his back and fired two rounds, which startled a flock of birds that flew up from where they had perched in the nearby trees. "Fuck off!"

The rounds had been fired high enough to not harm the prehistoric beasts, but they got the idea that this particular morsel would not provide an easy self-delivered lunch and backed away slowly.

Of course, he might have alerted his quarry that someone with a gun was on their trail, but he had to take that chance. He didn't exactly have the time to waste in a fistfight with the creatures.

Moving around the marshes gave him a better view of his surroundings, especially when he pushed toward where the larger trees made for firmer ground. The area he had wandered around in had been the thickest of the marshes. Circling the still water brought him to more open water.

The kind of open water that would allow a boat to move in. But, when he reached a higher location, he realized it was a land-locked lake from which water flowed out through narrow, shallow streams toward the larger marshlands, but this one was fairly isolated.

More importantly, though, he located a small cabin built on slats that kept it above the water and likely the alligators that infested the area.

"Seriously?" Taylor muttered in disbelief. "Who the hell would make the conscious decision to live here?"

"The kind of person who likes to dismember women with considerable privacy?" Desk suggested. He wondered if her expression was as deadpan as her tone implied.

"You make a good point." He shook the water and mud from his suit and started toward the cabin. It was still the middle of the afternoon and the heat could practically be seen shimmering from the overly humid landscape. He sweated copiously but the new suit was far less claustrophobic than his old one, and he had adjusted to worse heat and humidity in the Zoo.

He approached the cabin cautiously and kept his ear and eye tuned for any movement from inside or the area surrounding it. It wasn't only a cabin, he realized as he moved closer. The abode itself was mounted on the slats above the water, which led to a small jetty where a boat was tethered, but there was a smaller shed built where the land looked like it was a little firmer.

His careful scrutiny identified a driveway and tracks in the mud around it but no car anywhere nearby, which allowed him to assume with some confidence that the location was currently empty.

The tracks were fresh enough to tell him that whoever spent time there hadn't left that long before and would probably return soon. It seemed a logical deduction and better than the alternative that they merely liked to waste gasoline in the generator he could hear buzzing behind the cabin.

"I have a bad feeling about this," Desk said.

"How bad a feeling?"

"The serial killer kind."

"Well, we can't simply make assumptions like that these days." He felt he had to say that, even though he shared the premonition. "It could be they are enthusiastic fishermen in the area and headed off to get more tackle or whatever it is that they need."

"Haven't you ever gone fishing?" she asked.

"Have you?"

"No, but that's not the point," she grumbled.

"No, I never really liked the concept of waiting around for something to come along and nibble at what you have dangling. I've always been more of a go-getter."

"Is that another of your sexual innuendos?"

"Well, sure, it applies to sex too," he admitted. "But it's also a part of life. You don't wait around for nice things to happen to you. You have to go out and get them for yourself."

"It sounds like a good way to live your life," she said. "But I think we should return our attention to the matter at hand."

"Right. I'm supposed to find what might have left the bodies behind and honestly, this is as good a place to start as any. Whatever it was had to have at least passed through here, and that means there's a chance that whoever is staying here might have seen it."

"I have the feeling that this is a best-case, worse-case kind of scenario," Desk said. "What's the worst-case?"

"Well, if I had to guess, I'd say you're thinking the same thing I am." He spoke in a low tone as he approached the cabin as slowly and as quietly as he could.

"What, that it wasn't a Zoo monster that killed those girls?"

"Well, yeah. I guess the first thing that tipped me off was the fact that only women were targeted. Hungry mutants don't tend to be too selective about gender. But yeah, I don't think it was something goop-spawned that killed those girls. Whether or not it was a monster is still up for debate."

"How will we settle this debate?" she asked with what might have been clinical curiosity. He did notice the "we," however, and despite his inherent resistance, the thought of company was appealing in the circumstances.

"Well, I need to investigate further. Hopefully, I'll find something to either settle my suspicions or confirm them before the owners of this horror-movie-bait of a house get home."

"I'll try to alert you if I see or hear anything from here," she said.

"That would be appreciated. But it's not like this place is that big. It shouldn't take me too long to ransack it."

CHAPTER TWENTY-SEVEN

There weren't many things in the world better than time spent out with your friends to catch fish, drink beers, and simply not care about what happened in the world around you for a few glorious hours.

Wallace hadn't had too many friends before he'd started at Trellix Inc and certainly none who shared his enjoyment of taking a boat out on the open water to throw out a line or two. But, as it turned out, the people who worked at the IT firm were actually the same brand of geek he was.

Eventually, when he mentioned the fact that his dad had left him a cabin near a small lake that would allow them to catch anything from large-mouth bass to channel catfish, they had all agreed to head out. They hadn't caught much the first time, but they'd had a good enough time that a weekend trip had become a monthly tradition for their little branch of the firm.

A couple of the others had cabins and the like that provided similar outings and this month, it was his turn to host. As always, they intended to spend the weekend out there. Everyone brought their own food, drinks, and other vices they were into, as well as fishing rods, tackle, bait, and the accessories they would need for a successful fishing trip.

He really was excited about it—so much so that he had elected to take Friday off to arrive at the cabin a day early to set everything up. He had brought board games as well as other pastimes, and he would prepare the venue, spruce it up, and clean what he hadn't bothered to attend to when he had visited on the previous weekend without his friends.

The cabin admittedly didn't exactly have all the connections to the outside world. There was running water from a well nearby but there was no electricity and certainly no cables to provide even sketchy Wi-Fi.

He did have a satellite connection that helped with the Internet and the well had an electric motor that pumped the water out, but it all needed to be powered by a generator that needed more gas. It was annoying to have to drive back to the nearest gas station almost ten miles away when he realized that what he had wouldn't last them through the weekend, but there wasn't much in the world that could bring his mood down.

He pulled his jeep up to the cabin, stepped out, and hauled out the jerrycan of gasoline he had collected from the station. Utterly content with life, he strode toward the cabin and circled to the back where the generator purred happily, already working on charging the batteries inside the house and the shed in the back.

Unfortunately, it would take a while to bring them to full charge, and Wallace thought about getting solar panels that would keep the batteries charged even when he wasn't around.

It was something he needed to look into but maybe later in the year. He was due a raise and a bonus after helping with the development of the company's newest imaging software and would attend to it then. Some things were worth waiting for. The fact that he understood that so well was probably why he was so good at fishing.

On their last trip, he had caught a bass and it had been a delicious treat that fed all five attendees for dinner.

They still raved about it. His dad had taught him most of what he knew about fishing, which included preparing the fish after he'd caught it. The man certainly had left his impression and had, in fact, taught his son almost everything he knew about almost everything.

He missed him sometimes.

As he reached the generator, his gaze fell on the shed and his eyes narrowed when he noticed that the door stood slightly ajar. While he had spent a good deal of his last visit in it, he had made sure to lock it securely. It was where most of his equipment was stored and having it all stolen or ruined by a wandering animal would cost him thousands of dollars.

No, he hadn't forgotten to lock it. He was sure of it.

His first reaction was indignation, but it settled after a moment and he crept to closer the door, conscious of the fact that something or someone might actually still be in there. He scowled, thoroughly offended when he saw that the stainless steel lock intended to keep the wooden door shut had apparently been ripped off.

"What the fuck?" he muttered and edged closer when

movement out of the corner of his eye made him spin in alarm.

A man, tall and bulky, stepped into his line of vision. The intruder was dressed in a mud-spattered leather jacket and a motorcycle helmet and merely stood and watched him through the black visor.

"Shit!" Wallace shouted and ducked quickly into the shed. He had no intention to even bother trying to hide in there. The lock was broken and besides, it only locked from the outside.

His goal was something inside that he could use to defend himself. He ducked under the table in the back, hauled out the shotgun he had stored there, and loaded shells from the drawer before he thrust a few more into his pocket and rushed out again.

The biker hadn't moved from his position, although he did tilt his head when he saw the shotgun.

"I don't know what the fuck you're doing on my property," Wallace shouted, aimed the weapon at the man, and stepped closer. "But we live in a neck of the woods that it takes the cops a while to reach, so don't think I'll think twice about shooting you if you don't get the fuck off of my property right fucking now."

The man's head straightened when he came within three paces of him and drew the pump-action back.

"Do you think I won't shoot you, idiot?" he yelled and brandished the gun in an effort to be as menacing as possible. He wasn't a small man at a little over six feet and he went to the gym regularly. Keeping his body healthy was a part of keeping his mind healthy, and he was confident enough to not back down from a biker who thought he could wander around on his land.

"Fuck, I warned you!" he shouted but received no response except that steady stare. After a moment of hesitation, he pulled the trigger.

The gun kicked like a mule and knocked his aim up a little, but he could see the buckshot strike the man. He knew well enough to know that people catapulting away after being shot with a shotgun was pure film fiction, but he had still expected some kind of reaction.

The sound of metal striking metal was all he heard, and the biker didn't so much as flinch.

"What?" His disbelief was pushed aside when the man moved again and advanced on him. He pumped the action again and tried to aim the weapon, but the biker moved quickly—too quickly, he realized—and caught the barrel as he pulled the trigger almost by reflex. A full load of buckshot burst skyward and left his ears ringing.

The man's grip was inexorable, and while Wallace tried to put up a fight, it didn't amount to much. The weapon was yanked out of his hands like it had been held by a toddler, and the man looked at it. After a moment of contemplation, he grasped it with both hands, then squeezed and pushed until it was, impossibly, bent in half.

"What?" He gasped again and tried to back away. The biker drove a fist into his gut that thrust all the breath out of his lungs, picked him up like a rag doll, and tossed him the five yards between him and the shed.

He landed hard and ribs cracked to leave him wheezing for air.

"Jesus fucking Christ," he said once he was able to speak

again. "I…what do you want? I don't have much money, but the stuff in there is worth…like, ten grand. My jeep is in good condition too. Take that."

The intruder didn't respond, at least not verbally. He moved forward, caught him by the collar, and dragged him into the shed. Wallace groaned in pain as he was hauled into the back and deposited in front of the same table from which he'd retrieved his shotgun. In his hurry, he hadn't even realized that his laptop was resting on it, open and unlocked.

He absolutely knew he had locked that shit himself using code he'd developed in college that was meant to be unbreakable.

"What… You want my laptop?" he asked and looked at the impassive black visor.

Once again, his assailant made no answer and instead, reached over him to press play on the video that was queued on the screen. His heart jumped to his throat at the image of a woman lying on the ground, bound and trying to scream around a gag as he cut through her clothes with his scaling knife.

"I…I don't know how that got on there," he said quickly. "There are— My friends come to my cabin all the time and they use my laptop. They—"

The biker turned to look at him, and he didn't need to see through the visor to know that he wasn't buying it. There were hours upon hours of footage, as well as pictures and recordings, some of which had him talking. He had been careful to never let his face be caught on any of the images, but given that this wasn't a court of law, the standard of proof was much lower.

From where he sprawled, he could see the sun starting to set over the swamp through the open door. His heart dropped to his stomach considerably faster.

There was no way he would be able to bullshit his way out of this one.

The black visor stared at him while the sounds of the woman's screams filled the shed.

"Fine... Fucking...fine," Wallace said and scowled. "What do you want me to say?"

The silence seemed expectant, like the stranger waited for him to continue.

"They...they were hookers at first," he admitted and wondered at an odd sense of relief to finally talk about this to someone—anyone. "I picked them up in a rental car, drugged them, and brought them here to...be with me. When one of the bodies washed up, people started to panic that there was some kind of Zoo monster on the loose."

Now that he had started, there was really no way to stop. "The local news covered it, and there... Well, I had an opportunity. Hookers were fun but they were kind of used to it. They knew they deserved what they were getting and it felt so much more intense with the new girls. They... I don't know, I felt like our connection was so much more intense, especially when they realized I would make it look like a Zoo monster had taken them. I don't know how to explain it, but it was so...so real, you know?"

The relief he felt over finally letting it all out was overwhelming, and tears welled in his eyes as he looked at the emotionless visor that reflected his own image back at him.

"I guess you don't know what that feels like," he said and

relaxed against the wall of the shed. "Okay, so...fine. I confessed. What will you do? Call the cops and have me arrested? There's enough evidence in here to make sure I'm locked up for years. So do it. Get it over with. Maybe I can finally get treatment for my condition. Whatever the fuck it is."

The biker stood motionless for a moment before something weird happened. It looked like he was shaking at first, but the exaggerated movements of his shoulders suddenly started to make sense.

He was laughing.

"Don't you fucking laugh at me!" Wallace screamed and the blood rushed to his head. "You...you don't know what I am or what I feel. You don't know what it's like to be in my shoes."

"Oh," the man said and his voice had an odd, metallic quality to it, "don't get me wrong. I'm not laughing at you. I'm laughing at the...what's the word—irony?"

"What irony?"

"Okay, I do work for the FBI, and I guess their policy for dealing with sick fucks like you is to lock you up someplace dark and throw away the key." His nemesis continued to chuckle softly. "But see, I'm not into the whole arrest and due process crap. I'm in the hunt and kill monsters business and honey, you done made the cut."

Wallace opened his mouth and tried to think of some way to change the man's mind. He was great at bullshitting his way out of awkward situations.

Before he could get a word in edgewise, though, the large figure was already in motion. A fist collided with his jaw hard enough that he didn't even realize he was flat on his back until he noticed that he was staring at the roof of the shed.

That view was instantly replaced by the man's boot over his face and descending rapidly with a jerky motion. He tried to scream.

The sound of the fire consuming the damn cabin and the shed was music to Taylor's ears as he moved away. Thankfully, the sick fuck had brought enough gasoline for him to be able to start it without a need to coax it to life. Before too long, the whole place was ablaze.

Part of him protested that even that kind of funeral was too good for the guy. He had only seen enough of the footage to determine that he was the one who had killed the women who had been found—and many, many others besides, by his account. Desk had collected most of the recordings in case they needed them for evidence, but everything else went into the fire.

This wasn't vengeance, he decided as he made his way through the marshy wetlands to where Banks was supposed to wait for him. It was taking the garbage out. If the killer had ended up in jail, he would be locked up. The evidence all but guaranteed it. But there would also be the whole circus of the court case and that would turn the sicko into a damn celebrity.

There would be movies and TV series made of his story. They would interview him and make him famous—everything a lowlife like that wanted out of his life. It was too damn good for a piece of shit like that. Let him burn and let the cops think it was some kind of accident.

There would be a small funeral service and his friends and family would mourn, but in a few weeks, they would already start to forget him.

"Do you feel better?" Desk asked as he moved out of sight of the burning house.

"I don't think I'll feel better for a while," he replied and tried to keep his voice expressionless.

The agent waited for him at the SUV, from where she could clearly see the fire and the smoke despite the distance.

"How did your hunting trip go?" she asked and fixed him with a no-nonsense look.

"All's well that ends well." He eased his helmet off and placed it on the hood of his truck. "It's safe to assume that bodies won't appear around here anymore."

Banks narrowed her eyes and seemed to see through at least some of his bravado. "You know I can't simply take your word for it, right? I need to see a body or at least what's left of the body. I can't pay you otherwise."

"Well, that's fine. You don't have to pay me for this one." His voice was suddenly much softer than he'd meant it to be and he began to remove his armor as a way to avoid looking at her. "If you want, you can send one of your other cryptid assassins in to verify my work, but they'll find the same thing I did."

She shook her head, yanked her phone out of her pocket, and pressed one of the quick-dials. "Hey, Desk, would you mind telling me... Oh, come on, that's bullshit and we both know it. His suit lets you see through the HUD... So you weren't looking, is that it?"

Taylor froze for a moment. Was Desk keeping his secret for him? The thought made him realize that perhaps there was more to her than he realized. That, added to the fact that she'd made quick work of hacking into the killer's laptop, reminded him of their agreement. Maybe, he conceded, they had already begun the process of becoming a team.

After a quick series of insults, Banks pressed the end call button emphatically. "Well, I guess I'll have to trust you on this."

"And what a strange, terrifying new world that must be for you. Do you want to get a drink?"

"Fucking... Fine." She glowered at him but the effect was eroded by the anticipatory gleam in her eyes. It seemed the persuasive power of alcohol had its uses.

CHAPTER TWENTY-EIGHT

Taylor peeled out of his suit and climbed into Liz as Desk offered him the directions to the nearest decent watering hole in the area. He took the time to find a hotel to spend the night nearby as well as to take a shower and pull on a fresh set of clothes.

After wandering through the swamp for a few hours in a suit of armor, he was sure he could fell a water buffalo through its sense of smell alone.

It had been a long day, and he felt there would have to be many, many showers before he finally felt cleansed of everything he'd seen in that shed. It wasn't that he had a particular aversion to killing people. He'd killed his fair share in the Zoo and elsewhere during his time in the military. They had mostly been illegal bounty hunters who tried to cause trouble around the jungle or combatants in a military engagement, but still.

There were some things he had done on a regular basis that would shock people, but there were others he simply wasn't built to withstand. Inflicting pain like the son of a bitch had was something that didn't ring as healthy in his mind, and he couldn't help but feel a little infected and besmirched by what he'd seen. Admittedly, he'd felt no remorse over the three thugs who had tried to burn his building—and still didn't—but they had brought that on themselves. They weren't innocents and would have likely not given a rat's ass if he'd died in the blaze they tried to set.

He didn't even find out the fucker's name before he'd pounded his face into the ground. While he was sure Desk could probably dredge up ownership files for the cabin that would provide his name, it honestly wasn't worth the effort. It was done. In his mind, there wasn't anything he wanted more than to simply put it all behind him.

If it meant he wouldn't be paid for the job, so be it.

Once he was clean and in a fresh set of clothes, he headed down to the bar where Banks already waited for him. Or was already drinking, which seemed more likely, although she had her phone pressed to her ear and was too distracted to notice his approach.

"He isn't anything like that," she said as he entered earshot. "He's all brutish and a real man's man, the kind who wouldn't think twice about loving women and leaving them before they have time for a morning cuddle."

His eyes narrowed. That actually sounded a little familiar. He gestured to the bartender to set him up with whatever he had on tap, and the man nodded.

"Look, you need to know that he's bad news to any woman who has two brain cells to rub together and don't go anywhere near him," she continued, still unaware that he was nearby since her phone was on speaker.

"You try almost dying a couple of times, Niki," the woman on the other side of the line said. "When that happens, one's concept of long-term love does tend to get a little shattered—maybe even badly shattered. You're happy with a weekend of fun love."

"You're not in the Zoo anymore, Jennie," Banks retorted. "You need to get out of that mindset. And hey, I work in the FB-fucking-I. I've almost died many times."

"Sure, you have," Jennie said and laughed. "I'll let you get back to it. Love you, big sis."

"Love you too, you idiot." The agent hung up and turned to the bar to order another drink. In doing so, she realized that he stood less than two yards away from her booth.

She paused, cleared her throat, and turned her attention to the bartender to order another gin and tonic.

Taylor joined her without a word and waited for their drinks to arrive.

"If you have to know, that was my little sister," the woman said after she cleared her throat.

"Well, for starters, I'll simply go ahead and inflate my ego and assume you were talking to her about me." He took a sip of his beer and looked for the non-verbal confirmation that he was right. "In which case…ouch. It's accurate but still hurtful."

"She's a curious person and likes to know about the kinds of bounty hunters I have on my task force. She appears to have something of a romantic streak, and she imagines you're some kind of Wild West, Clint Eastwood-style hero who's all gruff on the outside but possesses a heart of gold. I need to remind her that movies are full of shit and the people who take the job of killing for money tend to be shitty people."

"Really?" He narrowed his eyes. "Because that's not what I heard."

"Oh, pray tell, wise one," Banks said and rolled her eyes. "What is it you heard?"

"Well, it seems like your sister might like to tease you, as I assume sisters do. But she actually sounds like she's the practical one of the two of you."

"How's that?"

"Well, you seem to think that my approach to women is an antiquated 'bang woman on head and she mine' kind of mentality." He deliberately adopted the Neanderthal voice she probably heard him speak in anyway—and would even he was a posh Brit who spoke the queen's English. "Jennie appears to know that it's less about simply taking what I want without care about what comes after and more about knowing what I need and that there are those out there who need the same thing. We both take what we need from each other and don't worry about unnecessary entanglements." He took a sip of his drink to emphasize his point. "It's entirely practical."

"It seems like you've put considerable work into rationalizing your behavior," Banks said with a smirk. "I would say you know it's wrong and that's why you feel the need to defend it to someone as unpractical as me."

"Well, it's obviously a defense mechanism, so of course I have to defend it," he said. "There's nothing about it that I'm ashamed of, but you have to think about how I might actually not be cut out to be with someone over the long term."

"You can always change that about yourself," she pointed out and raised an eyebrow in a challenge.

"Yes, and until that happens, I'll stick to the untethered enjoyment to which I'm accustomed." He grinned cheekily and raised his glass in a mock toast.

The woman shook her head and took a sip of her drink. "Whatever makes you feel better."

"There was another thing I noticed about this sister of yours."

"Do tell."

"She was in the Zoo?"

Banks appeared to have almost forgotten she had mentioned that. Her eyebrows raised quickly and her hand grasped her glass a little tighter as she gulped involuntarily.

Unfortunately, the special agent was the consummate professional and after a moment of shock and even a little fear, she was back her to her normal, unflappable self and took a second to toy with her drink.

"Yeah, she was in the Zoo," she conceded finally. "She's an evolutionary biologist and was somehow caught up in the hype of how the Zoo is the place to be if you're in that particular field."

"In fairness, that is accurate. It's a little more complicated than that, of course, but when you're out there, you are on the cutting edge of many scientific fields, including but not limited to evolutionary biology. It was mechanical engineering, in my case."

"Be that as it may, she was barely out of college and her heart led her to places where her brain couldn't follow. No, that's not a good metaphor. It's more like she volunteered to head into the Zoo before she could think about the decision. She ended up caught in too much pain and death and eventually, had to come home. So you'll have to forgive me for being a little protective of her."

"I have nothing against being protective over siblings." He raised his hands in a placatory gesture. "I didn't criticize you for standing up for your little sister."

"Then I'll be glad to hear you understand that I won't talk about my sister and her time in the Zoo—or any part of my personal life with you again." She fixed him with an unyielding expression.

Taylor raised his hands again. "Okay, sure. It seems a little unfair, though, given that you appear to know everything about my life."

"I've read your file," Banks said. "Mine is available should you need it. My knowing about your professional life is not the same as you knowing about my personal life."

"But you did have a nice little chat with Dr. Bedford, right?"

"That was a rare exception where your personal life intersected with your professional life," she pointed out. "You needed to be cleared psychologically to work on this task force. Your doctor needed to do that for you."

He sighed and shook his head. "Whatever you say. All I'm saying is that you might get a little tired of being up on that high horse of yours when you finally realize that you're the only one riding it."

She narrowed her eyes. "That...doesn't even make sense."

"I know. I thought I'd make it something clever like a joke about a high horse and riding, but it didn't come together in my mind. Unlike...you and..."

"Yeah, it didn't work there either." She grinned.

Before he could make a third attempt, she pulled her ringing phone out of her pocket. Her scowl told him that she might have expected a return call from her sister Jennie, but he could see the familiar blocked number instead.

She accepted the call and put it on speaker.

"Desk, you have Banks and McFadden here," she said and placed the phone on the table.

"Good, because I was about to call him as well," Desk replied.

"Is something wrong?"

"Yep, and I think the term the higher-ups in the bureau used was emergency. Yeah, they sent a memo to the task force about ten minutes ago about an emergency contract that opened in the Appalachians—and in more or less the same area the bear-bug monster was killed in. The assumption is that the one McFadden killed had babies or siblings or something. They're not sure yet since they don't have a clear image of what has done the killing there."

Taylor couldn't help a shudder when he recalled the beast in question and confronted the thought that it might have laid eggs somewhere—or birthed offspring. He wasn't even sure what it was, so either possibility and everything else between was an option.

"Why is it an emergency?" Banks asked.

"Because the word that it might be a creature or creatures from the Zoo has already begun to spread," Desk explained hurriedly. "There's a time constraint on this, so Fallon said he wants you on it immediately as well as the operative who's the closest."

"Which would be me," Taylor said.

"Correct," Banks replied. "We're on our way. Send us the coordinates."

"Already done and already waiting for you." The line clicked and they looked at one another.

"I'm…well, on my third drink so I don't think I'll be able to drive," the agent said. "Would you mind taking the first leg in the SUV?"

"I won't leave Liz here. What you can do, though, is hop into her passenger seat and we'll make it overnight."

The agent sighed, rubbed her temples, and finally nodded. "Fine. Let me get the bags I left in my room. Shit, I need to check out of the hotel too."

"That sounds like a plan. I'll meet you in the parking lot in…fifteen minutes?"

"Yeah, I guess." She looked unashamedly unimpressed by the whole idea. "And that truck had better be clean when I get in. I won't spend the night in a man-cave on wheels."

"Hey, she has a name, you know," he protested as they both paid their tab and headed toward the exit.

"I don't care"

CHAPTER TWENTY-NINE

Banks predictably had complaints to offer about Liz's current state, but she couldn't deny the fact that it was a comfortable truck to ride in. The shocks had been improved to the point where there wasn't even a hint of impact inside the cabin, even when they traveled the rougher roads in the area.

Once they reached the highways, it was considerably smoother, and she began to drift off slowly while watching a film on the screen.

Taylor pulled them into the auto-drive lane and adjusted his seat far enough for him to snooze for a while, which actually lasted until he could already see the first faint trace of morning in the sky. They were already most of the way there.

Low, forest-covered mountains already filled the vista he could see to the east, with one or two smaller towns pressed against them.

Zoo monsters aside, this area actually didn't look too bad. It had been one of the locations he had considered as a place to settle in when he returned. At the end of the day, the fact that he wanted to be somewhere far away from where the Zoo would be able to grow unabated had eventually led him to choose Vegas.

That and the sheer number of loose women. He couldn't ever forget about that.

As the sun started to rise, Banks groaned and shifted in her seat before she adjusted it. She grumbled something about her neck being stiff as she turned to look at him.

"Did you drive all night?" she asked. "Because I don't think this mission will be tolerant of you taking chemical help to keep you awake for it."

"I never admitted to that," he replied. "And to answer your question, no, I didn't drive all night. I turned the AI auto-pilot on and it kept us cruising while I slept with you."

"Oh, God, don't word it like that," she protested with a scowl.

"What, that I slept with you?"

"Yeah," she muttered and shook her head. "It's like a ghost placed a cold hand on my heart and squeezed over that possible future."

"It's accurate, though. And you can tell that ghost to calm down on the groping of your…uh, future or whatever that metaphor was. You're not my type."

"Is that so?" She raised an eyebrow. "Is that why I caught you and Zhang staring at my ass when I left that bar?"

"Well, you have a nice ass so it merited a stare," he told her unashamedly. "You can take that as an insult or as a compliment, whichever you prefer."

"I do have a nice ass," she conceded. "I've put considerable work into it too."

"Well, yes, obviously, but with that said, you're still not my type. You're looking for something I won't be able to provide, emotionally speaking. So, while I appreciate the ass and...other qualities, we really aren't suited to be together, physically, or otherwise."

"Oh." She frowned and rubbed her eyes. "Well, I guess that makes sense. And you're still an asshole, so while I appreciate the work you put into your body, you're not my type either."

"See how well that works for all involved?" he asked with a grin.

"Sure, whatever."

"Do you think we have time to get breakfast and coffee before we head into the mountains?"

"Yeah, but it will have to be quick," Banks replied after she checked her phone. "It looks like the situation has gotten worse and they need boots up there as quickly as possible."

By unspoken consent, they made a hasty breakfast of cold sandwiches, pieces of fruit, and cups of coffee to go. When they were on the road again, Desk directed them to the location of the emergency and they gradually moved away from the highways and into the mountains. Once again, it didn't look like there was much in the way of civilization in the area.

In fact, the only traces that humans actually passed through was the two-lane road they were on.

When the sun was halfway into the sky, they reached a group of cars assembled beside the road. Officers stopped all incoming traffic and sent them the other way.

Banks had to show her badge—with a little under-her-breath but colorful expletives—before the men who manned the line dragged the blocks out of the way and let them through. They disembarked and moved over to where the collection of regular police cars, flashing red, white and blue, and the FBI's SUVs were parked at the edge of the road that overlooked a shallow drop into the woods.

"Banks, nice to see you again," one of the FBI agents said. The tall man with a hint of male pattern baldness showing in his graying hair shook her hand. "I thought you might need to take a flight here."

"I decided it would be quicker and easier to drive up with my operative," she replied and gestured toward Taylor. "This is the operative I had closest at hand, Taylor McFadden."

"McFadden—our newest recruit. Of course." The two men shook hands. "I'm Jack Fallon, Special Agent in Charge and supervisor of Banks' task force. We... Well, there were doubts about bringing you on, but I have to say your resume speaks for itself."

"Thanks, I guess," he responded.

"Why hasn't the area been cordoned off?" Banks asked to bring them back to the subject at hand. "Turning cars away will only stop the least interested people who are heading in to watch the show."

"The area in question is actually over three hundred square miles," her boss explained. "We don't really have the people to cordon it all off so couldn't exactly stop the folks who are the most persistent from reaching the location."

"How did word about Zoo monsters spread, anyway?" she asked.

"Two Zootubers were making a film out here when

they apparently caught footage of some crazy beasts in the background of their video yesterday. It was eventually revealed to be nothing more than a viral marketing ploy, but before anyone knew that, a group of crypto-hunters headed in to see if they could bag themselves a monster or two. They were filming too, and they caught images of themselves being torn to pieces but there hasn't been any word since."

"Hence the emergency," she stated flatly, her expression one of irritation and disgust.

"Oh, yeah, a group of gun nuts heading into the wild to kill them some illegal aliens," Taylor said and laughed. "That'll totally not be misinterpreted when it reaches the news feeds. Do let me know how that goes for you."

"Shut it," she snapped.

Fallon shrugged. "It's a free country. People have been warned about the dangers of it, but there are those who think they're above such petty things as official guidelines. So, if they choose to head in, they are legally liable for anything that happens in there. With that said…"

"We still have to head in there and save their asses." Banks completed his sentence in a long-suffering tone as if she would prefer to buy popcorn and watch.

"Unfortunately, yes. So since you are here, why don't you suit up and head out there to earn the money we pay you, Mr. McFadden? It should be a good week for you with two jobs in quick succession like this."

Taylor narrowed his eyes and hesitated as he tried to make sense of the man's words. He had technically been a part of two jobs but he wouldn't be paid for the one in the swamp. Did the man merely not know about what happened? It seemed like the kind of thing a supervisor would be made aware of, especially if it had to do with the budget.

While a little confusing, it was also a question for later.

He returned to his truck, unloaded the crate with his new, lightweight suit, and began to assemble the pieces. Something that was lighter and easier to handle was also quicker to put on, as it turned out. He should have known about that but he had been surprised the day before by how quick and smooth it was to complete.

Of course, wandering through the swamp and beating a rapist, murdering prick didn't exactly constitute an actual test for the weapons and armor he would wear, but it at least helped him to get a little more used to how it moved and felt. It was quite literally like a second skin.

It was easy to forget that it was, in fact, almost a ton of hard exoskeleton armor that functioned with a mixture of hydraulics and magnetic coils, especially around the boots, that would allow him to move a little faster if he wanted to.

Well, until the point where he made some kind of gesture the suit then magnified to absurdity. That was when he was thoroughly reminded of the fact that he walked around in a suit that could kill him and others if he wasn't careful with it.

Taylor rolled his shoulders and took a deep breath before he attached the weapons Bobby had packed—an automatic shotgun along with two pistols that would work as sidearms and a machete-sized knife. The latter weapon wasn't necessarily the best thing to fight Zoo monsters with but it was better than having to use one of his guns as a club when the bullets ran out.

For not the first time, he wished he'd been in Vegas when they'd received the call, though. His assault rifle would have been his first choice, along with the mech suit, not the hybrid. If what he faced today was anything like the bear-mutant, he'd have his work cut out for him to simply stay alive. Hopefully, he'd learned a thing or two in that battle that would give him an edge this time around.

It took less than ten minutes to get the armor prepared. When Taylor pulled the helmet on and attached it to the suit, the HUD came online to display most of what was happening around him. He would talk to Bobby about finding a way to connect it to his phone via Bluetooth. Suits like these did have a satellite connection that allowed them to open comm lines when needed, but it wasn't quite like a phone.

Maybe someone had already come up with something that would enable them to connect a suit of armor to their phone and even let them control it that way.

Then again, that had too many ways to backfire. Maybe something else would be better.

He turned and frowned when Banks walked over to him in a heavy suit of her own. She checked the weapons it had been equipped with as she moved.

"And what the actual, literal fuck do you think you're doing?" he demanded, his eyebrow raised. She'd see it clearly enough as his visor remained up. "Are you even cleared to use that?"

The woman shifted like she was uncomfortable in it and the entire suit moved with her. "I had to be to take control of this task force. And I'll head in there with you. You need backup, and that's me."

"Um…no, I don't." He folded his arms obstinately. "There's a ton of ground to cover, and I'll do it faster if I don't have to teach you how to walk in that."

"I know how to work it," she said. "And I'll go in there with you. End of discussion."

"Why?"

She shrugged. "I don't trust you?"

Taylor sighed and shook his head. The day hadn't even started and he already had a headache. It didn't bode well for how the rest of the mission would go, but he clearly wouldn't achieve anything by arguing with her about it.

"Fine." He ran a final weapons and systems check before he turned to face her, his demeanor disapproving. "But if you fall and can't get up, don't think I won't mock you mercilessly for it."

"I thought that went without saying," she said. "I'm ready to go when you are."

"I'm— Let's go." He'd been about to say "good" but that was an outright lie. He would never be good about her tagging along like a clumsy armor-clad Mary Poppins to babysit him.

CHAPTER THIRTY

"You know," Taylor said after a fairly short but not entirely comfortable silence. "A more interested man than myself might think you were falling for me."

"What?" she asked and sounded genuinely shocked.

"Think about it. You haven't let me out of your sight and you charge into danger while you claim it's because you don't trust me," he said and grinned at her horrified expression that settled on her face. He wondered when she would close her helmet. "A less confident guy might misinterpret those signals as you trying to say that you really, really care about me."

"I really, really care about you not fucking this mission up," she retorted sharply and shook her head as if to avoid coming down to his level of banter. "When the media joins this particular circus, the kind of variables they add to the situation make basically any mission more complicated."

"Well yeah, people who come in to try to get themselves a Zoo beast to brag about do tend to complicate things as well," he admitted. "With that said, though, we're not coming in here to deal with them."

"The hell we're not."

"Well, I'm not, anyway. That seems like a symptom that should probably be looked at, but I'm the guy you send in for the cure. I'm there to cut the cancer out, not deal with the fucking nausea."

"That is an apt comparison, I guess. No one likes the scalpel that cuts into them, but it's still necessary, right?"

"Correct." He grinned. "That should be my nickname, by the way. The Scalpel."

"You already have a code name with the bureau and that's the Cryptid Assassin," she replied tartly. "And if there were ever a nickname for you, it would be something along the lines of…the Spiked Club or something. Maybe that wouldn't be anyone's first choice, but it does its job in a pinch."

"Blunt instrument does seem to be what I'm the best at," he conceded. "Well, when it comes to violence, anyway. I like working in the shop. Bobby and I were the ones who built this hybrid suit, actually. Well, he did most of the work but I did most of the testing. It's good fun."

"Sure it is," she said. "Right up until you charge head-first into the wall and get a concussion while you're liable for all the damages caused both to the suit and the building."

"That didn't happen to you did it?"

"I don't want to talk about it," she grumbled. "But yes."

"Damn." He fought a grin. "Okay, I can understand that they wanted you to be certified with the suits, but couldn't they do it somewhere outside where there was less shit for you to break?"

"It was a bureau training facility that was designated for training in the suits. So the cost wasn't too exorbitant, thank goodness, and they moved the next session into the woods. I broke a few trees too, but for some reason, no one cares about those."

"I beg to differ. There is a whole wad of Lorax-smoochers who care about the trees."

"Not like that."

"So, can I ask you something?" They spoke in low tones as they continued to push through the woods. "Nothing personal or anything like that."

"Is there anything I can say to stop you from asking?" she countered.

"Probably not."

"Then fire away."

"Well, I take it that supervisor Fallon likes to stay on top of the whole task force—managing the budget and calling you every time there's a hair out of place. Like he holds running the task force over you because it's about as much power he'll be entrusted with for the rest of his career."

"That sounds about right," Banks said, her tone a little impatient.

"So, when he talked about me getting paid for two missions in the space of a week, did he merely not know that I fucked it up with the mission in the swamp or did you not tell him about it?"

"Did you?" she asked.

"Did I what?"

"Fuck the mission up? Will there be more dead girls out in the swamps in the next couple of months?"

"Fuck no," he said forcefully. "Okay, there might be some by accident or something, but whatever it was that had killed those you had on file won't kill any more. But by fucked up, I meant that no body was presented for the bounty."

"I had some people look into the situation," she said cautiously. "In particular, the fire I'll go ahead and guess you started that destroyed a small cabin and a shed out in the boonies."

"I can neither confirm nor deny these allegations." He knew better than to talk to a cop about that kind of stuff. Or worse, a fed.

"Well, sure, I get that you'll plead the fifth. But the people who looked into the fire said there was a body inside. This was dead before it burned, apparently, and had its skull pancaked. And after a quick chat with Desk about it—"

"Goddammit, Desk, I thought we had an understanding," Taylor protested.

"It wasn't so much a conversation as her taking a peek into my servers," Desk said, immediately defensive. "Without my permission, I should add." Oh, so she knew how he felt now, did she? It wasn't pleasant to have someone where they didn't have permission to be.

"Whatever," the agent said. "With all the evidence I gathered, I now have a body and the confirmation from the freelancer that the deaths would stop. I saw no reason to not approve your payment."

"Wait—" He stopped and stared at her. "I mean…what? Why would you do that for me?"

"I didn't do it for you, dumbass. You did the job and you were paid for it. There's nothing more to it than that."

Taylor shook his head and continued to walk. "Don't you people in law enforcement usually like it when things are run by the book? All that due process crap?"

"You're not working a drug case, McFadden," she said acerbically. "You hunt monsters and are paid to do it. If that monster happens to be human, don't think I've changed my mind about it. Sure, some of our guys like to bring them in to be dealt with in the way the law demands, but to my mind, you dug for evidence, found the monster, and finished the job. Nothing more and nothing less."

He opened his mouth to say something, then thought better of it. While he doubted he would get the full payment for the job, he'd be a damn fool to complain about it. Until this moment, he had made his peace with the fact that he probably wouldn't be paid at all and really, all the satisfaction he needed was the assurance that the sick fuck wouldn't walk the face of the Earth anymore.

Any money he made on top of that was gravy to him. He would, of course, charge them through the ass for this job, though. There were all kinds of expenses. The way he was going, he wouldn't need to dip into his business funds to pay Bobby's salary for a while.

Taylor came to a sudden halt and raised his hand to tell Banks to stop as well. It took her a few seconds to see it but she complied and moved her hand slowly toward the weapon on her back when she saw how tense he was.

"What's the matter?" she asked with a furtive glance around them.

"You know how you get the feeling you know a place before you've actually been there before?"

"Like Deja vu?"

"No, because you've seen it before on film," he said. "Or, more accurately, on a shaky phone camera."

"What are you talking about?"

"I mean that I think this is where that hunting team was attacked."

"How can you tell?" She sounded openly skeptical. "It's not like they gave us a good view of the area with that shaky cam."

"Well, no, that's true, but you can look around and see more evidence that they were here." He pointed toward the trees around them. The bark had been damaged by what looked like a barrage from a handful of shotguns and a number of hunting rifles. If all the shots had gone in the same direction, he would have assumed that they merely had a scare and everyone had fired at a squirrel or something.

The firing pattern, though, was both random and wide-spread and had damaged at least a dozen of the trees around them. The evidence suggested they had looked around and fired wildly at a creature or creatures that moved quickly through the treetops.

And either these hunters were terrible shots, or the creatures were faster than could be imagined since he couldn't see any sign that they had been hit by the rounds fired.

"Shit," Banks said. "How many of the monsters do you think there are?"

"What makes you think there are more than one of them?"

"Well, you can see they fired all around here," she pointed out. "Logically, you'd think they would all aim at the same target if they faced only one creature, but it's all spread out."

Taylor scowled. It was a good point and he had looked forward to being able to explain it to her. It would have been a prime opportunity to prove how much more competent he was and take her down a peg or two at the same time. Still, now was not the time for an ego trip, so he simply turned to follow the trail of destruction through the forest. Now that they were in what he considered hostile territory, he sealed his helmet and nodded to her to do the same. She complied without argument.

It soon became apparent that the gunfire had begun to slow and became more and more sparse, probably as the shooters ran low on ammunition, he assumed. Either that or they were picked off one by one. He considered both and decided a combination of the two was as likely as either one.

These guys had thought the Zoo monsters would be like any other creature they could simply waltz in and shoot with impunity. They clearly hadn't considered the reality that they were the prey as soon as they stepped into the area.

There were tracks to follow on the ground too, mostly boot prints, but as they pressed on, he noticed where claws and pads had dug into the soft mud. Their sudden appearance told him that the creatures had sensed an easy kill and dropped from the trees to attack the hunters.

"Get down!" Banks yelled.

He spun to see what she was talking about and froze momentarily at the sight of what appeared to be one of the hunters, complete with the felt cap and bright orange blazer. The man stood not ten feet from him with a double-barreled shotgun aimed at him. He cursed himself for being so engrossed in tracking that he'd lost awareness of their surroundings. It was a rookie mistake and one he would never have made in the Zoo. He had allowed his irritation at having an unwelcome partner and the irascible need to upstage her to distract him—and if that had been the mutant they were hunting, she'd have possibly saved his ass to boot.

Still, this was a human—harmless in comparison—and although the man held a shotgun, he knew with certainty that at this distance, the shot would make little impression. "Don't shoot," he said once he'd activated the external speaker. "We're here to help—fuck!" The man ignored him and simply opened fire. Taylor felt none of the shots and, as expected, they didn't manage to pierce the outer layer of his armor.

"Don't get any closer!" the hunter shouted and fell back against the tree.

"Goddammit, man, we're here to help you!" the agent shouted and moved closer as he fumbled in his pocket. He tried to reload his weapon but his hands shook too badly for him to be able to push the shells into the appropriate chambers.

Taylor approached and closed his hands gently around

the man's arm. He tried not to injure him as he pulled him away from the tree.

"Don't get any closer." The hunter looked terrified as he tried to break away from his grasp.

"We're trying to help you, man," he said. "Calm the fuck down."

"No, you need to get out of here now." He tried frantically to move away while he struggled to reload his shotgun.

"Why?" Banks asked. "What are you still doing here?"

"Bait!" he said in a hoarse voice. "I'm bait."

It took Taylor a few seconds to realize what he had said.

"Oh, fuck." He gasped, took a step back, and yanked the shotgun from its holster on his back. "Oh…just fuck."

Her gaze followed his into the trees. His motion sensors told him that movement had begun in the branches all around them.

"Yeah," the agent said and readied her weapons. "Oh fuck about covers it."

CHAPTER THIRTY-ONE

There really wasn't time to think about what would happen next, even if he wanted to. Taylor knew they were outnumbered and out-positioned, and it looked like the monsters had the jump on them—literally.

He indicated for Banks to pull back with him and motioned for the hunter to do the same. The unfortunate man had finally been able to shove shells into the shotgun, but honestly, it was doubtful that he would be able to hit anything with the way his hands shook.

Which meant it was only him and a woman who, by her own admission, had charged head-first into a wall while learning how to use the suit she currently wore. Not only that, she had probably not been in one since she was certified for it until this very day. He had never seen her fight and had no idea how to coordinate with her while in combat.

Well, that left him. At least she wasn't shaking like she had taken a little too much cocaine and couldn't handle it like Hunter McHunterson.

Grimly, he checked his weapons. He had the shotgun, which he had three magazines for, and the pistols that he had two mags each for. And there was the machete too. He couldn't forget about that, given that there really was a very good chance he might need it.

That was all he had to fight what looked like two dozen of the creatures that looked hungry and very much like they wouldn't take much shit from the people on the ground below them. The only faint sliver of a silver lining in this fucked-up very dark cloud was that some of them chose to climb down from the trees rather than jump as he had expected. That many in a combined speed-jump would lower their odds dramatically.

They all looked similar enough that he could assume that they were from the same brood, at least, and were definitely, definitely Zoo monsters.

Or, at least, the kind of creatures that resulted from the goop being set loose into a forest like this.

He could agree that the location made it seem like they were somehow related to the bear creature he had encountered before, and there were a few similarities. It could be that they shared the same origins, although there was no way to tell what that might be. They had a similar rat-shaped head with the elongated jaw and the high-positioned eyeballs, and as they hissed and growled during their descent, he noticed that the bottom half of the jaws split down the middle too.

The rest of each mutant resembled an odd kind of armadillo, with a soft, mammalian body and an endoskeleton covered, for the most part, by what looked like a very insect-like exoskeleton. This was comprised of dark carapaces that were touched here and there with greyish-brown fur like the hybridization between the two creatures hadn't quite been successful but it was still alive to enjoy the results.

They were large but considerably smaller than the massive creature he'd previously encountered. From this, he was inclined to believe that they were the offspring of that same beast but had mutated into a different version based on available DNA. He'd read somewhere that armadillos could possibly spread to the DC area, so maybe some had made it there. Or someone might have left something made from the skin. Who knew what the goop was capable of extracting DNA from? Either way, the one good thing in all this was that they seemed to be young—which hopefully meant that they would have less strength than the parent and that the carapace was possibly not fully developed.

Tails flicked from the back of the creatures and moved much like rat tails, but looked like they had a stinger at the end.

Taylor remembered how close he had come to being impaled and poisoned by the bear monster. His thick armor had saved him by being barely thick enough, and he had been able to walk away from that fight unscathed.

Now, these creatures seemed to have similar kinds of venom in them and could punch holes in armor as easily. It seemed suicidal to simply stand there, but he needed to learn as much about them as he could before the shit hit what promised to be an industrial-sized fan. His life and those of his companions might well depend on even the smallest detail he could identify.

The armor he now wore could deflect most gunfire except maybe rounds that were designed to be armor-piercing, but he had no desire to test how it fared against the fangs these creatures had. He needed to make use of the mobility the lighter suit provided him.

"What do we do next?" Banks asked grimly. She sounded surprisingly calm.

"We hunt," he replied simply.

All he had to do was try to keep the monsters in check and make sure that she and the hunter didn't get their asses killed in the meantime.

It would definitely be a pain in his ass.

"Move to the left when I say so," he said to both her and the hunter. "Don't bother to ask questions, just move. Banks, you cover for this asshole and protect him as best you can."

"What will you do?" she asked and immediately ignored his injunction not to. Why was he surprised?

"I'll try to get them into a position where we can flank them," he explained, his focus on the beasts that moved slowly over the trees like they attempted to study the humans, unsure of what they were looking at. "Which means on the ground. Are you ready?"

She nodded.

"Okay. Go!"

Banks grasped the hunter by the hand and dragged him to the left. They rushed toward an open area clear of trees for a dozen feet or so while Taylor raised his shotgun into the air and aimed at the beasts that reacted to his companions' actions.

He felt a little bad for using them as bait, but he would

put himself in the same danger in mere seconds anyway, so there really wasn't a reason for guilt.

As the monsters moved, he kept his weapon trained on the one that seemed the quickest among them. It gained the ground first and surged toward Banks like she owed it something. He was certain that these were actually the spawn of the bear monster he had killed before. Maybe after laying eggs, it had needed more food, had begun to attack more and more creatures around it, and in doing so, absorbed their DNA and started to change. Perhaps these beasts had begun to do the same once they sampled the food in the area.

But that was a problem for the scientists to worry about. His job was to make sure they weren't on the menu and already, a few of them had completed their descent.

The AA-12 was equipped with a drum magazine containing thirty-two rounds that could be fired at around three hundred rounds per minute. He could effectively fill the air around them with flying lead if he wanted to.

And goddamn, did he want to.

Taylor pulled the trigger and the kick of the powerful weapon thrust into his shoulder. The mutants suddenly realized they were under attack. Two of them were shredded by the first couple of rounds while the rest reacted instantly and tried to take cover behind the trees.

The rain of lead didn't stop at the trees but ripped through them and the monsters that hid behind them. They fell and writhed hideously while they screeched and roared in pain.

It was a good start but it only lasted for a few seconds before the magazine was emptied. The smaller suit needed a little extra time to reload and the remainder of the creatures seemed to sense their window of opportunity. Many abandoned their slow descent and simply plunged from their higher elevation. He drew the sidearm from his hip and opened fire on the two that landed first. One shuddered and fell, clearly dead, while the other was wounded and screeched as it fell back and tried to escape the volley of lead.

The sidearm clicked and he tucked it into his holster and drew the second one clear. Banks realized that she needed to engage when other mutants began to converge on her. She raised her assault rifle and opened fire on the foremost creatures. Even the hunter pulled the trigger on his shotgun to empty both barrels.

Taylor couldn't tell if they did any damage, but the distraction was enough for him to reload the shotgun. As the monsters swarmed into the attack, he felt the comforting kick of the weapon as he fired systematically at both those on the ground and the few that remained in the trees. He did a fair amount of damage, some of it by felling the trees the beasts lurked in so one or two were crushed. Inevitably, he needed to reload, and as if they had anticipated the moment—like they had somehow identified this as a weakness—the monsters pushed into a combined assault.

"Banks, I could really use some help!"

She wasn't at all sure what she was doing there. Why had she elected to come out into the middle of the woods with

McFadden? There weren't too many people who liked the woods anyway, and Niki wasn't one of those on a good day.

So again, why had she insisted that she accompany him when he was more than capable of doing his job?

Hell, maybe she was falling for him.

"No, fuck no. Don't even start thinking like that," she shouted, reloaded her assault rifle, and opened fire at the aberrations that now seemed to have focused their attacks on Taylor and he shouted for her to help him. The hunter huddled behind her and tried to reload his shotgun again.

Maybe a damn double-barreled shotgun wasn't the best thing to use when hunting mutants.

She cursed the necessity to place her shots in a way that she wouldn't shoot Taylor. It would have been so much easier to simply tear through the creatures. Still, she must have done something right as they turned suddenly and rushed toward her. There weren't that many of them left, of course, but with each one that fell, those left seemed to become more and more rabid.

It wasn't that she didn't know how to fire an assault rifle, she reminded herself a little desperately. The problem was that these monsters moved in a way that looked unnatural and were somehow able to jump and bound off the trees for more speed as they attacked.

One fell with a handful of holes in its body, but the other two reached her. The hunter flung himself out of the way as she was knocked off her feet. She flailed in an attempt to keep herself from falling on her back.

The split jaws latched onto her arms and tried to bite and tear through. She twisted her arm violently and the action broke the first one's neck, but as she turned, the other had already moved to pin her down. It screeched and hissed when she tried to knock it away. The claws and fangs were latched on tight, and the only way would break free was to rip its head off. She was both terrified and enraged enough to do it but didn't have the angle for it.

The hideous tail tilted up and lashed down in an effort to punch the stinger through her armor. The first strike did no damage, but the second found a break in the plate, and she could feel a pinch as it dug in deeper and attempted to find something to inject its venom into.

"Shit!" She screamed and increased her fight to wrench herself free.

Suddenly, the creature stopped pushing. Something yanked it off, Niki realized and stared in abject horror when the fangs and head remained in place while the remainder was hauled free.

Taylor held the body, stood over her, and hurled it at the beasts that were still alive and on the offensive. He had dropped his shotgun and it looked like his pistols were empty too, which left him with nothing but what looked like a machete.

He bulldozed into the three remaining monsters with a powerful roar to hack, slice, and slash through them. His vicious onslaught left them in pieces while he seemed impervious to their attacks.

When it was over, he stood over the bodies and panted for breath. He made sure they were dead before he turned to where Banks struggled to push to her feet.

It was a little more difficult than she thought it would be. Maybe in all the biting and pounding, they had pulled some of the hydraulics out of whack. It wasn't until he strode up and offered his hand that she managed to stand.

"Are you okay?" he asked, both to her and the hunter who stared at them with a slack jaw.

"Yeah," Niki said and shook her head. "Well, now I understand what she sees."

"Understand what who sees?" Taylor asked and narrowed his eyes.

Oh, shit. Had she said that out loud?

"Huh?" She tried to sound bemused in the hope that she could avoid the truth. "Oh…nothing. I was thinking aloud. We need to call someone for a cleanup in the area."

"That sounds good." He obviously still needed to catch his breath. "We'll…uh, stand here and wait, I guess."

CHAPTER THIRTY-TWO

He rather liked the idea that choppers would come in —not exactly to the rescue because he'd taken care of that, but as part of the mission. They hadn't taken too many choppers into the Zoo. It was difficult enough to get shit on wheels to work in there with too many obstacles in the way to make it a comfortable ride along with the hellish vines that somehow knew to sabotage wheels, axles, and engines.

This was, thankfully, an entirely different scenario. It was nothing like the Zoo, and that was one of the reasons why he liked it. There weren't too many good things about being out in the boonies, but not having monsters on a regular basis was certainly one of them. And, of course, the absence of the kinds of trees with vines that would pick you up off the ground to either have you for lunch or kill you by dropping you from a dizzy height.

That and the view. He scrambled onto some high ground to make sure there weren't any more of the creatures. While he doubted there would be, his job right now was to be extra careful, and Taylor had begun to take it seriously. There was no way in hell he would let this place turn into the Zoo Two, after all.

The view around him was something else. It was the middle of the day and from the rock he'd selected as his high ground, he could see for miles in every direction. It wasn't all that far up into the mountains behind him but it was a view to kill for. It would hopefully only be monsters he killed, but he was flexible on that. His experience told him that humans often turned out to be shitty as well.

"Do you see anything?" Banks called from the bottom.

"Yeah, the choppers are incoming," he said. "I don't see anywhere for them to land, though."

"They won't need to," she said and used the comms in their suits. "They'll drop the people and equipment and they'll get to work."

"I really hope they don't expect me to do any of this cleanup work," he told her as he worked his way slowly down to where she and the hunter waited for him.

"Well, no. You're not paid for that," she replied once he reached them. "But I'm sure they'd always appreciate help, though. All the shit-fucking way out here and with this much work to get done, you have to know they'll hate every second of it."

"That's what the crews are paid to do, right?"

"Well, yes."

"And I won't be paid extra?"

"Nope."

"There you go. My hands are tied."

"You're the one who tied them but sure, okay," she said

and laughed. "Thanks for doing all the climbing there. I think the monsters took a bite out of my suit and the hydraulics were nicked or something."

"Nah, if the hydraulics were cut, you would see the fluid all over the place and you wouldn't be able to move at all." He shook his head firmly. "No, the chances are you simply need a little regulation. Probably around the hips —that's where most of the controls run and they get a little testy. Did you even calibrate the suit before you put it on?"

"No," she said defensively. "Did you calibrate your suit?"

"Of course," he snapped in response. "You don't get into one of these without checking every little detail of it. These were basically invented with Murphy's law embedded into their code. Anything you don't check will be what fails you when you need it most. That's almost a guarantee."

"Well, all right, then. The next time I head out into the field, I'll be sure to check every last inch of my suit."

"Yeah, that one is a little done for, though." Taylor tapped her shoulder. "The joints will be in a tiff, and of course, the connections around the hips were probably knocked out of joint. You won't be able to get much more out of that without repairs. Thankfully for you, I know a guy who works precisely in that field."

She laughed and shook her head. "I hate to break it to you, but I think the FBI has a contract with some of the larger companies to keep their suits in top—well, working shape, anyway."

"You see, that's what's killing America. The big corporations and monopolies kill the smaller businesses, the backbone of this country."

"Yeah, well, remember that next time you vote. Don't complain about it to me."

He tilted his head and focused on unexpected movement. They had gathered most of the bodies into a pile to make the collection a little easier, but he could see one of the beasts at the bottom wasn't quite dead yet. It now tried to drag itself toward the tree the hunter had hidden behind when they'd run into him.

"What?" the agent asked as he moved toward the pile, drew his machete, and delivered the killing blow. You could never be too careful with these beasts.

It had, however, appeared to move toward something, and as he approached the tree in question with her and the hunter beside him, he realized that a hole had been burrowed into it. Although fairly small, it was probably large enough for the monsters to squeeze through.

"What do you think that's about?" she asked.

"While they had a purpose for our hunter friend, I'm more or less certain it had nothing to do with being bait," he replied, his expression grim with sudden foreboding. He retrieved a flashlight from his pack, turned it on, and directed the beam into what he assumed was a den under the tree.

Sure enough, the light illuminated about three or four dozen tiny, shining blue spheres.

"What in the hell?" the hunter asked and made the sign of the cross over his chest.

"Well, if I had to guess—and I'm no specialist, so take my words with a grain of salt—I'd say that is a clutch of eggs. You were positioned directly over the den, probably as the first meal for whatever the hell would crawl out of there."

The man gaped, and his expression evidenced a mixture of terror and disgust.

"Yeah, it's not a nice way to go," Taylor said and moved away from the hole.

"What do you want to do with them?" the agent asked as she walked beside him.

"Well, if we had any scientists with us, I would say we should study them, learn everything we can about the monsters, and see what makes them tick. We could get your sister to poke them with needles to help us find a way to kill them more efficiently or whatever it is that evolutionary biologists do."

"It's not that, I can tell you that much. Without any researchers here, what do you think we should do?"

"Well, I say we blow it the fuck up and kill them all before they have the chance to hatch and attack us. What do you say?"

"That sounds great to me, but how in the hell can we blow it up? We don't have any explosives on us, remember."

"Damn it, you really didn't check your suit before you put it on," he complained and turned to face her with his arms folded. "You have a rocket launcher mounted on your back. Most of the larger power armor suits do. You call it up using the HUD, prime, aim, and fire. I assumed you simply held back in case the fighting got too bad, but now I realize you actually didn't know you had them."

Banks flipped him off, and the gesture caught him by surprise because he really hadn't expected it. "Yeah, and you can go fuck yourself. How do I activate it?"

"Key the button at the right side of your chin and that should give you manual access to the weapons on your suit. I seem to remember the older suits had actual buttons in the helmet. Once there, you should be able to call up— ah, there we go."

He backed away quickly as the shoulder-mounted rocket launcher came up from her back. The hunter pulled away as well, anxious to avoid being blown up accidentally.

"You simply click the button again to prime, and it'll use your eyes on the HUD to lock onto the target." Taylor kept his distance as she turned to aim at the den.

"How many should I fire?" she asked.

"You have four in the barrel so...fuck it. Fire all four." He turned to the hunter. "You might want to take cover. Oh, and cover your ears too."

The man nodded and raced behind a nearby outcrop of rocks with his hands already over his ears.

"Well...fire in the hole, I guess," Banks said when she finally managed to lock onto the target. Four successive whooshes followed one another in rapid succession as the rockets were launched toward the den.

Her suit did its job well and delivered the payload dead on. The powerful detonations were enough to decimate the whole area and topple the tree as well. The dust and debris settled slowly and the rumbled echo of the explosions were superseded by the steady thump of rotor blades as the helicopters he had seen earlier swept in to hover overhead.

"Is everything all right down there, Special Agent Banks?" asked a man through their comm line, likely one of the pilots.

"Yep. We merely finished a little business down here. There's no need to worry," she replied. "You can send your people down. Everything's dead down here but us. Oh, and we have a survivor too."

"You two and the survivor can mount up in the helo once everyone's off," the pilot replied as a series of lines snaked out and a group of men in military garb began to descend, carrying heavy packs of equipment.

It took them a few minutes to set up but once they were finished, Taylor, Banks, and the hunter all hitched themselves to the ropes and were wound into the choppers that were held steady by the patient pilots until everyone was on board.

"Okay, I get to decide my own fee for this mission, right?" Taylor asked. "I decide how much I want to be paid and send you guys an invoice along with all the expenses or something."

"Sure," Banks replied as the helicopters turned to head back.

"So, my thought is that…you know, with more than one monster and doing most of the work myself, I should probably make far more than your average contract, right?"

"That sounds about right," she said, seemingly distracted.

"With all that said, I think the reasonable rate for this mission is about sixty grand. What do you say?"

"It sounds fair. Send us the invoice when we get back."

He paused and let a moment of silence pass between them.

"I really thought you would offer more resistance to the price tag," he said finally.

"You did good work out here today. Far be it from me to keep you from getting paid a fair amount."

"Good. Because it was good work that I did out here."

"That's what I said."

"And don't you forget it."

CHAPTER THIRTY-THREE

"No, I'm not calling it Mechs-R-Us," Taylor said and looked up sharply from the piece he was working on at the table.

"I'm only saying you haven't come up with a good name yet so we might as well choose a name that's marketable and go with that until we get a better one," Bungees replied. "Mechs-R-Us has a ring to it that people will recognize. It's nostalgic, you know?"

"Our marketability won't be based on the fucking name." He narrowed his eyes. "It'll be based on the fact that we do good work in a market that has all kinds of demand but no supply. That's what's marketable about it."

"I'm only saying think about it. You need to be open to new ideas once in a while, you know that?"

"Yeah, well, that's not a new idea," he snapped. "That's trying to cash in on an old one."

"Disney's done that for years and they're still making billions."

"Well, we're not Disney."

It was an argument but not one that would prove problematic. The two of them had tried to think of a name for the company for as long as they had been open and still hadn't settled on one they both liked, not even during the couple of weeks since the mission in the Appalachians.

Banks had been true to her word and paid what he asked for and on time. That gave them what they needed to continue with the renovations to the strip mall while they worked on the mech suits that had been shipped in from the Zoo.

It had been good, hard work, but they had finished them on time and sent them out without hiking the bill too high. Now, they waited to hear how the mercs liked the work. Everything was reliant on this first job and if they liked it, they would refer them to the others in the Zoo.

If they didn't, he might as well cash out and move on.

Still, he was confident with what they'd managed to do. The suits had arrived in almost irreparable condition, and thanks to Bobby's ingenuity, they'd cut down on dead weight by twenty-percent, repaired all the armor, and added a couple of the magnetic coil alterations on top of that. They'd also managed to keep costs below what they would charge out there in the Zoo, even when factoring in the shipping.

The suits worked better than ever and the invoice sent billed the mercs a little over thirty grand apiece for the work and the pieces they needed.

"We will probably never be finished with this place," Bobby said. "What's the point of naming it anyway if it'll crumble around us the whole time?"

"Don't be melodramatic," Taylor retorted. "The prefab they built this with will outlast you, me, and probably the rest of this damn country. I swear to God, they could nuke us all and in a million years, aliens will come along and still find this building standing."

"Now who's being melodramatic?" his friend challenged and ducked when a handful of bolts were thrown his way.

"I'm going to look to see if they've sent word on the suits," Taylor said, moved away from the worktable, and stretched his back. "The shit should have been there for a few hours by now so they should have something to say, at least. Are you good to keep working here?"

"I'm only playing around with Liz. It's not rocket science."

"Yeah, well, you've tried to stick nitrous up her ass so it might end up being rocket science," he yelled over his shoulder as he wandered out of the garage and into the grocery store. They had put considerable work into the whole building, but Bobby was right. It would take forever to get it into perfect condition.

Hell, he didn't know if it was even possible to do so but damned if he wouldn't try. He felt he owed it to this little place if it would be both his home and his place of business. His friend had even suggested he move in as well, and that actually wasn't a bad idea.

He would obviously take the rent out of the guy's paycheck, so it had advantages.

Taylor still needed to think about what kind of vehicle he should choose as a city alternative to Liz, and more and more, he liked the idea of a motorcycle. There were Harley shops in the city where he could maybe buy something used and work on it like he had with Liz.

His gaze settled on the laptop and the new messages that waited for them. He wasn't too surprised to see that some them were from the merc companies in the Zoo.

"Mechs have exceeded expectations." He read the short note out loud. "Invoice payment outgoing. Looking forward to doing more business with Mech Repair Taylor McFadden in the future."

Mech Repair Taylor McFadden was the name he had used as a stand-in for the paperwork. It was even worse than Mechs-R-Us, in his opinion.

"We'll need more help," Taylor said as he scanned the future orders they were considering them for.

Another message waited for him with no address and no title.

It was short and to the point. *Pick your damn phone up!*

He could guess who it was from, though. There weren't too many people in the world who could leave a message like that in his inbox.

Sure enough, there were fifteen missed calls on the phone he hadn't taken into the shop with him.

He had no sooner picked the phone up when it rang again.

"McFadden here."

"Taylor, it's nice to talk to you again," Desk said. "How are things with your business."

"Never better," he replied. "How can I help you, Desk?"

"There's a job in California," she said. "Hollywood Hills, in fact. Are you interested?"

Taylor looked at the orders coming to them from the Zoo and grinned.

They would definitely need more help.

"Send me the details. I'm on my way."

The story continues with Silent Death, coming January 23rd, 2020.

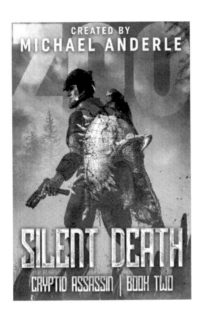

"Vickie, would you mind answering that?" Taylor asked, soldering gun already in hand and glasses in place to keep him from blinding himself.

"Sure," she said, picking the receiver up from the cradle. "Who the hell has a landline these days?"

"*We* the hell do," Taylor grumped. "Answer the phone."

He could almost hear her eyes rolling as she pressed the

receiver to the side of her head. "McFadden's Mechs, how can I help you?"

It wasn't a great name, but he wasn't going to be complaining, turning to his work, but keeping an ear out for the conversation, or the one side of it that he could hear.

"What?" Vickie asked. "No, I'm not a secretary. Why, are you a janitor? I mean, yeah, all janitors are men, right, so all men must be janitors, are you kidding me right now?"

Taylor raised an eyebrow. Maybe work could wait. He wanted to hear what Vickie had to say to whomever was calling her.

"*Yes*, it was a sexist question, thanks for asking," Vickie replied. "Now, do you want to try again? Hi, this is Vickie from McFadden's Mechs, how can I help you not be a sexist a-hole this afternoon?"

Well, that was one way to go about it.

Taylor could hear the man on the other line laughing, which was better than them getting offended and hanging up, sure, but Taylor pushed himself up from where he was working and walking over to where she was still on the phone.

Special Agent Niki Banks has called in a favor, and now Taylor has a young hacker with an attitude as an employee. Along with new monsters to kill, a business to get off the ground, a relationship with an annoying FBI Handler to … deal with Taylor is becoming a surrogate male figure for a role he didn't want.

But may be the best man for the job.

Pre-order your copy new for delivery on January 23, 2020

Thank you for reading this story far enough to find my author notes in the back!

Cryptid Assassin is 'edgier Michael Anderle' writing where the door might not be open to the bedroom, but it isn't closed, and adults talk about things that adults talk (and kid) about.

Plus cussing...lots and lots of cussing.

Because (and this is only a personal opinion) cussing is fucking hilarious at times. Also, in my group of friends, a bunch use it like salt for spicing.

For example (from https://english.stackexchange.com/questions/155664/how-many-different-parts-of-speech-can-the-f-word-be-used-as)

· Noun: "Fuck you, you fuck."
· Pronoun: "I hit fuck over there with a baseball bat."
· Adjective: "And they leave a fuck stain on my couch."
· Verb: "They fuck all the time."

· Adverb: "She fuck(ing) screams so loud, I got a noise complaint."

· Conjunction: "I take Viagra, fuck I last all night."

· Preposition: "Come fuck me later."

· Interjection: "Fuck! I stubbed my toe."

Below is a transcript from a video link provided by Tilak which was variously attributed to Osho, or George Carlin, and even from across the pond to Monty Python.

• Ignorance: Fucked if I know.

• Trouble: I guess I am fucked now!

• Fraud: I got fucked at the used car lot.

• Aggression: Fuck you!

• Displeasure: What the fuck is going on here?

• Difficulty: I can't understand this fucking job.

• Incompetence: He is a fuck-off.

• Suspicion: What the fuck are you doing?

• Enjoyment: I had a fucking good time.

• Request: Get the fuck out of here.

• Hostility: I'm going to knock your fucking head off.

• Greeting: How the fuck are you?

• Apathy: Who gives a fuck?

• Innovation: Get a bigger fucking hammer.

• Surprise: Fuck! You scared the shit out of me!

• Anxiety: Today is really fucked.

Further, I'll end with this research link which shows that "Swearing is Actually a Sign of More Intelligence – Not Less."

https://www.sciencealert.com/swearing-is-a-sign-of-more-intelligence-not-less-say-scientists

With the obligatory summation of the research:

Instead, swearing appears to be a feature of language that an articulate speaker can use in order to communicate with maximum effectiveness. And actually, some uses of swearing go beyond just communication.

So, please provide a good fucking review if you would like for either this book, or another favorite fucking author and have a fucking great weekend coming up!

Michael Anderle

OTHER ZOO BOOKS

BIRTH OF HEAVY METAL

He Was Not Prepared (1)

She Is His Witness (2)

Backstabbing Little Assets (3)

Blood Of My Enemies (4)

Get Out Of Our Way (5)

APOCALYPSE PAUSED

Fight for Life and Death (1)

Get Rich or Die Trying (2)

Big Assed Global Kegger (3)

Ambassadors and Scorpions (4)

Nightmares From Hell (5)

Calm Before The Storm (6)

One Crazy Pilot (7)

One Crazy Rescue (8)

One Crazy Machine (9)

One Crazy Life (10)

One Crazy Set Of Friends (11)

One Crazy Set Of Stories (12)

SOLDIERS OF FAME AND FORTUNE

Nobody's Fool (1)

Nobody Lives Forever (2)

Nobody Drinks That Much (3)

Nobody Remembers But Us (4)

Ghost Walking (5)

Ghost Talking (6)

Ghost Brawling (7)

Ghost Stalking (8)

Ghost Resurrection (9)

Ghost Adaptation (10)

Ghost Redemption (11)

Ghost Revolution (12)

THE BOHICA CHRONICLES

Reprobates (1)

Degenerates (2)

Redeemables (3)

Thor (4)

Printed in Poland
by Amazon Fulfillment
Poland Sp. z o.o., Wrocław

58457526R00221